"Who are you?" Grace asked.

"I'm just a man."

"Of course." Grace sighed. He would be as evasive as he was elusive.

He came in close, closer than he'd ever been. In the space of one wild heartbeat, his knuckles brushed across her cheek. Then his hand curled against the side of her face. Grace forgot to breathe.

Amazingly, he came closer still. She never thought to protest as he touched his lips to hers, too briefly. Yet nothing could have lessened the searing heat or the power of his touch. Grace made a helpless little moaning sound, deep in her throat. She reached for him, trying to hang on to him, to the moment.

He lifted his head, and then bent toward her again, his breath brushing across the side of her face. His mouth ended up near her right ear.

"Ah, Grace," he whispered. "I'm no angel. No saint, either."

And then he was gone.

Dear Reader,

Once again, Silhouette Intimate Moments has rounded up six top-notch romances for your reading pleasure, starting with the finale of Ruth Langan's fabulous new trilogy. *The Wildes of Wyoming— Ace* takes the last of the Wilde men and matches him with a pool-playing spitfire who turns out to be just the right woman to fill his bed—and his heart.

Linda Turner, a perennial reader favorite, continues THOSE MARRYING McBRIDES! with *The Best Man,* the story of sister Merry McBride's discovery that love is not always found where you expect it. Award-winning Ruth Wind's *Beautiful Stranger* features a heroine who was once an ugly duckling but is now the swan who wins the heart of a rugged "prince." Readers have been enjoying Sally Tyler Hayes' suspenseful tales of the men and women of DIVISION ONE, and *Her Secret Guardian* will not disappoint in its complex plot and emotional power. Christine Michels takes readers *Undercover with the Enemy,* and Vickie Taylor presents *The Lawman's Last Stand,* to round out this month's wonderful reading choices.

And don't miss a single Intimate Moments novel for the next three months, when the line takes center stage as part of the Silhouette 20th Anniversary celebration. Sharon Sala leads off A YEAR OF LOVING DANGEROUSLY, a new in-line continuity, in July; August brings the long-awaited reappearance of Linda Howard— and hero Chance Mackenzie—in *A Game of Chance;* and in September we reprise 36 HOURS, our successful freestanding continuity, in the Intimate Moments line. And that's only a small taste of what lies ahead, so be here this month and every month, when Silhouette Intimate Moments proves that love and excitement go best when they're hand in hand.

Leslie J. Wainger
Executive Senior Editor

Please address questions and book requests to:
Silhouette Reader Service
U.S.: 3010 Walden Ave., P.O. Box 1325, Buffalo, NY 14269
Canadian: P.O. Box 609, Fort Erie, Ont. L2A 5X3

HER SECRET
GUARDIAN

SALLY
TYLER HAYES

Published by Silhouette Books

America's Publisher of Contemporary Romance

With special thanks to Bob Pappano
for so generously sharing his expertise.

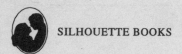 SILHOUETTE BOOKS

ISBN 0-373-27082-8

HER SECRET GUARDIAN

Copyright © 2000 by Teresa Hill

Visit Silhouette at www.eHarlequin.com

Printed in U.S.A.

Books by Sally Tyler Hayes

Silhouette Intimate Moments

SALLY TYLER HAYES

lives in South Carolina with her husband, son and daughter. A former journalist for a South Carolina newspaper, she fondly remembers that her decision to write and explore the frontiers of romance came at about the same time she discovered, in junior high, that she'd never be able to join the crew of the *Starship Enterprise.*

Happy and proud to be a stay-home mom, she is thrilled to be living her lifelong dream of writing romances.

IT'S OUR 20th ANNIVERSARY!
We'll be celebrating all year,
Continuing with these fabulous titles,
On sale in June 2000.

Chapter 1

Dr. Grace Evans was bent over her supply cabinet—a beautiful antique that once held hymnals—when an odd shiver snaked down her spine.

She dismissed it as a minor annoyance. After all, she had real problems to worry about. The hymnals were long gone, riddled with bullets and burned for what little heat they generated. Most of her supplies were gone, too, but with snipers lining the hills on three sides of town, she was unlikely to get more anytime soon. Unfortunately, she had no shortage of patients.

And then she felt it again—that distinctive, tingling sensation. As if she were being watched.

No...more than that.

Her breath caught in her throat. Excitement, dread, intense curiosity rushed through her.

He was back!

She straightened, her gaze sweeping the remains of the bombed-out church they'd been using as a makeshift clinic for the past seven weeks. Since the Red Cross had pulled its people out of this troubled corner of Eastern Europe and an International Relief Council's medical corps team—consisting chiefly of Grace and her friends Jane and Allison—had moved in.

There was hardly any electricity in the city, hadn't been for the entire time they'd been in residence at the church. Even if they had electricity, much of the ceiling was gone. There were no light fixtures left, no bulbs. Not much of anything, except sick, injured, tired, hungry people with no place to go.

It was dusk now, the city bathed in shadows, quiet save for the occasional burst of gunfire.

Grace had wished for a lot of things since she came here. An extra pair of hands. More antibiotics. More pain medication. A world where no one ever shot at anyone else.

Now she added one more thing to her list. *Light.*

She wished for just a bit of it. So she could see him.

Grace worked up her courage and turned around. There he was, just as she'd imagined, broad-shouldered, slim-hipped, long-legged. Dressed all in black, he blended perfectly with the night, an air of mystery surrounding him, a slight smile Grace sensed more than saw on his lips.

It *was* him.

Oh, there was no way she could be sure. Because he always came to her in the dark. That part had puzzled her as much as anything else about him. Surely, if he were an angel, he'd come in the light.

He never stayed for long, never even let her get a good look at his face, and truly, he seemed to be a different man each time he came to save them. Although, the fanciful part of her that still wanted to believe in some bit of magic liked the idea that he was indeed one entity.

She'd tried to convince herself it was something in his voice or maybe the faint but familiar scent that clung to his skin or maybe the way he walked, but in truth it was nothing as concrete as that. It was a feeling. More than that—an unshakable certainty deep in her soul that recognized something in him, something that was so much more than any of the physical characteristics he'd been so stingy in revealing. She knew him somehow, in a way that made absolutely no sense, but there it was. She *knew* him.

She also sensed that he didn't want her to recognize him, that he was deliberately trying to confuse her.

The first time she'd seen him, he spoke in an impeccably proper British accent, his tone clipped and a bit frosty, with the bite of authority that would not be denied. He seemed quite unassuming for a man of his size, until he opened his mouth and started issuing orders.

Grace had been a medical student at the time and she hadn't cared for taking orders from someone she didn't know, someone who had no authority over her. But she had to admit he got them out of Kuwait in the nick of time. Conditions had worsened dramatically within hours of their departure, had become impossible within days.

Two years went by before she saw him again. She was in Afghanistan, and he was little more than a voice in the darkness, speaking with a decidedly Irish brogue. Through the shadows, she saw that his hair was likely down to his shoulders when it wasn't tied back into a ponytail at the nape of his neck, and that he had a full beard—convenient for shielding his face. He wore a black cape that time, or maybe just a plain overcoat. The cape better suited the stories that had grown up around him, so a cape it had become in her own mind. And again, he'd warned them that it was time to go. Right before the fighting began in earnest.

And then came her first visit to the former Yugoslavia. He'd sounded American, seemed even more imposing, as if he'd grown more powerful and more certain of himself in the intervening years. Of course, he was the stuff of legend by then.

Grace's guardian angel.

Her friend Jane dubbed him that long ago, and it had stuck.

Late at night, when they had no more patients to see and there was nothing to do but talk, Jane—the medical corps' unofficial historian and best storyteller—launched into her tale of the mysterious man who watched over Grace and her team. The man who always appeared out of the shadows with a timely warning.

Grace had no idea who he was or where he came from. But it was as if he had a sixth sense about her. As if he watched over her and her staff day and night, intent on keeping them safe.

Lots of people had made her promises they hadn't kept. He'd never promised her anything, and yet she trusted him completely. She'd come to rely on him in ways that made no sense. Things got scary in the field, and Grace would start looking for him. She always figured if he wasn't around, she and her staff were okay.

She knew it was sheer folly, believing in anything she couldn't quite see and didn't understand. But everyone she knew believed in something. People around her wore crucifixes and Stars of David on little gold chains around their necks. Allison had the dog tags her father had worn in Korea, where he died. Jane had a rosary. Grace had *him,* her mystery man.

As he moved smoothly and silently down the hallway, an unfamiliar rush of heat flooded her cheeks. She spent a lot of time in war zones, in the villages, with the people left behind and caught in the middle with no place to go. Most of the men were either old or sick or injured, and she saw them as patients, not as members of the opposite sex.

But her mystery man made her remember man-to-woman stuff. How interesting it could be, how it could tug at a woman so and leave her feeling empty deep inside and needing things she thought she'd long ago forgotten and maybe never really understood at all.

Grace found that she very much liked watching him walk down the hallway of the ruined church. There was something about the way he moved, the sense of control, of purpose, of power and direction. He was a man who seemed absolutely certain of where he was going, and she thought she could have stood there, watching him put one foot in front of the other, for days. She couldn't remember the last time she'd taken a minute to admire a good-looking man.

Her would-be angel paused in an arched doorway five feet away, his face still in shadows. He gave a formal nod of his head and greeted her and Allison and Jane, who'd come up behind her, in perfectly accented French. "Mesdemoiselles."

Grace was good with languages, but she'd never been able to distinguish the accents he adopted from a native's speech. She figured he must have been raised in a bilingual household, learning from the cradle to straddle two cultures and blend seamlessly into either one. Of course, that still didn't explain how she could have alternately sworn he was English, Irish, American and now French.

But it was him. Definitely him.

He nodded his head at her, then off to the right. "A moment of your time, Doctor? Please?"

Behind her, two middle-aged, no-nonsense nurses giggled. Honestly, for a moment it was as if they were all fifteen and he'd come to ask her to the school dance. Grace had to remind herself they were in the middle of a war zone, and she was cold and tired and no doubt ragged-looking. He was no boy with a crush on her, and this was not a social occasion.

None of which did anything to lessen the nervous little flutters in her stomach.

She heard fevered whispers behind her. Jane, who'd been with her for years, explained to Allison, *"Grace's guardian angel."* Allison, whom they'd known only for a few months, added in her sultry Southern drawl, *"That man is no angel."*

He heard them, too. Grace could have sworn she saw a hint of a smile cross his lips as he turned and walked past a thick pillar candle that served as the only light in the dim hallway.

She followed him. It never occurred to her not to. She would have followed him anywhere.

He led her to the back of the church and outside. There was a little stone terrace, surrounded by a low fieldstone wall, still lined with plants and shrubs. The stars were out overhead, the night air chilly and stinging her cheeks. He kept to the back wall, staying in the shadows even then, leaving frustratingly little of himself for her to see.

Until tonight, no one but Grace had ever seen him, and there were times when she honestly thought she had made him up, that he was nothing but a figment of her imagination, a kind of sixth sense. She was tempted to reach out to him, just to make sure he was flesh and blood, and not sheer illusion. But she settled for asking, in French not nearly as polished as his and a voice weakened by awe and wonder, "Who are you?"

A faint smile stretched across his lips. "I'm just a man."

"Of course." She sighed. He would be as evasive as he was illusive.

Still smiling, he asked, "You're disappointed?"

"No." She was glad he was here. There was so much she wanted to ask him. But she doubted he was going to satisfy her curiosity.

"I'm afraid it's time to go, Grace."

Her eyes narrowed, surprise and a deep rush of pleasure overriding everything else. He'd never called her by name before. She blinked up at him, ridiculously happy over this one, little thing. He knew her name.

"Grace?" he repeated. "I said you have to go."

"Oh… Tomorrow?" she stammered like a school girl, so eager to please.

"At first light," he insisted. "Take the coast road, then veer south. Don't stop until you cross the border, and don't come back."

"All right."

"You went back into Afghanistan six weeks after I told you to clear out."

"Yes." He'd known that, too? And it had annoyed him? Her chin came up. "I have a job to do."

"Which you can't do unless we manage to keep you alive, now, can you?" he said evenly. "You have vehicles? Gasoline?"

She nodded. They stockpiled gas for this very reason. Her heart broke just a little for every one of the people they would leave behind. She'd never be able to do enough. And why, she wondered, looking away, could he save her and not them all?

By the time Grace turned back to him, he was leaving. She called out desperately, "Wait."

He faced her once again. She saw his shoulders rise and fall in one long, smooth breath. Hers wasn't nearly as steady.

"It was you in Kuwait, wasn't it?"

Still, he said nothing.

"And when Yugoslavia was falling apart the first time? You got us out?"

Again, nothing.

"How do you always know what's going to happen?" she tried.

"It's my job to know," he said simply.

"Know what?" When trouble was about to erupt? Or when *she* was in trouble?

"Everything," he claimed, not trying to hide his amusement any longer.

Grace frowned. In her wildest, most fanciful of dreams, she had decided he was a savior of her very own, his skills and attentions honed in on her and her alone. Which was silly. She was just a woman. A doctor. One of many trying to make a difference.

"But…your job? What is it?"

He shrugged elegantly, carelessly, mysteriously. "I do all kinds of things."

"For whom?"

"All kinds of people."

"But—" she began.

He came in close, closer then he'd ever been. In the space of one wild heartbeat, his knuckles brushed across her cheek. Then his hand curled against the side of her face. Obviously he was no illusion.

Grace forgot to breathe. His thumb stretched out to brush across her bottom lip, which was suddenly trembling. She felt a twinge of awareness all the way down to her toes, a flash of heat deep in her belly.

If she hadn't felt it herself, she would have sworn it was impossible for something as insubstantial as one touch, one brush of a man's thumb, to cause such upheaval in a woman's body, but there it was. She could no more deny it than she could deny the fact that he was standing here beside her in the darkness. The aloofness dissipated, and almost reluctantly, he smiled, his teeth a flash of white in the otherwise darkened night, and there was power in his smile, she found.

"You've grown into a real beauty, Grace," he said, in English this time, with the faintest hint of a Southern drawl.

"What?" she said breathlessly.

"You," he said soberly, still touching her. "You're beautiful."

No, she thought, *I'm not.* But he made her feel just that. The sound of his voice, the touch of his hands, as much as his words, made her feel utterly appealing.

Grace wanted to hold on to the moment, to stop time, to make the world dance to her tune for just a second. *Hers and his.* She wanted to memorize all his nearly indistinguishable features, the hard line of his jaw, the faint curve of his mouth, those smoldering dark eyes. She wanted to remember the enticing scent of his skin, the firm touch of his hand, that silly jolt of anticipation humming through her veins.

And she didn't want him to go.

"Who are you?" she said again, desperately needing an answer.

"I thought you knew, Doc." Amusement was rife in his voice then. "Someone appointed me the guardian of all the beautiful, stubborn, redheaded, do-gooder lady doctors who don't have the sense to stay out of war zones."

Mesmerized, Grace just stood there, frustration and a pervasive, near-paralyzing sense of awe preventing her from doing anything else.

"Couldn't you find a nice, simple natural disaster?" he suggested. "A flood, an earthquake, maybe a plague to contend with? I'd sleep better at night knowing no one was shooting at you, Grace."

She colored a bit, imagining him lying down at night, rumpled white sheets in stark contrast to what she thought must be sun-browned skin, miles of it. She imagined him tossing and turning, thinking of her as she often thought of him. Worrying over her, and her, Grace Evans, being the last thing he thought about before he fell asleep.

"I can't stop doing what I do. People need me. They depend on me. Besides," she mused, "I've got you. To look out for me."

"I might not always be here when you need me. I worry that one day, I'll be too late." He frowned, all teasing aside. "Let's not have any misunderstandings about this, Grace. There's nothing magical about me or what I do."

She sighed. She believed there was something decidedly magical about him, as would any woman alive, she imagined.

"I told you, I'm just a man," he said, smiling faintly again, the charm back full force. "And I have to warn you, your friend was definitely right about one thing."

"What?" she asked.

Amazingly, he came closer still. She never even thought to protest as he touched his lips to hers, too briefly. Yet nothing could have lessened the searing heat or the power of his touch. She made a helpless little moaning sound, deep in her throat. A hungry, happy, needy, surprised sound, and she reached for him, trying to get closer, trying to hang on to him, to the moment.

He lifted his head briefly, his eyes so big and so dark, and then he bent toward her again, his breath brushing across the side of her face. His mouth ended up near her right ear.

"Ah, Grace," he whispered. "I'm no angel. No saint, either."

And then he was gone.

Grace grabbed for him, but he slipped away, right through her fingertips. Like a puff of air, he seemed to dissolve into the night, swallowed up in the darkness and the cold.

She just stood there, her hands trembling, her shoulders heaving as she worked hard to take it all in. She told herself she couldn't have imagined anything so vividly. Nobody kissed her in her dreams. Nobody whispered seductively sweet, teasing words into her ear. Nobody felt so wonderfully big and warm and safe, in her dreams.

He was real. She could go back inside and Jane and Allison would pester her questions, because they'd seen him, too. Because he was real.

Just a man, he'd said.

No way, she thought.

And he was watching over her? Why? That part absolutely fascinated her. As far as she knew, there was no mysterious corps of men hired to look after anybody, no mythical beings at all.

She laughed at the thought, and she desperately wanted him back. She wanted to know his name, to see him one time when no one's life was on the line. Putting a trembling hand against her lips, she realized how very much she wanted him to kiss her again.

He'd said she was beautiful. No, that she'd *grown* into a beautiful woman. Which meant what? That he'd been watching over her? Ever since she was a little girl?

Grace laughed. The sound bubbled up out of her. A soft

chuckling that went on and on, until she had to sit down, weak and spent and trembling.

If she'd been anyone else, she'd have worried that the stress and fear of living in the middle of what would soon become all-out war was getting to her. But Grace didn't get scared, and work like this was all she'd known from the time she was a little girl. She'd grown up just like this.

And he'd been watching, even then?

She rubbed her hands against her arms, the chill getting to her now, and looked out across the top of the trees to the sky, wondering where he was right now and if he was still watching. Somehow she thought he was.

Suddenly, she heard footsteps and excited whispers behind her.

"Well?" Jane asked. "It was him?"

"Yes," she admitted.

"And he's gone now?" Allison asked.

"Yes."

Then Jane. "Are you okay?"

Grace nodded.

"Who is he?"

"He wouldn't say."

"Where did he come from?"

"I wish I knew." She'd track him down if she could.

"Sweetie," Allison said, "you look like you've been hit upside the head and the world's kind of spinning all around you. Are you okay?"

"I think so."

"What did he do to you?"

Grace would never hear the end of it. She knew it. But she was too surprised, too overwhelmed, and she couldn't hold it inside. "He kissed me."

Stunned silence greeted her revelation.

Jane cocked her head to the side, then felt Grace's forehead. "No fever," she said, holding up two fingers. "How many?"

"I'm not sick, and nobody hit me over the head," Grace said, pushing her away. "Do you think I'd have to be delusional to believe a man kissed me?"

"No." Jane looked offended. "I didn't mean that at all. Although, I know you, Grace. You have a sex life that would make a nun proud."

"That bad?" Allison chimed in.

"Oh, yeah," Jane insisted, turning back to Grace. "Are you sure he didn't cast a spell over you? You still look a bit dazed."

She felt that way, too, and no matter how odd it sounded, found herself compelled to ask, "You both saw him, right? Tall, dark and handsome? A bit dangerous, maybe? He was here? Just now?"

Jane looked even more concerned.

Allison giggled and took Grace by the arm. "Come on, sweetie. Let's go inside. Somebody needs to check you over. I think you've got a fuse on the fritz. But don't worry. We'll take good care of you."

"I'm fine," Grace insisted. "I'm just…surprised. That's all. He knew my name. How would he know my name? How does he always know where to find us and when we have to go? Why does he even care?"

"So he's like a stalker now?" Jane suggested.

"No," she insisted. "I don't know what he is, but he says we have to leave."

"And we're going?" Jane asked.

"Yes."

"Because he said so?"

"Yes," Grace admitted. "I know it doesn't make any sense. I know nothing about this makes sense. But he's always been right about these things."

She believed in him, and she didn't believe in anything or anyone.

Grace looked up at her two friends. Jane still looked worried. "Are you going to write me up?" Grace asked. "Send me off for a psych consult when we get back to London?"

"I don't know. Do you need one?"

She sighed. "I don't know."

But she needed him. She needed him to come back. To tell her his name. To kiss her about a dozen more times.

"So," Allison said, devilish delight in her tone. "He *kissed* you...."

"Yes." Grace blushed.

"And you liked it?"

"Yes."

She put her arm around Grace's shoulders. "Come tell Mother Allison all about it."

Grace ducked under the arm and turned to go back inside. "Come on. I promised we'd be out of here at first light."

Reluctantly, she packed up her team. Grace stopped the small convoy just across the border. At the request of the UN's officer in charge, she told him what she could about the situation they'd left behind. He told them it wasn't public knowledge yet, but within hours, UN Security Council-authorized military strikes would begin against the rebels trying to take control of the area.

Grace and her team had known that was coming. Even when they'd gone in, weeks ago, they'd known. But military powers tended to talk about things for a long time before taking action, and a lot of innocent people got hurt in the interim. People who needed the kind of help Grace and her team had to offer. So they always stayed as long as they could, sometimes too long.

Grace could tell by what she saw at the border that the time for diplomacy had passed. Military action was indeed imminent.

And *he'd* known. The tall, dark, handsome man, who thought she'd grown into a beauty and had kissed her until her brain short-circuited, had known.

Grace thought about asking the British commander if he'd

sent anyone into the city to warn people like her to get out, thought about asking about *him,* her mystery man. But what would she say? She could barely describe him, couldn't even be sure of his nationality.

He'd saved them one more time. And she didn't even know his name.

Chapter 2

Eighteen months later

The communications technician frowned at his computer terminal, which was emitting an unsettling beeping noise he'd never heard before outside a training exercise.

"What the hell is that?" he said to the senior man sitting next to him in the room where communications were monitored twenty-four hours a day.

"Bad news," the second man said calmly.

A message, clear and concise, flashed across his screen, a level-five flash directed to his superior's superior.

"Geez." The technician read the message twice, blinking in disbelief. "I thought the president had to get shot or something before I'd seen an L-5 flash."

"Close to it," the second man said. "What's it about?"

Puzzled, he said, "Some lady doctor."

The printer was spitting out the message, even as they spoke. The second man picked it up and read it himself, cursing and shaking his head. "The boss is visiting today. I think he's on the firing range. Keeping us all humble, I'd bet."

The first man took the message back. Procedure called for it to be delivered immediately, by hand if possible. "I'll see to it."

"Rodrigez?"

"Yeah, skipper," he said, already turning to head to the firing range.

"Let me give you a little tip. You don't want to hand that to the boss while he's got a loaded weapon in his hand."

Rodrigez frowned, not at all sure how he might get his boss to put down his weapon before handing over the message.

He was almost out the door before the second man called after him. "Tell the boss I'm pulling together any info we've got on the situation down there, and that I'll find him a plane."

Surprised, Rodrigez said, "You think he'll go down there?"

"He and the lady go way back. He'll go."

Two hours earlier

Grace, Allison and Jane stared intently at the murky image on the television screen. There was Grace, two days before, calmly explaining to the camera how little she could do to save the people painstakingly making their way to the IRC clinic in the tiny Central American country of San Reino, because she simply didn't have the necessary medical supplies.

As the camera panned down the rows of makeshift cots, past the painfully thin bodies of children and adults in desperate need of help, the IRC's medical director, Peter Baxter, shouted, "Are you seeing this?"

"Yes," Grace said into the static-filled pay phone connection. She'd given an interview to an American television journalist two days ago. And now all hell had broken loose. "I don't see the problem."

"Keep watching," Peter said.

Her face gave way to that of the serious-looking journalist, who said bluntly that medical supplies from all over the world, sent by well-meaning people trying to avert disaster in Central America, were likely being stolen by the country's rebel dictators, then sold at hugely inflated prices on the black market to fund the rebels' military operations. It was the kind of news that dried up donations all over the world and ultimately made her job much harder.

"I didn't tell him that," Grace shouted into the phone. "I didn't."

She'd wanted to, because everything the reporter said was likely true. She knew exactly where her supplies were going. But Grace hadn't said any of that, because she knew it wouldn't do any good. The reporter went on, about greed and frustration and the tragedy of a country's citizens being betrayed by its own people.

"Come on." Grace waited. "There's got to be more to it than this."

There wasn't. The reporter had let Grace complain and then added his own conclusions, from his "anonymous sources," that her supplies were being stolen for gun money, and one thing ran so smoothly into the next, it looked to all the world as if it had all come from Grace. End of story.

Beside her, Jane groaned. Allison whistled her trouble-is-coming whistle.

"I didn't tell him that," Grace said again into the phone. "I swear."

"All right. I believe you. But I'm probably the only one who's going to," Peter warned.

"The kicker is, I still have no supplies, Peter."

"I understand. But infuriating the local officials is not going to help."

"Neither has anything else I've tried," she complained.

"Hey, do you want out of there?"

"No," she said.

"Because if you can't do this job, I'll take you out."

"Peter, I can do this job."

"You're sure? I could send someone for a couple of weeks. You could take a break. How long has it been since you've had some time off, Grace?"

"I don't need time off. I just need supplies."

"Okay. I'll find a way to get them to you."

"Thank you," she said, not sounding at all grateful. Grace sighed. "I am sorry, all right? I don't want to make your job any harder, either."

"Then be careful, okay. And watch yourselves. There's a tropical depression that popped up yesterday. You might get hit with another hurricane."

"Great." She hung up the phone and frowned.

"That bad?" Allison said.

"No." She'd been bawled out before, by men far more stern and imposing than Peter Baxter. Granted, she normally handled things with a bit more diplomacy than she had this morning's grilling by Peter. But she was okay. She could cope with all of this. Grace always found a way to cope.

"I noticed you didn't tell Peter about your little chat with the locals this morning," Jane, her conscience, said.

"No, I didn't." Why add fuel to the fire? Peter was upset enough already. "This will all blow over. You'll see."

The three of them strolled down a narrow, crowded street in the capital of San Reino. The tiny country in Central America had been crippled by devastating floods and mud slides following a hurricane that had stalled off the coast three months before, dumping torrential rain on the area for days on end. They were working in the countryside, near the coast, under the most trying of conditions—understaffed, overwhelmed and desperately short of supplies—and Grace was tired. Desperately tired. That was the only excuse she had for her little show of temper this morning with the provincial governor, who'd sent troops to her clinic to "escort" her and her staff to his headquarters. Grace hadn't even thought of arguing at the high-handed tactics.

She'd tried to swallow her temper once they arrived. But the man—Milero—had been so smug, making a show of apologizing for the difficulties she and her team faced in trying desperately to help his people. He'd assured her that he wanted her organization here and would do all he could to help her by putting an end to the irregularities with the delivery of her supplies. But his tone clearly said something else, delivering the kind of veiled threat that made Grace's blood boil. Clearly, he was furious at her and her organization.

"You really think I came on too strong with our so-called friend this morning?" Grace asked. "What was I supposed to do? Smile and nod and look contrite?"

"He could kick us out of the country if he wanted to," Jane warned.

"He won't." Grace's pride was smarting, her temper still short. "If we were gone, who would he steal supplies from?"

Allison chuckled.

Jane persisted. "You could be careful. I know you're never afraid, but you could think of the rest of us. The man scared me, and I'm scared for you now."

"Come on," Allison said. "Grace is right. All of this will blow over. And we can't be in real trouble. If we were, Grace's mystery man would be here."

Grace rolled her eyes. The legend lived on. It simply refused to die. Just like her memory of his kiss. She'd drawn his face a million times in her mind. There were times when she'd be in a city somewhere—a civilized place—and she'd catch sight of a dark head in the crowd, and think just for a moment it was him. That he was indeed watching over her and knew she was looking for him, wishing for him to appear.

She was frustrated enough today that she was ready for a fantasy man. Ready for him to drop from the sky and carry her off with him, to somewhere cool and clean and untroubled.

A holiday, Grace thought. Peter was always pestering her to take a holiday.

Where would she go?

Anywhere with *him,* she decided.

"Good Lord, look at her face," Allison said. "You're not holding out on us, are you, Grace? You haven't seen him lately?"

"No." Much to her chagrin, he hadn't appeared out of thin air, at least not anywhere near her. Not for more than a year. Her life had been downright predictable. He'd told her to go find a nice, safe natural disaster, and a string of them had fallen into her lap—as if he commanded the forces of nature, as well.

"You're still grinning," Allison said. "You never tried to find him?"

"How could I? I don't know anything about him."

"Oh." Allison sounded disappointed. "I thought you might be telling us a story about that, too."

"I didn't make him up, and I don't know anything about him. I swear."

"If she did, she'd have disappeared with him by now," Jane said wryly.

"You know something," she admitted, "you're right."

They were still laughing as they turned the corner onto the main street, a hot, dusty, bumpy ride back to the clinic site awaiting them. Grace was distracted, thinking about him. Irritated with him. A man shouldn't be allowed to kiss a woman like that, then disappear for a year and a half. Especially a woman kissed as seldom as Grace.

Shaking her head, she continued on. Traffic noises were constant, raucous and unpredictable. She barely paid attention to the squeal of tires forced to stop too quickly. Even as she sensed a real commotion behind her, she wasn't really alarmed.

Maybe she had put entirely too much faith in her so-called guardian angel, because she hadn't worried about anything really bad happening to her, even before he first showed up. Death was something she hadn't feared from the time she was a girl. Not since she lost everyone who mattered to her. So she was only mildly interested in the commotion that erupted around them.

Allison screamed first. Turning, Grace saw that her friend had been thrown to the ground. Vaguely, she realized the crowd on the streets had fallen back, creating a cavern of sorts—a line of people, the building, the cars, her friends and her in the middle of it.

The men in front of them had submachine guns. Grace knew the make and model. She'd gotten up close and personal with a lot of weapons.

Jane went hurling sideways next, knocked out of the way by a burly-looking man dressed in fatigues and a pair of army boots. Dark-complected, dark-haired, with a bushy mustache and of indiscriminate age, he could have been from any number of factions of Central American rebels, freedom fighters, militia or military. Everybody fought for some cause in San Reino. Chaos reined.

She'd known that, and still, she hadn't been afraid.

Grace knew she'd feel so stupid about it later, but she actually looked around for *him.* Her angel. He'd speak Spanish here. Flawless Spanish.

Of course, it was broad daylight, and he didn't venture out in the light. Now, when she needed him most of all, he was nowhere to be found. Would that be his excuse, she wondered? The light?

Grace gasped, near-hysterical laughter threatening to erupt from deep within. She fought it, let loose a scream instead. Because one of the rebels was reaching for her, and if they were going to take her off a public street in broad daylight, she wanted to make sure as many people as possible saw them, saw her, and remembered. Maybe someone wouldn't be afraid to tell what happened to her.

The man closest to her hooked a beefy arm around her waist and flung her toward the waiting car, the back door open, the motor running. Someone was gunning it. Ready. She would simply disappear. It happened all the time in Central America. Kidnapping had become a favored sport.

She fought again, getting her arms out, pushing against the frame of the car they intended to use to take her away. That was the first rule in this sort of situation. Don't let them take you. She got slammed against the car frame for her troubles, the impact knocking the breath from her lungs.

The man shoved her down, her chin connecting painfully with the top of the car before he backed up long enough for her head to slide in. He shoved one more time. She went sprawling on the floor of the back seat.

He jumped in beside her. The door slammed. The engine revved. The car tore away from the curb. She was still screaming, still trying to draw as much attention to herself as she could. She rose up on her hands and knees, and her captor backhanded her across the mouth, so hard she hit her head against the back of the seat. The tinny taste of blood filled her mouth.

It was done. They'd taken her.

She could hardly believe it, even when her kidnapper pressed a dirty cloth, wet with some chemical, across her mouth and nose. She fought him, knowing it was a losing battle. The way she was gasping for breath, it wouldn't take long for the chemical to do its work. Already, that seductive sense of calm and quiet was calling to her, weakness invading her limbs and making her head spin.

But still, she fought, because she was mad, almost as mad at her abductor as she was at herself.

Mad at another man, as well, the one who hadn't come in time to save her.

* * *

They'd bound her ankles together with duct tape while she was unconscious. Her hands, too, she found as she slowly came to. Her arms were stretched behind her back in a hold that was painful; they'd gone tingly, almost numb, from poor blood circulation. She was moving in an awkward way she couldn't comprehend, her head bouncing, the world bouncing around as well.

And then she realized she'd been flung over a burly shoulder. Her head hung over the man's back, bobbing as he walked.

Grace's mouth was painfully dry. Her head hurt, and she felt nauseous. She was scared to open her eyes, to see where they'd brought her, to imagine what they were going to do to her.

The odd, insistent sound of the wind made her curious. She wasn't even sure it was the wind. Opening her eyes, she found that they'd taken her to the coast. The sound she heard was a combination of the wind and waves, and she was being taken down a dock. Not deep into the mountains of Central America, mountains that swallowed people up so completely at times.

Grace shuddered. She was honestly and truly scared. She'd been so very foolish to think she was safe, protected, that someone was magically watching over her. She laughed a bit, or maybe the sound was a cry, a sob.

The whole situation held an air of unreality. She was on a beach. Normally, she loved the beach. And she wasn't supposed to be afraid. Not ever. They could kill her, and she would just be dead. It wasn't as if she hadn't been in situations dozens of times before where death was a distinct possibility.

Honestly, the only real difference between death someplace else and death here was the time frame involved. In a war zone, it was often fast. She knew, by the expressions on the faces of the dead bodies she saw, that sometimes people weren't even aware of what was happening. They didn't look surprised. They must have been alive one second, gone the next.

How frightening could that be? There would be no time to be afraid, no time for regrets or pain.

But these people who had her now...she could imagine them toying with her, dragging things out. She might have days to anticipate all of the bad things.

Grace deliberately closed her mind to the idea. She let her body go limp, blacked out again.

She came to as she was being carried into what looked like a fortress, complete with a thick rock wall.

She'd feared they'd dump her in a tent in the mountains or maybe a hole in the ground. She'd heard stories of another kidnapping victim, held for weeks in a hole in the ground.

But she was in a stone fortress, saw the thickness of the walls.

They went down a narrow stone stairway for a long time. She was in a castle—one complete with a dungeon, she feared.

It was dark here and amazingly cool. She hadn't been cool the entire time she'd been in San Reino, but she was now. Cold, even.

Grace shivered, unable to steady herself or to calm her fears.

She heard her captor grunt as he unceremoniously dumped her onto the stone floor. Her head slammed against it. She exhaled raggedly, instinctively curling into a ball to preserve what little warmth her body possessed.

There was a conversation going on above her in rapid-fire Spanish. Normally, it wouldn't be any problem for her to follow. Now it was simply beyond her. She gave up, gave in. Fatigue overcame everything else—thirst, hunger, pain, cold, arms that had gone numb, even the fear. And Grace slept.

She dreamed about him, dreamed that he came for her. An avenging angel, roaring into her tomb, flinging off attackers

left and right as if they were nothing but the most minor of
annoyances, their power no match for his. He was big and
strong and furious, and they cowered in the face of his superior strength.

Grace smiled as she watched him come, knowing he would
succeed. He could do anything, after all. She wasn't even
mad at him for messing up earlier and letting them grab her.

"Grace."

She could hear him call her name in that deep, smooth-as-
silk voice of his that seemed to warm her from the inside
out. He was so close now. It was almost over. Everything
would be all right.

"Grace."

"Hmm?" she murmured.

"That's it. Come back to me, sweetheart."

She sighed, not nearly as cold anymore. She'd found a
source of heat, of strength. He was going to save her.

"Grace."

Her eyes slid open, fatigue still dogging her. Lethargy.
Weakness. *Drugs,* she supposed, feeling as if her head were
stuffed with cotton balls. She couldn't think through all the
fluffy white stuff.

"Don't scream," said a barely there voice near her right
ear. "Don't move. Don't make a sound. The guard's coming
back. Grace?"

She said nothing, didn't even think the voice was real. But
a hand slid across her mouth. A real one? She panicked for
a moment, thinking he was going to smother her, and started
to struggle, but she was indeed pathetically weak at the moment, and her hands and feet were still tightly bound. He
controlled her easily, his hand firmly over her mouth, his own
lips next to her right ear, and when her confusion subsided
a bit, she grew still.

"Shh," he whispered. "It's okay. I'm not going to hurt
you."

The voice was different now. So quiet. More an impression inside her head than real. So different from the rich, full voice in her dreams.

"Shh."

It was *his* voice. Her absent savior.

There was only one problem. Grace didn't think she was asleep anymore.

Still, she heard someone, felt someone in the darkness beside her. Which probably meant she was hallucinating.

He soothed her with his almost-hypnotic voice, and unless Grace was mistaken, he was lying on the floor behind her. Either that or someone had turned on a furnace aimed directly at Grace's back. It felt so good. He left one hand over her mouth, firm but unthreatening now, and with the other, he pulled her hair back from her face, tucking the strands gently behind her right ear. Then he ran his hand down her arm.

She felt only the vaguest impression of his touch. But she liked it. It helped, having him touch her this way. Having him talk to her.

Grace blinked three times to convince herself her eyes were actually open. It was pitch black inside the room, except for a sliver of light coming from under the door. To her cell. In the dungeon. In the fortress by the sea.

Surely she was dreaming. There was no man whispering soothingly to her and stroking her hair. It was sheer illusion, fleeting comfort, although she'd take all she could get. But she couldn't let herself trust in it. She couldn't fool herself anymore.

"He's gone," the voice said, still nothing but the faintest of whispers but sounding disconcertingly real.

How did a woman ever really know, Grace wondered, what was real and what she merely imagined? Which demons lived and breathed and which existed only in her mind? She'd been through so many things, seen so many horrors, and she'd never had a reaction quite like this to stress.

Tentatively, she tried to flex her bound hands. Because if

he was real and here behind her, she should be able to touch him, if he was flesh and blood.

She couldn't be sure exactly what she managed to do with her hands. It hurt simply to try to move them. But then her hand was enveloped in warmth.

"Grace?" There was heated breath at her right ear. "I'm going to take my hand away from your mouth. Don't scream."

The hand slid away. He rose up, leaning over her, until his face was next to hers. His cheek was rough, and there was something faintly familiar about the smell of his skin. He leaned over her, one arm on the ground above her head, the other around her side, his hand turning her face up towards his.

She was enclosed in luxurious warmth. She itched to move closer, to climb on top of him, let him take her body into his, until she was a part of him and she wasn't alone or scared anymore.

"I'm dreaming," she whispered.

"I'm still the stuff of your dreams?" He was close enough that she would have sworn she felt his answering smile. "And here I thought you'd be mad at me."

Grace went still. Blinking up at him through the thick, oppressive darkness, her mouth desperately dry, her throat tight, she whispered, "Who are you?"

"Just a man, Grace. Did you forget?"

It was too bizarre, his words an eerie echo of those used by the last man who'd come to save her. That man had been real. She remembered. She hadn't been the only one to see him. But this one...this time...

"Tell me who you are," she cried, sick of all the games.

His arms tightened around her. "You know who I am, Grace."

"I don't. I've never known. Never understood."

"But you know who I am. The one who watches out for you. You know that, even if you've never known my name."

Tears seeped out of the corners of her eyes. She'd even entertained the idea that he might truly know who she was, although she'd successfully hidden that truth for years. But no one knew…

"Why are you doing this?" she asked. "Why are you here, and why can't I ever see you? What kind of game are you playing?"

"Shh," he said, the sound falling over her like a balm. "I can't explain now, Grace. I don't have time. It's almost morning."

"And you don't appear in the light," she said, near hysteria now. Her savior, thwarted by a little fact of life called the sun.

"Grace?" He whispered urgently now. "I'm doing the best I can. I'm sorry. It's so much less than you deserve, but it's the best I can do under the circumstances."

"I don't understand," she said, weeping. Her head was throbbing, her arms numb, half of her body freezing to death, and she was obviously hallucinating. But the power of the hallucinations frightened her. She was lucid enough to know she'd been drugged but had no idea what they'd used, and there were things on the black market that could fry someone's brain in seconds.

"I know you're not real," she insisted. The worst part was how very much she wanted to believe the whole illusion.

"Aren't I?" he said.

"No." She went to shake her head back and forth, but it hurt too much, and she started to cry even harder, her sobs coming out as long, shuddering breaths that shook her to the core.

"Oh, sweetheart. What can I do?"

"Nothing," she said. He couldn't do anything, because he wasn't real.

"You're freezing." His hands were back, running up and down the front of her body. "Does anything hurt? Can I roll you over? Get you off this cold floor? Would that help?"

Anything would help, she thought. Anything at all. Light. She'd wished so hard for light the last time he'd been with her. She'd wished for so much over the years, and seldom gotten any of it.

"Tell me if I hurt you," he said. "Tell me if I need to stop."

He rolled her in one smooth motion until she was lying on top of him. Her head fell to his chest, and her arms were still tied behind her back, but one entire side of her body was pressed against the length of his. His arms tightened around her, and somehow her cold toes became wedged between his calves. His body was muscular and firm, not at all soft but more yielding than the stone floor, and he was so warm.

She wept from relief and fear. He let her, telling her how sorry he was and urging her to be quiet.

Grace was still so confused, but better. Everything was better with him. Finally, she said, "I'm going to wake up, and you'll be gone."

"Not gone. Just hiding. Until tonight."

"I was right. You are afraid of the light."

He swore softly. "Grace, I can't let anyone see me. It has to be a secret that I'm here. Do you understand?"

"But you're not real."

"Ah, Grace." He sighed. "They hit you on the head. You know that, don't you, sweetheart? I felt the bump."

"Yes."

"And they drugged you?"

"Yes."

"You're confused—"

"Yes."

He dropped a light kiss on the top of her poor, bruised head, taking such tender care of her.

"I'm no illusion, Grace. No angel, remember?"

"I still don't know what you are," she whispered.

"I'm the man who's going to get you out of here," he

said unequivocally, as if he had no doubts, as if he'd tolerate nothing less than the universe bending to his will.

"Promise?" she said, feeling like a child in need of the illusion of reassurance that came from nothing but someone's word.

"I'll do it or die trying," he said.

It seemed too truthful a response, too starkly real, for a man who was sheer fantasy. But she couldn't ponder the inconsistencies of that now. Utterly weary, she snuggled closer, her cheek pressed against the soft cloth of his shirt.

"I'm so tired."

"I know, sweetheart. Go to sleep. It's the best thing for you now."

"You'll be gone, won't you? When I wake up?"

"Hiding. Just hiding."

"Gone," she said forlornly. He'd dissolve into the darkness, just like before. If she could have gotten her hands free, she would have clung to him and never let him go. "Just take me. Take me now."

"I can't, sweetheart. It took me too long to get here. Too long to find you. It's almost dawn. I can't get you out of here in the daylight. It's a fortress. On an island. It's going to take time for us to get away. We'll need all night to do it. Tonight, I promise. As soon as it's dark."

"Now," she insisted.

"Grace—"

"Do you know how long a day is? How many minutes? How many seconds of light?" They could do anything to her in the space of a day.

"It's a risk, I know. But it's our best chance. It would be suicide to try it now. I'd give my life for yours, but I'm no good to you dead, Grace. Do you understand that? Your best chance of getting off this island alive is with me, which means I have to stay alive, too. So I have to play the odds. I've looked at this every way I know, and believe me, I don't like it. I don't want to leave you. But I don't know what else to do, and I honestly don't think you're in any shape to argue with me right now. I don't believe you're thinking clearly. So you just let me to do the thinking, all right? You just do what I say and try to trust me. Because I can fix this. I can get you out of this mess.''

Grace lay with her body draped over his. She tried to breathe deeply, steadily, tried to calm down and think clearly, and he was right. She couldn't. She didn't even have a way of knowing if he was real or not. As to whether he'd come back for her…that was even more impossible to say.

So she lay there against him, soaking up his warmth and the reassurance of his presence.

There was really nothing for her to decide, anyway. Even if she'd conjured him up inside her own head, he'd made her feel better for now. He'd beaten back the panic that threatened to engulf her and taken away the worst of the chill. He'd soothed her with those amazingly big, warm, gentle hands of his, and he'd given her reason to hope.

He would get her out. Or die trying.

She puzzled over that, nearly asleep by the time she muttered, ''Angels can't die, can they?''

''Ah, Grace,'' he said, sad and so weary-sounding. ''I've messed it all up, haven't I?''

''Messed up what?''

''You and me.''

''Have you?''

''I just didn't know how to go about it. Watching out for you was fine, as long as I didn't have to get too close. But then I did. You needed me, and…I'm afraid I messed up.''

''I believed in you,'' she said, even if it was silly. ''I thought you were coming to save me.''

''I am. I'm here.''

''I looked for you as they were shoving me into the car.'' She laughed weakly. ''It was so stupid. I feel so foolish. But I kept thinking you were going to come charging out of the crowd and save me.''

His arms tightened around her. "I'm sorry, sweetheart. I should have been there. But I'm here now."

"Just like all those times before?"

"Just like that," he promised.

"You kissed me," she said drowsily, sinking toward oblivion. "Before—"

"I shouldn't have done that, either, Grace."

"Why not? I liked it."

"So did I."

Grace sighed, sinking deeper. "I'm so tired."

"I know. Go to sleep, sweetheart. Try not to be too afraid when you wake up. Even if you can't see me, I'll be here. I'll be watching over you, Grace, and I'll be back."

Chapter 3

Of course, it had been a dream.

Grace knew the minute she woke up. She hurt too badly to be hallucinating anymore.

The reality was that she'd been drugged, hit over the head, was weak, thirsty, hungry and scared. None of those things led to particularly clear thinking. Obviously, she'd had a dream. A fear-induced dream, where she felt safe and protected. It was merely her mind's way of coping with a bad situation. She'd conjured up a hero, a savior, to get her out of this mess. If it wasn't a dream, it was pure hallucination.

Still, when she'd awakened moments ago, alone on the cold stone floor, shivering, her head pounding, her mouth painfully dry, she'd looked for him. She couldn't call out to him, because she still didn't know his name. But she looked for him. She remembered so clearly him urging her not to be afraid, not to think he was gone just because she couldn't see him.

Not that it helped at the moment.

Her eyes tried to cut through the oppressive darkness to

find some sign that she might not be alone. But there was none. He'd been nothing but a way for her to get through long, frightening hours without falling into a blinding panic, and he'd served his purpose. She'd survived. She wasn't screaming or crying or climbing the walls.

Now she had to face the unknown all by herself. She didn't want to think about what might happen.

Looking around, she noted the walls must be thick, because she could hardly hear a thing, save for the occasional footsteps of the guard. He paced past the door to her room every fifteen minutes or so. Sometimes she thought she could feel his eyes staring at her through the narrow window on the door. As the day wore on, she pivoted around in a circle, inch by inch, using her bound feet to propel her, saw that the room held a cot in the corner, some blankets stacked neatly on top. She would have killed for one of those the previous night. There was what looked like a utilitarian bathroom through a doorway in the back corner of the room. Boxes of supplies stacked along the back wall. Not much else.

It appeared a place where someone might hole up in times of trouble. From an attack, maybe? A shelter, in case of bombing?

She could understand a man like Milero—the one she believed was responsible for her kidnapping—having his own private bomb shelter. He'd likely have a fortress, as well. Maybe she hadn't been hallucinating about that part. Maybe that was real.

Grace was thinking it over when she heard the lock give on the door behind her. It opened.

The walls and the door must truly be thick. They'd muffled a great deal of sound. People talking, in rapid Spanish. People walking along the stone steps. She heard it all, until the door shut once again.

Someone walked toward her. Grace saw a pair of worn black boots caked with mud, camouflage pants and shirt, the shadowed face of a man. She frowned. It wasn't *him,* the man she wanted, needed.

The guard nudged her with his booted foot, telling her in Spanish that she was being permitted ten minutes to use the facilities. Fresh clothes would be made available to her and, in the end, a bit of food and water, if she cooperated and didn't cause any trouble.

She nodded her acceptance, managed not to flinch as he pulled out a wicked-looking knife and sliced through the thick bands of tape at her wrists and ankles. The pain in her arms and shoulders was excruciating. She cried out as he pulled her roughly to her feet. Her muscles weren't cooperating the way they should, and she had to lean heavily against him as he walked her to the door of the small bathroom and shoved her inside. He flipped a switch, flooding the room with light, nearly blinding her, sending excruciating pain through her head. A bundle of clothing landed on the floor beside her feet.

Ten minutes, he decreed. If she made trouble, there would be no food.

Grace wasted a whole minute huddled against the floor, then somehow managed to get moving, to take care of her most basic needs. The room was surprisingly clean and stocked with supplies—soap, toothbrushes, toothpaste, shampoo, towels. She'd been correct in thinking this was some sort of bomb shelter, a room kept ready for times of trouble.

She scrubbed her face, her teeth, fumbling with the most basic of moves because of the damage done to her arms while they'd been bound behind her back, and then she got into the crude shower, hoping the cold water would clear her head. She scrubbed her body as best she could, her knees weak, her whole body trembling. Then found herself sliding down the wall of the shower, to curl into a ball on the floor, crying, the water streaming over her.

She couldn't get up. Didn't have the strength. Her whole

body hurt, her head especially, and she was afraid. Desperately afraid and alone.

She gasped when the shower curtain was yanked back, the guard leering at her. He shut off the water, hauled her roughly to her feet. Grace made a feeble attempt to cover herself, but he batted her hands away, made guttural sounds of appreciation deep in his throat, laughed a bit, his hands coming out to run roughly over her breasts. She flinched, her skin crawling at his touch, and she thought about spitting in his face, wondered if the satisfaction she'd feel from that small bit of rebellion would be worth his angered response. Honestly, she didn't think she had the strength to do much more than spit in his face. Maybe the power to blank out what was happening as best she could, but he would do what he wanted with her. There was no way she could run away, no way to fight. She had never been this helpless.

The man moved menacingly closer. She saw him reaching for the button of his trousers, felt bile rising in her throat. And then he stopped. Someone else was in the room, she realized. Someone was shouting, words she didn't understand. Something about trouble outside. A disturbance. For a second, Grace thought it was *him,* saving her again. Then she shook her head at her own foolishness, her desperate need.

The guard looked murderously angry at the interruption. He motioned toward the clothes. She picked them up, and he pulled her out into the main room, giving her a disgusting look of anticipation, saying something about "later," before disappearing, locking the door behind him.

Grace fumbled into the clothes—a rough, shapeless, mud-colored cotton shirt and drawstring pants. Then she got onto the cot and climbed under the blanket, wondering how long it would be before the guard would be back to finish what he started and where she might find the strength to fight him.

And then she thought of the other man, her savior, and of sweet, empty promises in the dark.

* * *

They brought her food—some soup and bread—which she ate very, very slowly, despite her hunger. Because she wasn't sure how her stomach was going to react. She forced herself to go slowly with the water, too, knowing her body could only take so much at one time.

An old woman brought the food, a woman who eyed her with suspicion and maybe a bit of concern. Grace figured she had nothing to lose. She asked the woman, "Where am I?"

The woman frowned, looked nervously at the door and lowered her voice. "The compound."

"Whose compound?" Grace whispered.

"You will know soon enough. He will be here tonight. They say he comes for you."

Grace felt a chill race down her spine. A man with a compound, a dungeon, coming for her. A savior who was not.

Earlier, when they'd let her get cleaned up, she thought she'd be making a videotape for them to use in their ransom demand, that they'd want to show what humanitarians they were, treating her so well. But maybe they'd done it for the man who owned the compound. Maybe he preferred to terrorize clean-smelling women instead of dirty ones. She shuddered once again.

"He's coming tonight?" she said.

"*Si*. If the weather, it does not get too bad."

Weather? she thought, thinking of the guardian angel she'd once believed commanded the elements, thinking of the string of natural disasters that had fallen into her lap after he'd urged her to go find one.

"What's happening outside?" she said.

The old woman said something indecipherable at first. "Hur-r-ree?"

"Hurricane?" Grace said.

"*Si*. Hurricane."

Grace laughed. The old woman looked at her as if she'd lost her mind, and obviously, Grace had. She needed help, and it seemed someone had sent a hurricane her way.

* * *

Grace was back on the cot, legs and arms bound once again, her head spinning from the drugs she suspected had been in her food, when her cell door opened once again. She tried to see through the awful blackness to the face of the man walking toward her.

The faint odor of tobacco gave him away. It was the guard from this morning. Come back to finish what he'd started, she suspected. She was too stubborn to surrender without a fight. He'd have to undo the bindings at her ankles to do what he wanted. She'd have a chance, wouldn't she? She'd had some training in self-defense, and she wasn't as weak as she'd been that morning.

He locked the door behind him. She thought he was already reaching for the buttons on his clothes as he walked ominously toward her.

Grace let out a slow, shaky breath. If she couldn't fight him off, maybe if she made him mad enough, he would hit her. Maybe she would pass out. How awful could it be, if she never even remembered it?

She bit her bottom lip to stifle a scream, refusing to give him the satisfaction of seeing her cower before him.

Closing her eyes, Grace remembered a promise—a soft, sweet promise. *Try not to be afraid. Even if you can't see me, I'll be here. I'll be watching over you, and I'll be back.*

But her angel wasn't coming back. He wasn't going to save her now. Nothing was. He was nothing but an illusion, after all. In front of her was the guard, brandishing a knife once again. For the bindings, Grace told herself. He wasn't going to cut her.

She did scream when he reached for her to cut the bindings at her ankles, and she did manage to kick him, getting in one good blow before he fell on top of her, pressing her down onto the cot. He backhanded her once, the blow stinging against her cheek. She was disoriented for a minute, her head spinning, but unfortunately she didn't pass out.

She roused to find him pulling at her clothes, lying heavily on top of her and grunting. Grace had waited too late for the mental games. She couldn't seem to find any kind of distance from the situation, any kind of barrier to bring down in her mind, and he was so heavy. She was suffocating. She couldn't budge him. She didn't think there was anything at all she could do.

She opened her mouth to scream again, in anger and frustration, no self-control left, and she must have opened her eyes again, too.

So she saw it all.

Or all there was to see through the blackness.

She saw the shape of a man taking form out of what she could swear was nothing but air. It was as if he fell from the sky, from the heavens.

One minute there was nothing, and the next, he was there.

He moved soundlessly, landing on his feet, almost on top of the cot she lay upon. He pulled the guard off of her in one swift, deadly motion, then lowered the guard soundlessly to the floor.

Grace stared, thinking she was honestly losing her mind. There was no other explanation. Unless she'd just been saved by a man who had fallen from the sky. Right after he'd finished conjuring up the hurricane she needed, Grace supposed.

Suddenly, there didn't seem to be enough oxygen in the room to suit her. The guard hadn't made a sound, and she wondered if he was dead.

Guardian angels didn't kill people, did they? And nobody literally dropped out of the sky.

She felt a hand touch her shoulder, cried out a little, the sound as measly as a whimper. She'd been reduced to this.

"Grace?" He turned her over gently and used a knife to free her hands, then moved to check her ankles, found they had already been freed.

Her angel swore. She puzzled over the incongruity of that. He'd saved her with stealth and speed, but in doing so had taken another's life. She was scared enough that she had no regrets about what he'd done. She wondered if he did, if he had a conscience. A soul. If he needed air to breathe and had blood running through his veins.

He ran his hands over her again, gentle, swift, impersonal hands, but she didn't want anyone touching her. She flinched as his hands moved over her rib cage near her breasts.

He swore again and stopped. "Grace, is anything broken? Does anything hurt too much for you to move?"

"Everything hurts," she said.

"Can you walk? Crawl? Could you run if you had to?"

"Crawl? Run?" She laughed a bit, near hysteria. "My hands are numb. My arms. My shoulders."

He started rubbing them, trying to work some blood back into her limbs, some feeling, work out some of the soreness. She gasped, because it hurt. Suddenly everything hurt.

"How long have you been tied up like this, Grace?" he said, his voice insistent, a bit impatient.

"I don't know," she said, angry now. Who the hell did he think he was? What kind of rescue was this going to be? Exhausted, she closed her eyes and pleaded with him, "Make me disappear."

"What?"

"I want to disappear, like you do. Into the darkness." Into nothingness. She thought it would feel good, to feel nothing. To be nothing.

"Ah, Grace," he said, swearing again, sounding as weary as she felt.

"Please? Make me disappear."

"I can't, sweetheart. But I can drag you out of here, if I have to."

She shook her head, shook off his strong, insistent hands. "You just appear out of thin air. I've seen you. Just now, it was like you fell out of the sky."

"It's the ventilation system, Grace. There's a vent and an air duct, right up there."

"What?" she said. Ventilation system?

"Those bastards. They drugged you again, didn't they?"

"I think so. Maybe with the food." Actually, she couldn't think at all. Nothing made sense. He'd come out of the ventilation system? Like a mere mortal?

He lifted her off the cot. She swayed unsteadily on her feet, and he hauled her up against him, holding her close in a grip like iron. She felt steely muscles, in his arms, his abdomen, his thighs. He had shoulders a mile wide, and possessed the kind of strength she'd only dreamed of, and for a moment, it was all hers. It was as if he'd infused a bit of his strength into her, by holding her so tightly. Or maybe he was simply trying to reassure her, to show her the might of the man fighting on her behalf. Either way, it worked. She found it immensely reassuring. She decided there wasn't anything in this world he couldn't do when he set his mind to it.

"I'm getting you out of here," he promised, just as he had the night before.

"If this is a dream," Grace said. "An illusion—"

He took a breath, his massive chest rising and falling. She felt every bit of the movement, through every pore of her body, the way she was clasped against him.

"Do I feel like an illusion?" he asked.

"No," she said, starting dangerously to believe in him once again.

"Then let's go. There's a vent about three feet above my head. I'm going to lift you up, but you're going to have to help me. Pull yourself up."

Up she went, into an inky blackness, a nothingness. No, she realized, just a dark, narrow tunnel.

"Go right," he said, pushing her ever higher.

Grace did, pushing with arms still half-numb, pushing until she was lying in the rectangular tunnel that reminded her of a coffin. She didn't like it one bit.

"Watch out. I have to get in there," he warned.

She made room by rolling onto her side, her back against the tunnel wall. He inched up beside her, until they were side by side, facing each other, the space curiously void of air and uncomfortably warm.

"I don't like it here," she complained, only then realizing how childish she sounded.

He smiled a bit. She could feel it. He was that close.

"Then let's get you out of here, Grace."

"How?" she whispered, putting her faith entirely in him.

"I was hoping you'd be able to crawl," he said soberly.

She gave it her best shot, but her muscles simply couldn't take her weight.

So, in the end, he maneuvered until he was lying on his back and drew her on top of him, as she could have sworn they'd lain that first night in her cell when he'd been trying to warm her.

She'd never understand how he did it, was still having trouble believing it was all real, but she lay on top of him, and he pushed with his feet and his arms and, inch by inch, got himself and her out of there.

Chapter 4

Grace woke to blackness once again. She thought perhaps she'd been blinded at first, it was so complete. But eventually, she calmed down, waited, and the faintest of shadows took shape. None that made any sense. But shapes, all the same. She wondered if she was doomed to live the rest of her life in the dark, if she'd ever see clearly again.

She found herself lying on very hard ground. What felt like a rock, actually. But there was something soft beneath her head. Someone had brought her a pillow, but left her to sleep on the rock? Alone in the dark?

It made no sense.

Her head hurt terribly. Her mouth was dry, her stomach sickeningly empty. She still felt as if she had cobwebs in her brain; it was still so hard to think.

Drugs, Grace remembered. She'd been drugged.

And she'd had the oddest dreams.

Of him.

Nightmares, too. Of being kidnapped?

Grace's heart started pounding. She felt each and every beat in her aching head, like a series of rhythmic blows.

Groaning, she closed her eyes.

That's when she became aware of the storm. It had been nothing but a dull, painful roar at first, but now she was able to break it down into distinct sounds. Rain was beating down somewhere. Not on her. She was perfectly dry. Warm, even. Blessedly warm.

On a rock?

No, she realized looking all around her, a cave. The faint shadows made sense now. It wasn't a room with curving walls and a rounded ceiling, but a cave.

Somewhere outside it was raining viciously, the wind positively howling. She shivered as a gust of it hit her in the face, and all around her she heard an odd crinkling sound. She flinched, and the crinkling erupted again.

Grace was wrapped in a noisy, crinkly thing.

She pinched a bit between her thumb and forefinger, rubbed back and forth. It was a blanket. A very, very thin, shiny, noisy blanket. Which, oddly enough, made sense. She'd seen them before. Well-equipped soldiers had them. The fabric was a space-age innovation. Very lightweight, very thin, very warm. Sometimes she'd been able to beg and borrow some for her patients.

Looking around, she saw what seemed to be a neat stack of supplies off to her left against one wall, a passage to her right that must lead to the outside, judging from the noise and the wind.

There was nothing else. No mystery man.

Her heart lurched once again. Had he been real? The question would not leave her alone. Was he someone who existed only inside her head, or a flesh-and-blood man?

The mind was a truly powerful thing, Grace knew. So were fear and stress, which could play tremendous tricks on the brain. So could drugs.

She had definitely been drugged and grabbed off the streets

of San Reino. She had vague memories of a dungeon. *A dungeon?* And a man.

That was it.

Was she even awake now? Or was this part of her illusion? Her nightmare?

Despite all her years of medical training, she could come up with no definitive test of whether or not she was awake, whether she was alone in a cave or delusional.

She was considering her next move when she realized she was not alone. Grace hadn't heard a thing. He'd crept up on her as silently as a ghost. Or an illusion.

At first, he was nothing but a big, spooky shadow coming at her out of the darkness with a wicked-looking submachine gun strapped across his chest. He peeled off the weapon, then seemed to shed something else, she feared his skin. Then she saw that it was merely rain gear, dripping-wet rain gear. She could smell the moisture on him.

Peeling off the poncho, he stood there dressed in what might be camouflage, and he either had enormous feet or he was wearing big, heavy boots. Probably that shadow at the side of his waist was a pistol. He seemed incredibly tall and broad and strong as he stood staring at her through the blasted near darkness.

"It's all right," he said, almost before her fears had a moment to take hold. "It's me."

Of course, she thought. It would be *him*. It was dark, after all. Safe for him to come out, and she was thoroughly confused. No need to worry she might make sense of him now or ever figure out who he was.

"Grace?" he whispered.

She made a vain attempt at wetting her painfully dry lips in hopes of being able to talk. He must be a mind reader. Because the next thing she knew, he knelt beside her, his big, strong hand supporting her head and neck. Cold, wonderfully wet water slid into her mouth and down her parched throat.

She was painfully grateful, wanted to gulp it all down. He wouldn't let her.

"Slowly. You'll make yourself sick."

Grace frowned. She knew that. Her stomach was rolling even now. But she was so thirsty, she didn't care.

He eased her back down, sat on the ground beside her. "So, you finally decided to wake up."

"How long did I sleep?" she whispered.

"Round the clock. It's almost midnight."

She took that in, considered. Had she been sleeping? Or unconscious?

"You scared me," he said softly.

He had an amazingly pleasant voice. Full and deep and moving over her senses in a way that had her feeling warm all over. And he was speaking English, she realized. A familiar American English with that hint of the South. The same voice he'd used to tell her she'd grown into a real beauty. Right before he'd kissed her a year and a half ago, a continent away, then disappeared.

It was the first time she'd ever heard him use the same accent twice, which made her wonder if this little part of him was real. Had he merely slipped up? Or was he finally going to stop playing games with her? Finally tell her who he was and what in the world he'd been doing with her all this time?

It was probably a foolish thing to be considering at the moment, given how little she knew about her own predicament. But that was the first thought that ran through her muddled head.

She forced herself to be practical, something that was normally second nature to her. "I was kidnapped?"

"Yes."

"In San Reino?"

"Yes."

"When?"

"Two and a half days ago," he said.

She'd lost two and a half days? Grace felt sick once again.

They could have done anything to her in two and a half days.

She remembered being shoved into the car, hitting her head as she went. Remembered the dirty cloth pressed against her nose and mouth, the bitter taste of the drug. She remembered her wrists and ankles being bound, checked automatically to make sure they still weren't. She found no tape, but sores left in its wake.

She remembered the guard…shoving her legs apart and climbing on top of her.

"Aah!" All the breath went rushing out of her body.

"It's all right," her mystery man soothed. His hand pressed against her shoulder, his thumb making little circles on the upper part of her arm in a soothing yet impersonal touch. "They don't have you anymore."

"You got me out?"

"Yes."

So it hadn't been a dream after all. At least not all of it.

Then she remembered something else.

"And the guard? You killed him?"

"Yes."

"You…" *Couldn't have done anything less drastic?*

"It was the only way to get you out of there," he said, as if that was the only thing that mattered to him.

He's rescued her once again, and she still didn't know who he was, still wasn't convinced this was real and not a dream. God, if this wasn't real…if she was still back in that cell in the dungeon…

"Grace?"

"Am I ever going to see your face?" she asked.

"Does it matter so much? It's just a face. I told you, I'm just a man."

"Are you?"

"What else would I be?"

"Oh, I don't know. My friend Jane calls you the caped crusader."

He laughed. Beautifully. She thought she remembered that laugh. She wanted it to be the same one. It would mean he was real.

"I must be out of it," she whispered.

"Why do you say that?"

"How am I ever going to know if this is real? If you are?"

"I kissed you, Grace. In the courtyard of the church. I held you in my arms. You felt that. Didn't that seem real?"

"No," she said. It felt better than any reality she'd ever known. Much better than any romantic encounter she'd ever had, despite the simplicity of it—merely a kiss—and despite its briefness. In the past year and a half, she'd wasted so much time dreaming of him and nothing but a kiss.

"It didn't?" He seemed indignant at the thought.

"It doesn't matter," she lied. Ridiculous as it was, it mattered to her. But it wasn't the point. Not at the moment. The point was the panic she couldn't quite shake, the unreality of the situation, her utter confusion. "I just...I don't understand you at all. Nothing about you. I never have. I can't even be sure that you're here, that you're real, and because of that, I'm wondering if I'm losing my mind right now. Because I can't make sense of any of this."

"Shh," he soothed. His hand went to the side of her face, her neck. His thumb brushed across her lips. "It's all right."

"No. It's not. And I won't be quiet," she protested. "You don't understand. You can't have any idea how I feel right now. How confused you make me."

"I'm sorry, Grace."

"I could be dreaming this whole thing. I could still be back in that cell. Did they have me in a cell? In a dungeon?"

"You're not far off. The basement level of a stone fortress."

"Dammit," she whispered. It had been real. The cell. Probably everything that happened there.

"Hey, I got you out of there, Grace. A day ago. You've

been sleeping ever since. You've been right here with me, and I would never do anything to hurt you.''

"Who are you?" she cried.

"An American."

At last. She actually knew his nationality. "That narrows things down considerably."

He laughed again. Briefly. Irritatingly.

"It's not funny," she cried, the fear coming through loud and clear in her voice.

"I'm sorry. I've never been drugged before, but I have been hit on the head. I should have remembered how disorienting it can be. I'm an American, Grace, and I'm going to take care of you. I promise you that."

"And you're real? All of this is real?"

He frowned, leaned closer. A sliver of light flared between them and then it was shining in her eyes as he stared down at her.

She winced. The light hurt. And she couldn't help but be surprised. He had a light. The man who never showed up except in the blackest part of the night had a tiny flashlight.

She was utterly intrigued, fascinated with him yet again, and he was obviously wondering how hard she'd been hit and how much of the drug was still in her system. Which she'd think would be her main concern, as well. But it wasn't. Hers was him.

He leaned back, the light extinguished. She had the childish urge to steal it and shine it in his face. Finally, she'd be able to see something of him, and maybe she'd feel better somehow. She could put a face to her mysterious, nameless American stranger.

"Your pupils are a bit sluggish," he said.

Grace was not particularly surprised, given the depths of her confusion and the time she'd lost, the utter fascination she had at a time like this with the idea of actually seeing him.

She was irked with him, as well. "Not that you've given me cause to be confused," she complained.

He frowned yet again. She could feel it through the darkness. He was looking down at her and frowning.

"I want to sit up," she said.

"I don't think that's a good idea."

"I'm the doctor here. I want to sit up." She wanted to see the world from an upright position, was hoping so many things would fall into place when she did.

He gave an exasperated sigh, but he helped her. She was cradled against that big, powerful body of his for a moment, his arms tight around her back, as he helped her slide into a semisitting position and pushed something soft and bulky behind her, for her to lean on.

"Don't fall over and crack your head again," he ordered.

Grace wasn't about to admit it was a distinct possibility. The world hadn't quite righted itself. Her surroundings were still spinning.

"Okay?" he said.

She frowned, wishing it was. Truth was, she was still spooked, rattled, downright scared. It wasn't going away. "No."

"Oh, hell. Here." He handed her the flashlight. She was so stunned, she didn't do anything at first. Then he handed her something else. Something slick and smooth and heavy that she grasped easily within her right hand.

"Careful," he said, when she went to hold it up to her face to see.

He aimed the light at it. At a knife. Not the kind she used. A big one with a mean-looking blade. Before she could say anything else, do anything else, a tanned, muscular forearm was shoved toward her, highlighted within the narrow stream of light.

"Go ahead. Cut me."

"What?"

"You want to know if I'm real?" he said. "Cut me. I'll bleed."

"I...no," she stammered. She couldn't just sink a knife into his flesh. She wasn't that crazy, was she? So much so that she needed to cut a man just to prove he would do what any human being would in that case. He'd bleed. Because he was a human. Not an illusion. Not an angel of any kind. Just a man.

"Go ahead," he urged. "My blood's as red as yours."

"It's not necessary."

"I think it is, sweetheart." He took the knife from her and before she could stop him, slid it across his skin.

Grace gasped.

He didn't so much as flinch. Not a millimeter. But he did bleed.

"Dammit," she protested. "I told you it wasn't necessary."

She tugged at the long shirt she was wearing until she had the ends in her hand and quickly pressed the cloth over the small cut.

"I can't believe you did that," she said.

"You needed to see it," he said, as if that meant everything. She needed; he provided.

Grace remembered being in her cell with him, the second time, when she'd begged him to simply make her disappear. He'd said he couldn't. But that he'd die for her. That he'd save her or die trying.

She could fathom that. A man willing to die for her? Bleed for her?

She stared up at him, feeling now the warmth of his skin beneath her palm.

"You didn't have to do that," she said again of the cut. She didn't want him hurt. Not for her.

He had the nerve to laugh. "Grace, it's nothing."

But it wasn't. She knew that. He'd cut himself, just to prove a point to her.

"I don't want you hurt," she said, because she didn't. She didn't know who he was or why he was here, why he was watching over her. But she didn't want him hurt.

"Sweetheart, I've got more scars on my body than you could count—"

"I don't want you hurt," she insisted.

"Okay," he said gently. "If that's what you want, I'll do my best, Grace. I want to keep you happy."

His hand closed gently over hers, pulling it and her shirt away from him. Briefly, matter-of-factly, he smoothed the shirt back into place. His big, warm hands were gone almost as quickly as they'd come. She was vaguely aware of the fact that she wasn't wearing anything else at all and that his hand—accidentally, it seemed—grazed the sensitive skin of her belly. Aware too that they both gave a small start at the contact.

His arm, absolutely impersonal, came around her back, and he eased her down until she was lying flat, something soft against the back of her head and neck again.

It was ridiculously good just to lie back down. She had a million more questions, but she was so tired.

He was arguing with her about something, she realized vaguely. He was an incredibly annoying man.

Eating. That was it. He wanted her to stay awake and eat.

She couldn't. She was exhausted. She couldn't even lift the flashlight still clutched in her hand so she could finally see his face.

She woke to that infernal blackness. That cursed, stubborn, maddening blackness, and was disoriented, but for merely a few seconds. If she was in a cave with that man—a man who'd bleed for her and maybe even die for her—and she'd really been kidnapped, her head was finally clearing.

She shifted a bit on the rock-hard ground. The blanket rustled, and her head protested yet again. She remembered the blanket well. How could anything so slight make such a racket?

The wind was still blowing. It was still raining like the devil outside. It was damp in the cave, and there were gusts of air and an unnerving, howling sound. Probably the wind rushing past the mouth of the cave.

She thought about trying to walk or even crawl to the entrance. If only she could see. Anything but this awful darkness. But as she shifted on the hard floor of the cave, she realized why she was so wonderfully warm. He was asleep behind her.

She remembered thinking, that first night after she'd been taken, that someone had lit a furnace and aimed it directly at her face. Not a furnace, it seemed. Him. He generated heat like no man she'd ever met before.

His arm, big and muscular and hard, was looped around her waist in a hold that wasn't tight but absolutely unrelenting, and heat spread from that point, too. He was lying on his side, right up against her, holding her, and she was on her back, tucked against his side.

It was not at all an unpleasant way to sleep.

She thought about the fact that she still had no idea who he was, except that he was an American and that he'd rescued her once again. She thought about the fact that she was alone with him, somewhere in the darkness yet again, but closer to him than ever before.

She went to turn onto her side, to see if she could make out anything of his features, but he wouldn't let her. His arm tightened around her. It cupped her rib cage, and he turned her himself. Until she was on her side, too, facing away from him, their bodies pressed even more tightly together.

She let the weight of her body sink back against his, from the top of her head to the tip of her toes. Now that she thought about it, her feet were freezing. She found a gap between his ankles and burrowed between his calves with one foot, then the other.

He swore softly. "How can anyone possibly be that cold?"

"Sorry."

He laughed a bit but let her feet stay where they were. "Are you okay?"

"Yes," she said, realizing that despite everything, she was.

"Your head?"

"Not as muddled."

"Good. Try to sleep a little longer. It's still early."

His head was pressed against the side of hers, which was resting on one of his arms. His breath, steamy hot, rushed past her ear, causing her to shiver once again. In answer, he pulled her even closer. She was fascinated by how big he was. How tall, how wide, how hard his entire body was. Vaguely, she remembered sleeping on top of him that night in her cold cell. He'd been not much more than an impression of sheer power and heat, and she'd thought of nothing but being warm and safe.

But her brain wasn't so muddled now. She was very much aware of the fact that he was a man. A big, strong, tough man. Gentle, when he chose to be. Fast and deadly when he did not.

She had a quick flash of memory of the guard, the knife, and shivered once again.

"You can't possibly still be cold," he murmured. "And I know I said I'd do anything for you, Grace, but right now, the only other thing I could do to warm you up is to strip down to my skin, strip you, too, and wrap that blanket around both of us. It would be like an oven, but…"

But?

She shifted against him once more, not looking for warmth, just trying to get a bit closer. Just for the sake of being close and the reassurance that came from it. And maybe so she could feel those delicious muscles in his powerful chest, his rock-hard abs, his…

"Oh," she said.

They were caught together like two spoons in a drawer. Against the fleshy curve of her derriere was something very hard, as well. Instinct, shameless, thoughtless instinct, had her pressing even closer.

He swore softy in the darkness.

She didn't shiver this time. It was more like a minor earthquake that shook nothing but her own body.

He still held her firmly, but he eased his lower body away from hers.

"Sorry," he said. "I can't quite help that. Not..."

Not when a woman was wrapped around his body. "I understand."

She went to move away from him, but the arm at her waist didn't give an inch.

"You can stay. I can't control the reaction, but I don't have to do anything about it. I'm not going to hurt you, Grace."

"I know," she said.

"The guard?" he asked. "He scared you, but that was it, right?"

"Yes."

"You're sure?"

"Yes. You got there in time." One more time, she realized.

"And you're not afraid of me? You're not afraid to be here with me like this?"

"No."

"You're still shivering," he said.

"I'm not cold," she admitted, thinking that told him all he needed to know. He was thoroughly, she would guess painfully, aroused, and she was trembling in his big, strong arms.

Despite everything she'd been through and how tired, how weak she was, she couldn't help but react to the overwhelming feel of his body pressed so tightly to hers. She felt boneless and tingly and hot all over at the moment. She didn't want to budge, unless it was to get closer.

"Then sleep here," he said, accepting everything and seemingly dismissing it, as well.

They weren't going to do anything tonight. Except…what? Snuggle? That was much too tame a word for it.

It made Grace a little dizzy, and not because of anything wrong with her head. It made her think of a dozen, thoroughly shameless possibilities of things they might do on another night, in the cool, deep darkness, before they were through.

She eased against him once more. He was still impressively aroused.

"Sorry," she said. "I'm sure that's…uncomfortable."

His mouth was practically pressed against her neck and she definitely felt a grin.

"Grace," he said, in that beautifully deep, slow, heated voice of his. "I've fallen asleep more nights than I can remember wishing I had you right here in my arms. Just like this. It's not exactly a hardship—"

He broke off abruptly, seeming to realize at the same moment she did, just what he'd said. She refrained from making any jokes at all, though she wondered, if he felt that way, why hadn't he come to her? He seemed to always know where she was, after all. She doubted she would have resisted.

"I still don't—"

"Go to sleep, Grace," he murmured.

"But—"

"Sleep. For now. I'm not going to disappear this time. Not anytime soon, at least."

"Promise?"

He kissed her softly, his warm mouth against the side of her neck. She shuddered against him. It felt so good.

"I promise," he said.

And she realized too late what a leap of faith she'd taken.

She never asked anyone to promise her anything, and yet in the space of two and a half days, he'd promised her the world, and she'd put her faith wholly in him.

She was too tired to even think of the fact that there was a reason she never asked for promises, not from anyone. She simply let herself drift off in his arms.

Chapter 5

It was merely gloomy when Grace woke the next time. She was immensely grateful for the grayish half light. Her gaze hurried from one spot to the next, confirming what she believed she'd seen the night before.

A cave. A small stack of supplies that looked to be military-issue, some of it quite sophisticated. She'd been up close and personal with soldiers from all over the world. She knew.

Her mystery man was a soldier. She believed he must be, but she hadn't known for sure. Not until right now.

Grace sat up gingerly. Her head didn't really hurt anymore. The blanket was no longer loud enough to annoy her, but the wind and the rain were. Would it ever stop howling and pounding that way?

She felt a bit dizzy, a bit weak. No surprise, given how little she'd eaten or drunk. Her stomach was empty and protesting that fact. Her mouth was dry. But her brain seemed to be working just fine for a change. Apparently, whatever drugs her captors had given her hadn't fried her brain, as she'd feared.

She was alive, awake, thinking clearly. Hungry, thirsty. *Alone.*

The last part bothered her a great deal.

She searched the parts of the cave she could see. No mystery man.

But he'd promised, she remembered. He wasn't going to disappear this time. Grace had a thing about promises. She didn't want any. Normally, she would never have asked. She wouldn't have let herself trust him or anyone else to keep those promises. Life had taught her that; she'd learned her lesson well.

So, she hadn't been thinking clearly the night before or back there in the cell in the dungeon. Otherwise, she would never have asked him for any kind of reassurances. And she shouldn't be this upset or uneasy now because he wasn't here.

She certainly didn't need to panic, either. She'd been on her own, more or less, since she was eleven, had been in almost every major natural disaster and war in the last ten years. She knew how to take care of herself. Normally, she did it very, very well.

She set out to do just that. First, she found the canteen he'd left by her side, and that's when she found his note—unsigned, of course—wrapped around the canteen. Obviously, he knew she'd wake up thirsty and reach for this.

He was out patrolling the perimeter and warned her not to leave the cave without him, that it was dangerous, booby-trapped, he wrote. Grace frowned and looked around the cave. They had a perimeter? And booby traps?

Which meant, if he didn't make it back, she was stuck here forever?

She pushed her fears aside and drank from the canteen, slowly so she wouldn't be sick. She pushed her blanket down and saw that she was in a T-shirt. A drab, olive-green one that was long enough to almost be a dress. And she wasn't wearing anything else.

Which meant he'd undressed her. Completely.

Because of the rain? Had they traveled for what seemed like forever in the rain? She'd been so out of it, hardly aware of anything. Except that they hadn't stopped moving and she'd thought her head was going to fall off—wished it would—and the rain had been incessant, moving horizontally, it seemed. Eventually she'd been soaked through and through. That's how she'd gotten so cold.

It seemed odd. They were in the tropics, after all. But anyone who was wet enough, long enough, especially in a strong wind, turned cold. And he'd done the right thing to strip her.

As a doctor, she knew just how impersonal a thing it could be, taking off someone's clothes, assessing his or her condition. Still, this was a man who'd had her trembling early this morning, just by pressing his hot, heavy, hard body to hers.

Grace felt her cheeks go hot. What an odd time to be attracted to a man. She hadn't been near one in any kind of romantic way in…well, since the last time she saw him. She was a woman devoted to her work. It kept her on the road and in desolate areas for long stretches of time and left little time for things like men. Which had always suited her just fine.

Oh, she had nothing against men. She just didn't find them at all necessary to her day-to-day existence. Which was why her reaction to him left her unsettled. Especially that she was dwelling on her physical reaction to him when they were obviously in real trouble here.

She didn't even know where they were, but they must still be in danger. Why else would they be hiding out in a cave with him prowling the perimeter and—

Grace froze, a sickening kind of fear invaded her already-protesting stomach.

Someone was here once again. She was actually afraid to look up for a moment, afraid of what she might see. Odd, because until this happened, she couldn't remember the last time she'd been truly afraid. She'd faced so many things with nerves of steel, and they seemed to have totally deserted her now.

"Grace," he said. "It's all right. It's me."

It was the voice she remembered. The man. Her savior. Flesh and blood, but still her savior.

Grace lifted her head and found him standing in the tunnel that must lead to the outside world. Through thoroughly insufficient light, she could see him more clearly than ever before, and he was every bit as big and imposing as she'd always sensed he was.

At the moment, he was covered in a military-style rain poncho. A big, square piece of dull green plastic that hung from his shoulders, a hood shielding his head and much of his face. The German-made submachine gun she vaguely remembered seeing was strapped across his chest, and he was dripping wet.

He slipped the weapon over his head and placed it by his side, stripped off the rain poncho, too, and then she saw that he was armed to the teeth, like a man in the middle of a war going on patrol. He had a pistol, a Sig Sauer, she thought, strapped to his right side, at least two knives, some kind of radio, fancy binoculars and a lot of ammunition.

Grace had seen her share of big, tough guys. She'd met a lot of cocky soldiers in her day, and it usually took much more than a well-toned set of muscles and an attitude to impress her.

But this man… She swallowed hard and her throat was parched once again. He looked every inch the warrior.

She studied his face greedily, thinking it seemed impossible that after so many years, she was finally seeing him. Not in the bright light of day, but more clearly than ever before.

He had thick black hair with just a hint of what she found a very attractive gray sprinkled sparsely throughout. He wore it short. Not precision, military short, but in a thoroughly no-nonsense way. His eyes were just as dark, his face not without the signs of age, but he wore them all well, too. She guessed he was in his early forties, though built like a man ten or fifteen years younger. His skin was what she thought must be a permanent coppery color, from long exposure to the sun, and his mouth… Well, she had no business concentrating on that wide, full, sensuous-looking mouth. Or thinking about how it had felt on hers, either.

Truth was, she was blown away by the reality of him. Utterly captivated and fascinated and a bit dizzy, as well.

She sensed a raw power inside of him, something that might explode at any moment, and it had nothing to do with the weapons he carried. It came from him, that sense of strength and speed and determination that made him so dangerous, made her feel so safe.

She'd always believed he could do anything, even before she had a clear look at him, and now she knew she was right.

"You remember me, don't you?" he said, without a touch of amusement. "Last night? The things we talked about? I'm not going to hurt you, Grace. You're safe with me."

Grace realized she'd been gaping at him with her mouth hanging open and promptly closed it. Opening it only long enough to offer a hoarse "Yes."

He grinned at her.

"How do you move without making any noise?"

"Years of practice." He unhooked his belt and shed most of his paraphernalia, then came and sat on the floor beside her, his big hand going to her forehead. "How's your head?"

"Not bad. Not at all."

"Good." He stared into her eyes. "Pupils look good. No more woozy feeling?"

"I'm hungry. A little weak. But that's to be expected."

"We can take care of that," he said, going for his stack of supplies behind her.

She propped herself up against the back wall of the cave,

the blanket wrapped around her from the waist down, and sipped slowly from his canteen while he pulled an MRE out of one of his packs and heated it up in one of those little ovenlike cardboard sleeves. She wrinkled her nose just a bit when he tore open the so-called meal and she took it from him with only a hint of distaste.

"Hey, they're a lot better than they used to be," he claimed.

Grace wasn't picky about her food. She couldn't afford to be, given the way she lived. Still, she liked it to be real.

She bit into something that tasted like rice and kept eating because she knew rice should sit easily on her poor stomach. It was warm, and it had some flavor. She tasted something that was probably supposed to be a bit of shrimp, which struck her as ridiculous. Shrimp and rice-flavored…what? She didn't even want to think about it, and either she was starving or it was truly pretty good.

He handed her the canteen and she sipped between bites, until the food took the edge off the shakes she had. She found she could only eat about half of it and decided not to push it.

"Done?" he asked, then took what was left and finished it himself. "We may be here for a while. We can't afford to waste anything."

Oh. She looked around her at the cave. And him. And wondered just what *a while* meant. But she decided the most logical place to start was by asking, "Where are we?"

"Milero's compound. On a private island in the Caribbean Sea, about forty miles off the coast of Central America. His fortress, as you called it, is on the other side of the island, seven and a half miles by foot from here."

"Oh." Seven and a half miles didn't sound like a reassuring distance to her. "Milero—he controls the whole island?"

Her mystery man nodded.

"Does that mean we can't get off?"

"I'll get you out of here, Grace. Just not anytime soon."

She nodded, thinking of the incessant wind and rain. "Because of the storm?"

"It's a Category 3 hurricane at the moment," he explained.

"Oh." She remembered now. The old woman who'd brought her food had told her a hurricane was coming. She'd thought the man who stood before her had somehow arranged it, just for her. "You can't handle a hurricane?"

His gaze narrowed on hers. She thought he might check her pupils again, especially when she started to laugh.

"I'm sane. I swear," she claimed, not at all convinced that she was. A man who commanded the elements? She'd actually wondered about that. "I was just thinking of the last time I saw you. In Bosnia. You told me to go find a nice, simple natural disaster, and I happened upon a string of them."

"And you thought I waved my hand and conjured up the earthquake in Russia, the floods in Nepal and the mud slides in San Reino?"

Grace took a breath as he rattled off exactly where she'd been in the last year and a half. Which was a whole other subject that fascinated her as well.

"I entertained the thought. Briefly," she admitted. "I've imagined just about everything in the world where you're concerned."

Which was more than she cared to tell him when he wouldn't tell her anything. But he claimed they'd be here for a while, and he'd promised he wasn't going to disappear without a word this time. There would be time, at last, for all the questions she had about him. Whether or not he'd answer, she'd at least get to ask. For now, she really needed to know what kind of predicament they were in.

"So you can't actually snap your fingers and turn off the hurricane," she said wryly.

"Not even for you, Grace. I told you. I'm just a man."

She reached for his hand and turned it over, exposing the underside of his forearm, and there was the thin line, the wound she was looking for. The one from last night, when he'd cut himself just to prove a point to her, to settle her rattled nerves and maybe to keep her from getting hysterical. She'd never been hysterical in her life, but she must have been rattled enough to worry him greatly.

"Need another demonstration?" he asked.

"No." The scar was enough. She let go of his hand, and he withdrew it. "And you should cover the cut."

"I did. Must have lost it in the rain this afternoon."

"It's afternoon?"

"Almost six."

Which meant she'd slept for hours yet again.

"Have you been getting any sleep at all for the past month, Grace? Are you that exhausted?"

"Maybe," she admitted. They'd been particularly short-handed in San Reino. She'd pushed herself to the limit, maybe beyond that.

She wondered if he was going to scold her for that, as Jane might. But he didn't. She had a feeling he knew all about pushing one's self to the limit, that it was something he'd done all his life.

"So," she said, "you didn't conjure up the hurricane and you can't make it go away. We're going to wait it out?"

He nodded. "No choice. Our only way off this island is by boat or aircraft, and nothing's going up in this."

Okay. They were stuck here. "How long?"

"You remember the storm that caused the mud slides? The one that came right up to the edge of the coastline and sat there for days?"

She nodded. Hurricanes brought with them tremendous amounts of rain. But they usually had some forward motion to them. The rains were heaviest for the period of the time the innermost portions of the storm passed through. Which could still be enough rainfall to cause widespread flooding.

The hurricane this summer that struck San Reino and much of Central America had stalled off the coast, trapped by an unusual pattern of prevailing winds. It just sat there and dumped torrents of rain on a seventy-mile stretch of the coast, weakening areas to the point where the ground started moving, mud flowing much like water normally did. It had wiped entire villages off the map and created one of the most devastating natural disasters Grace had ever had the misfortune to see.

"We've got another hurricane doing the same thing," he said. "It's stalled practically on top of us."

"For how long?"

"The outer bands of the storm reached the island not long after you and I did, and then it lost nearly every bit of its forward motion. The eye of the storm still isn't close enough to put us under hurricane-force winds."

She was stunned. And a bit worried. "That howling outside *isn't* hurricane-force winds?"

"Not quite," he said, amazingly calm.

Grace had never been in the midst of a hurricane, but she'd seen the aftermath. Trees thrown around at will, landing in piles this way and that like tiny spears of wood in the children's game pickup sticks. Houses simply gone or reduced to rubble. Flooding. Cars thrown around. People, too.

"Hey," he said with a whisper of a smile. "We'll deal with it. Whatever happens."

She managed to smile back. "You're prepared for anything?"

"Of course," he said, as if she'd insulted him by even insinuating that he might not be. "We knew it was coming when we put the mission together."

"We?" She looked around again. "We're not alone."

"There are two other operatives on the island—"

"Operatives?"

"Yes."

"Soldiers?"

"Not exactly."

She frowned. Game time wasn't over. Even now, he wasn't going to tell her anything about himself. "But—"

"Two operatives. One other hostage. An American businessman."

That was interesting. As far as she knew, the American military didn't involve its soldiers in the rescue of businessmen who found themselves taken hostage in Central America or anywhere else. At least, it didn't acknowledge involving its military in such operations.

"Milero had the two of you in separate areas of the compound," he continued. "We split up to get you out, had supplies stashed in a second hiding place on the island, and the other team found it easier to get to the second spot than here. They'll stay there until the weather clears."

"Oh." So they were alone. "How long do you think it will be?"

He shrugged easily, as if it didn't matter at all. "I wouldn't have thought the storm would just sit on top of us for this long, but it has. The forecasters are stumped."

"You've been hearing weather reports? Here?"

He nodded.

She was developing serious envy of his equipment. Anything that could receive a signal through a hurricane…

"We'll just have to wait it out," he said.

She nodded and thought about days alone with him in a cave. *Nights*. With a man who wouldn't even tell her who he was.

"You don't have somewhere you need to be, do you?" he asked.

"Actually, I do." Another hurricane meant more flooding, more mud slides, more sick and dying people.

"Someone else is going to have to take care of this one, Grace."

"It's my job." One in which she took great pride. One for which she felt a great responsibility.

"It's someone else's turn to deal with it."

"I think that would be my decision," she countered.

"No," he insisted, a hint of steel in his voice and an amazingly irritating sense that he somehow had the right to tell her what to do. "Once I get you out of here, there's no way I'm letting you back in San Reino."

"You've got to be kidding."

"I mean it. You're not going back. Not after that bastard snatched you that way. Good God, he could have done anything to you. One of his goons nearly did."

Grace glared at him. "Who in the world are you to even imagine you can tell me what to do?"

"It's time someone did," he said, at his most maddeningly arrogant. At least, she hoped this was his worst.

Grace laughed at him. She couldn't help it. "I don't even know you. I don't have any idea who you are. I don't even know your name. Let's start with that. If you think you're going to dictate terms to me, I have some of my own. Who are you?"

He remained stubbornly silent.

"What? You could tell me, but you'd have to kill me?" she said flippantly.

"Not after I've worked this hard to keep you alive. Although, at the moment, the idea is tempting. I wonder sometimes if you have a bit of common sense."

"And I suppose you never put yourself into dangerous situations?" She laughed. "You've been in the same places I have for the last ten years, in case you've forgotten. But then, that would be your job, I suppose. You're just doing your job?"

He glared right back at her.

"And exactly what," she asked, "would make it acceptable for you to stick your neck on the line, but unacceptable for me to do the same thing?"

"I take carefully calculated risks. You see people shooting at one another, and you can't wait to get there."

"Funny thing about that—people who shoot at one another happen to need doctors, and I am one."

"You're reckless, Grace. You know it."

"I am not." Fearless, according to her friends. She wasn't sure what she truly was, didn't even want to think about it.

He just stared, daring her to lie to him again.

"Oh, and you're not reckless yourself?" she cried. "Just how is it that you think we're different?"

"I give a damn about whether or not I stay alive," he roared. "I'm not sure you do."

Grace wouldn't say anything to that. She couldn't.

That would be the other possibility, the one she didn't want to consider. Reckless, fearless, or someone who really didn't give a damn whether she was alive?

She had to take a second, because her chest hurt. She felt like someone had slammed a weight down upon it. "I..."

"You're really not going to try to deny it, are you?"

Grace stared at him, thinking again of the all-knowing, all-seeing, superhuman being she'd once thought he was. He couldn't possibly know, she told herself. The whole conversation was ridiculous. He couldn't know what went on inside her head. Especially when she fought so hard not to acknowledge it, even to herself.

But he always knew where she was. He always knew when she was in trouble. How could he possibly know?

"Who are you?" she cried.

"I told you. I'm just a man. An American..."

"Right. A man. An American. Not exactly a soldier..." she said, helping him along. "Then what? What do you do? Who do you work for?"

"I'm here...with some friends. Who work for an agency of the U.S. government. I could tell you the name, but it wouldn't mean anything to you."

"You're telling me they're spies?"

"It's a counterterrorism unit. Top secret."

"And these people happen to be your friends, and you're...what? Coming along for the ride?"

"They'd already been given the job of getting the American businessman I mentioned out of here. They knew the area. They had a mission planned, were ready to go. And then Milero took you. I..."

"What? Said you'd just come with them? Grab me at the same time?"

"Something like that."

Of course. He'd just invite himself along on a top-secret mission by a top-secret, nameless agency, and they'd just say yes?

She let that one alone. What was the point? Asked instead, "Why?"

"Because I didn't want that bastard to kill you."

"Why? What am I to you?"

"Someone who irritates me half to death," he roared. "Unfortunately, I'm bound and determined to keep you alive, although I wonder if I'm up to the job, at times. Why do you make it so hard on me, Grace?"

"Why do you even try?" she cried. "What could I possibly matter to you?"

"You do. You matter a great deal to me."

"Why? You keep telling me you're just a man. Well, I'm just a woman. A doctor. That's it. There are tons of women doctors in this world."

"Not like you," he claimed.

"There are," she insisted. "There are hundreds of doctors in the relief organization I work for. If you were a soldier all these years, you had to have come across dozens of them. You can't tell me you watch over them, just like you watch over me."

"No, I don't."

"So why me?"

"I happen to think you need looking after. That you deserve it."

"Why? I'm just one person. A very ordinary person. There's nothing extraordinary about me at all."

"Of course there is," he said.

The quiet seriousness of his tone, that bit of—what? Admiration? For her? It stopped her cold.

Grace thought perhaps she understood part of this now. Although it simply couldn't be. She'd successfully hidden her identity for years. He couldn't know. Could he?

But he said he had friends in some super-secret American spy agency. Friends he could just call and invite himself onto their mission. What kind of man had friends like that?

A man who could find out things? Things he had no business knowing?

Grace backed away from him. She had a wall inside of herself, a door she'd always been able to close at will. It slammed shut right then.

She didn't really need to know anything about him. Not if it was going to lead to this. To him wanting to know all abut her, or maybe telling her what he thought he already knew about her.

"Okay," she said. "You can watch out for me. For whatever reasons you like. And you can keep all the secrets you want."

"What?"

She frowned and looked around at the cave, considering her current state. She was so upset she was shaking. She was also tired and cold and filthy, and maybe she could do something about those things and ignore the rest of it. Ignore the things he made her think about, the things he made her feel.

She looked up to find him staring at her and quickly looked away. "I don't suppose you have a bar of soap I could use?"

"What?" he roared.

"And something I can clean my teeth with?" That would be heavenly, she decided, determined to change the subject, to end this conversation about her and whatever he thought he knew. She didn't want to talk about it. He couldn't make her.

"You've got to be kidding me," he said, obviously intent on still trying.

"No."

He stared at her, as if he might look right through her. Was that how he knew? Could he look right inside of her? See all her secrets?

"Please." She closed her eyes, so tired. "I just want to clean up. I think I might feel like a seminormal person if I could just clean up."

He kept right on staring. She feared he was going to press the point. But he finally gave in, turned his back and went to search through his supplies.

She could finally breathe freely again. Her heart was finally slowing to a normal rhythm.

Let him keep his secrets, she decided. And she'd keep hers.

Chapter 6

He directed her to the makeshift bathroom he'd set up in one of the deeper passages of the cave, gave her some water and things to wash with, another of his T-shirts and a pair of his boxer shorts, the best he was able to do for clothes for her on such short notice.

He'd been too busy convincing his brother-in-law to let him come with the team, so he could get Grace. Too busy arguing that it didn't matter if he wasn't part of their organization and he hadn't been in on the lengthy background preparation they'd already undergone. Or that the plan they'd devised had nothing in it about rescuing a woman snatched mere hours ago. And what was a little thing like a hurricane heading their way, when Grace was in the clutches of a devious bastard like Milero?

He'd talked his way around all of those things, and he was here. He'd gotten her away from Milero, and she would be okay. *This time.* Now, if he could talk some sense into her…

Oh, hell. That was the problem. He couldn't.

Which meant he'd be back right here with her before long,

either getting her out of some jam or trying to make her leave another hot spot before it erupted. He'd been doing it for ten years now, ever since she headed off on her first mission with the IRC's medical corps, when she was just a med student. He worried it was never going to stop, that she wasn't.

God, when he'd gotten the message that morning that Milero had her...

It was the closest he'd come in years to losing control.

He'd always been so careful with her. As careful as he could be and still keep some distance between them. While she'd been so damned reckless her whole life.

Well, obviously he hadn't been careful enough. He'd been lulled into a false sense of security, thinking she was contending with nothing but a mud slide, and he knew Grace. She could handle that easily. Disaster was her forte.

As long as nobody was shooting at her and there were no bombs going off around her, he tended to back off. Which was obviously a mistake.

God, if that man had killed her...

As it was, the guard had hurt her, nearly raped her. His killing the guard had shocked her, but anything short of that would have risked his chances of getting Grace out undetected, and he would never do anything to put her at even greater risk.

And now, here he was, trying to save her and trying not to touch her, to kiss her, and tempted beyond belief. Just like he'd been tempted that night in the bombed-out church when she just couldn't seem to let him go, and he couldn't bring himself to walk away one more time without saying more than a few words to her.

She'd had the funniest ideas about him. She and her friends. She was so curious, so alive, so interesting. So beautiful.

He hadn't lied. He lay awake more nights than he cared to remember thinking about her, wishing he had her in his arms. Ever since he'd been foolish enough to give in to the impulsive desire to kiss her in the courtyard of the church.

All this, he thought. Over a kiss.

Over a woman he could simply never have.

He'd told himself that for so long. It was pointless to ever get this close. To give in to his fascination and admiration for the beautiful, stubborn, incredibly generous and talented woman she was.

He was closer to her now than he'd been in so many years, stuck here with her, the elements conspiring against him.

Dammit, he'd gone beyond just wanting to keep her safe. He'd like it a lot if she was happy, and he feared she wasn't. Content with her work, committed, busy, but happy? He'd never allowed himself to linger close enough to see or to ask.

But he suspected he'd gotten the answer from the look in her eyes when he'd told her the difference between the two of them was the fact that he cared whether or not he stayed alive, and he feared she did not.

"Ah, Grace."

There it was. He'd finally asked, and as far as he was concerned her answer was loud and clear. And he had to find a way to help her deal with it. There certainly didn't seem to be anyone else around to do it for her.

How was he going to do that? To fix this, when it was every bit as bad as he feared?

She complained that he wouldn't even tell her who he was.

As near as he could tell, she was a woman who'd lied to the whole world about who *she* was for all of her adult life.

Grace felt halfway human again, once she'd cleaned up a bit. She was used to roughing it, so the conditions didn't bother her. They had food that was edible, water and adequate shelter. Nothing to complain about there.

The only real problem was him. He left her feeling so edgy, so unsettled. It was the energy inside of him, that feeling that with him, things could simply explode at any mo-

ment. Grace placed a great value on control. Or at least, controlled chaos. She prided herself on staying cool under
pressure, on being the one people turned to for direction
when all hell was breaking loose around them. She knew all
about disasters.

She just didn't know much about men, and he seemed like
a particularly dangerous one. So she approached him with
great caution, as she might walk up to the bars of a tiger's
cage. She would treat him like that, she decided. She'd been
to Africa. She'd seen tigers on the prowl. She'd try hard not
to do anything to catch his attention, to interest him. To make
him think of making a meal of her.

Grace frowned. Even while she was trying to concentrate
on staying away from him, she'd been thinking of him eating
into her, metaphorically. Digging into her soul. Getting to
her. And somehow it had all gotten turned around in her
head, the image turning sexual instead.

Him devouring her.

He would be insatiable, she thought. What would that be
like? Being with an absolutely insatiable man? She'd never
really considered it before.

''What in the world are you thinking?'' he said.

''What?'' She blinked up at him, lost in thoughts of him,
insatiable, devouring her. *Damn.*

''You had the oddest look on your face.''

''Nothing,'' she lied. ''It was nothing.''

He didn't believe her, of course. Because somehow he did
see right through her. She didn't even want to think about
that.

He waited a long time, watching her in a way that had her
fighting not to squirm. She didn't have to let him know he
was getting to her.

Finally, he let it go and said, ''Feel better?''

''Yes. Thank you for the clothes.''

She felt his gaze rake over her, too slowly for her own
comfort, saw the slight tightening of his jaw, which did funny

things to her insides. He liked looking at her. She hadn't known many men who simply liked looking at her. Or if she had, she'd never noticed. She was usually so matter of fact in her dealings with them. She either patched them up and sent them on their way, or she watched them die. Some, she worked with, considered them friends and colleagues. She really couldn't think of any men who fell in between. Friend, colleague, patient. That was it.

Grace looked around for something to do, something to say, and one of his weapons caught her attention. They were in danger. There was a nice, diversionary subject for them.

"Do you think Milero's men are looking for us?"

"I don't think so. Not in the middle of this. But we won't take any chances."

This. The storm. The relentless wind and rain. Sometimes it faded into the background, became merely a dull roar, and then she'd hear a gust or a crackle of a branch hitting the ground and it would leave her unsettled all over again.

"They know there's no way we can get off the island now," he said. "They'll wait it out. Wait us out. Sooner or later the storm will end, and we'll have to make our move. They know that, too."

"So when it's over...we'll just try to get out of here before they find us?"

"We *will* get out of here before they find us," he said.

Yet another promise. She should have stopped him right there and told him, *don't promise me anything. Don't.* She found it disconcerting that she didn't. She was also scared to get within arm's length of him, afraid that if she did, she might want to be even closer. She was thinking more clearly, and her memory of the last few days, from the kidnapping forward, was coming back to her, more vivid than ever before.

She had been so scared. Scared like she hadn't been since...well, since her whole life fell apart. She was hovering around that part of her brain where she hid the really bad things. The worst. In a place she never went. *Never.*

Grace sensed movement, looked up and found he was right in front of her. So very close she could feel the heat coming off his body. He managed to move more silently than any man she'd ever known, and it was just one of the many utterly disconcerting things about him.

"It's all right to be scared, Grace. Especially after what you've been through. It's all over but the shouting now. I'll get you out of here," he whispered, his big hand at the side of her waist, then sliding around her, pulling her to him, settling her gently against his hard mountain of a body.

She remembered this feeling. The sheer might of the man, the strength. Back in her cell, he'd held her up against him like this, as if to show her more clearly than any words could have that everything was going to be all right. He was going to get you out of this, and she thought he was a man capable of doing anything he set his mind to.

She let her head rest against his shoulder. Barely, she fought the urge to bury her nose against his neck, against the tantalizing strip of browned skin. But her hands found his waist, slid around his well-muscled back. As always, he was deliciously warm and so very solid. There was such reassuring bulk to him; he was an all-together substantial man.

And there was more, as well. Her breasts were crushed against his hard chest, her legs against his equally hard thighs. She remembered the way it had felt, when he'd been so obviously aroused the night before, how it made her go hot and cold all over and set her to trembling from head to toe.

Not that he'd touched her in a sexual way at all. He was just standing there holding her, comforting her. His big hands traveled in slow, soothing strokes up and down her back, but other than that, it was as if he was barely even breathing. As if he'd been caught in the same spell she was.

Unnerved by how much she wanted to stay with him,

maybe get even closer, she stepped away. He didn't try to stop her, didn't protest in the least. Instead he stood, unmoving, staring at her.

"Sorry," he said finally.

"It's—why?"

"I don't want to make you...uncomfortable."

She frowned at him. He was a master at making her uncomfortable, on so many levels. But she didn't think she needed to elaborate on that. Let him think it was merely sexual or about her being afraid. Grace ignored both what she'd said and what he'd done. She looked around the cave, fighting the urge to pace.

"I guess we just have to wait," she said, thinking she'd just stay away from him, stay out of his arms, try not to be drawn into conversation with him.

Which meant there truly was nothing to do. She was lousy at doing nothing, at being still. One thing about her job, it seldom left her time to think about anything other than the crisis at hand, which was one of the things she loved about it. She stood there, growing more agitated with every minute that went by. She looked toward the back of the cave, thinking about exploring.

"Have you been back there?"

"Of course," he said, as if it were an utterly ridiculous question. She supposed it was, considering who she was talking about. He was obviously a man who left nothing to chance.

"Does it go very far?" she tried.

"No. There's no place to run to, Grace. It's just you and me and the rain."

She nodded, thinking he knew what she was doing, knew what was wrong. Of course *he knew*. And he wasn't going to leave it alone.

She felt her heart accelerate in a way it seldom had, a hard, painful out-of-control thudding. She felt hot and a bit sick to her stomach and panicky. Grace never panicked.

"I don't suppose you have a deck of cards with you," she suggested, failing miserably to distract him because her voice was positively weak and she was breathless.

"Sorry. I guess I'm not prepared for every possibility. I never worried about you being bored."

Her head dipped downward, hiding her expression, her embarrassment. She was being petty, whining. She hated women who just sat around and felt sorry for themselves, particularly when they didn't have any good reason for doing so. When they had perfectly acceptable lives.

Grace's life was normally fine. Busy. Challenging. Meaningful. She felt ashamed that she'd worried about being bored when he'd risked his own life to save hers.

"How long are you going to run away from it, Grace?" he asked.

Her heart started thudding again. Even more strongly than before. *He knew.* And he wanted to talk about it.

She eyed him warily. "I don't know why you're doing this...."

"Because I'm worried about you."

"Well, I'm fine. Stop worrying."

"Grace, I've always worried."

"I can't imagine why," she lied. "I don't want to know why. Nothing gives you the right to dig into my life."

"I'm in your life now. You and I are stuck with each other."

"And I'm grateful for what you did," she said. "But saving my life doesn't give you the right to... To..."

"What?" he asked. "To try to keep you from being so careless with it?"

"I'm not going to debate my life choices with you. I'm a doctor. I've chosen to work with the IRC. I go where they send me, where I'm needed."

"Just following orders? Is that it?"

She nodded, thinking that was it. He'd stop. But she should have known the man never stopped.

"And that doesn't scare you?" he asked. "All those tight spots over the years? All those people admiring you because you're so fearless?"

She glared at him.

"That's right. I know what they say about you."

How? She wanted to scream it at him, but she couldn't. She'd promised not to ask. Of course, he wasn't following the deal. Not at all.

"What is the point in all this?" she asked finally. "What do you want from me?"

"I want you to talk to me."

"About what?"

"Your family."

She barely covered the shudder that ran through her or the thing that felt like a kick in the gut. She put the question right back to him. "And you're going to reciprocate?"

"Okay."

"Fine. Although, I don't know what there is to tell," she hedged, using the old, standard lies. "I'm an only child—"

"No, you're not."

Grace paled, her gaze darting to his, then darting just as quickly away. She was desperate now. Desperate. "My parents were already in their forties when I was born, and they're both dead now. That's it."

"Very ordinary people? Totally normal, everyday life, huh?"

"Yes," she lied, the word not much more than a hoarse squeak.

He sighed heavily, exasperated. "Give it up, Grace. I told you. I know."

"Know what?"

"Everything."

He couldn't, she told herself. Maybe the bare bones of it. From old newspapers and magazine articles, if he'd made the connection to who she really was. Maybe even from what she imagined could be in classified documents, if he was who he said he was and had friends in high places.

But he couldn't know the whole of it, the reality.

"This is none of your business," she said.

"I'm afraid it is. I've watched you come too close to dying in the last few days. I couldn't handle that, Grace. So I'm making it my business."

"You can't make me talk about it," she said, hating the childishness of the threat. *You can't make me.* God! She was lost if she'd been reduced to this.

He was on her in a flash. He moved so fast, she hardly even blinked before he had her by the arm, holding her, not tightly enough to hurt, but in an infuriatingly no-nonsense grip. He wasn't letting her go.

"No, I can't make you talk. But I can make you listen. Dammit, I'm through watching you try to throw your life away."

"I'm not," she insisted.

"It's cowardly, Grace, and it doesn't become you at all. Because you're one of the bravest women I know. One of the strongest, the most determined I've ever seen. And I admire everything about you. But this."

"Let me go," she said through clenched teeth.

"No. I didn't see it before, because I didn't want to see it. I hated the thought of it, and I suspect you don't want to see it, either. But there it is. Do you want to die? Is that it? Or are you just not interested in living?"

"I'm fine," she insisted.

"Think about your father," he said. "Think about what he'd want from you."

Grace started to cry. Damn the man, he had her crying now. "My father would be very proud of me!"

"For everything but this, he would. He would be so proud. But he couldn't stand the idea of you placing so little value on your own life."

"I don't," she argued, still crying.

"Oh, sweetheart. You know you do."

His entire face softened, those big, dark eyes locked on hers, a sad, tender smile on his lips. One of his hands cupped the side of her face just as tenderly.

Dammit, she thought. He was going to be kind. Wretchedly kind. She knew it. Just as she knew she couldn't stand that at the moment.

Grace saw her chance and she took it. She wrenched away from him and turned and ran, with him yelling after her. The opening of the cave wasn't far. She stumbled out into the torrent of rain and the howling wind. The island was heavily treed, and there was a ton of brush underfoot. She flew across it, thinking only to get away. She had to get away from him and all his questions, all his accusations, all that he knew.

"Grace! Stop!"

She didn't. Until she stumbled over something, and he roared at her yet again. He was practically on top of her by then, swearing and yelling and pinning her body between his and the tree that she nearly ran into when she fell.

She tried to get away, and he tightened his hold on her, pressed her even more tightly against the rough trunk of the palm tree, and she finally gave up her struggle, just stood there feeling miserably weak and sobbed.

It was a horrible place to be. His body so hard, so insistent behind hers, holding her in place against the unyielding trunk of the tree. In rain that never slackened, just fell in torrents, and terrible gusts of wind. She was soaked already and getting cold. She couldn't stop crying, couldn't move, just couldn't deal with him or any of this anymore.

"Let me go," she sobbed. "Just let me go."

"I can't," he claimed, his lips against her right ear.

"Why not?"

"You're getting off this island alive if it's the last thing I do," he said.

"Fine,," she said. "I will. But right now, I just want to get away from you."

And then she started to cry harder. Uncontrollably. Inconsolable. Like a weak, gutless woman, the kind she absolutely despised.

She leaned her forehead against the tree, and he leaned his head down against hers, his mouth somehow finding her neck, rain running off of it. His body completely surrounded hers, holding her so tightly she could scarcely breathe.

"Shh," he soothed, soft, soft lips against the sensitive skin of her neck.

Grace was so surprised. There were times she would have sworn there was nothing at all soft about him, not anywhere on his body. She should have known better. He'd kissed her once before.

She felt his heart thundering, where his chest was pressed against her back. He was breathing hard, as was she, and she couldn't be sure but she thought he was shaking as well.

The wind roared right on. So did the rain, seeming to encompass them both, leaving them all alone in this little sliver of the world.

She was wrapped in utter misery, and in his tight, unwavering arms.

"You can't just dig inside of me this way," she cried. "You can't."

"I'm sorry, baby. I'm so sorry."

"You have no right, dammit. Especially when I don't even know who you are."

"I'm sorry—"

"I don't even know your name, dammit. Why can't you tell me your name?"

"Sean," he said. "It's Sean."

She shivered, thinking, *Finally*. She had a name at least, and it seemed no secrets at all from him. Grace sagged against him, all her energy gone, but that was all right. He held her fast, and after a moment, he turned her in his arms and molded her body to his.

His kiss, when it came, simply wiped away everything else. The rain, the wind, the anger, the tears. Everything.

It was as devastating as any storm she'd ever witnessed, as powerful and as all-encompassing. It was as if the whole world must have sat up and taken notice.

He'd captured her, enslaved her, with nothing but the heat and the need of his mouth on hers. He kissed devastatingly, thoroughly, his tongue sweeping through her mouth. Taking possession like a warrior, a conquering hero.

What in the world would she do with a hero? What use could he possibly be? After all, she would have sworn no one could save her. Not from herself. Not from the secrets she held so tightly inside.

But for now she wrapped her arms even more tightly around him, never wanting to let him go. Never wanting to lose this feeling. Of being plastered against him, all that strength and heat and need. Of wanting to be a part of him, absorbed into him.

It was as if she were soaring. As if she'd gone from the lowest of lows to the highest of highs. If she could just have him touching her this way, she thought life certainly might be worth living.

He made her want to take all those nasty risks. The huge ones. Caring about someone again. Needing them. Depending on them. Believing all those promises so many people carelessly made.

Grace arched against him, unable to get close enough. She felt hard, hot muscles everywhere, and tasted such heat, such need. She wasn't sure if she ever would have stopped. He could have had her, right here in the rain with her back pressed against the tree, if that's what he wanted. He could have her anywhere at all, as long as he could make her feel like this.

So alive. She'd never known it was possible to feel so startlingly alive.

She was still in a daze when he finally lifted his head, still struggling for every breath, still flush against him, enough to know he wanted her, too. Badly. Desperately, it seemed. She fought the urge to snuggle closer to the hot, hard spot between his muscular thighs, to wrap her legs around his waist and beg him to take her, fast and hard, right here. It would be like nothing she'd ever experienced before.

"Grace!" he muttered, shaking his head and looking at everything but her.

He was trembling, too. She loved the fact that she could make him tremble with need, as he made her. And she didn't want to let go of this feeling and go back to her real life, back there in the cave with him and what he seemed determined to say to her. She didn't want to hear it.

He started to back away from her. She hung on for dear life.

"We have to get inside," he said, his voice low and strained.

She clutched at his shoulders, cursing the blasted rain that was so thick, she could hardly look up at him, could hardly see. "No, we don't."

"Grace—"

"No!"

"Yes, dammit."

He didn't give her time to argue. He swept her up into his arms. She thought he'd haul her into the cave, which was only about fifteen feet away. But he didn't. He stood there, carefully surveying the scene.

His heart was still thundering, she realized, his arms steely and wrapped tightly around her. As if he still thought she might bolt?

"What's wrong?" she asked.

"Milero's a careful man. He knew the caves were the best hiding place anyone could find on his island. We cleared half a dozen booby traps from the entrance before we set up camp here, and I think we got them all," he said tightly. "But I can't be sure."

Chapter 7

*B*ooby trapped?

"Oh, God." All the breath left her body.

She remembered now. He had warned her, in the note. She'd forgotten all about that as she'd run heedlessly out into the rain, away from him.

Suddenly, she understood his anger, his fear. God, he'd called her worse than reckless, and she'd argued the point. Only to prove it to him and herself not a moment later.

Was she truly that careless with her own life?

Her gut said no. She'd simply forgotten about his warning. He'd pushed too hard, and she'd been too angry, too desperate to get away. Which was no excuse. He'd warned her. The danger here was very real.

"I'm sorry," she said, knowing it wasn't nearly enough.

He didn't say anything, merely picked his way carefully through the brush. She didn't see how he could ever find the way. There was no path. The island's terrain was junglelike. Thick with trees and vegetation, and so much debris the wind had brought down, and it was nearly impossible to see with the rain beating down on their faces.

But he did. He was muttering under his breath the whole way, cursing and talking about damned, reckless, stubborn women.

A moment later, they were inside. Just enough to be out of the rain. He stopped there, set her on her feet, then turned his back to her and leaned against the wall of the cave, as if his legs would barely hold him at the moment. It was the first time she'd ever seen the smallest hint of weakness in him. She wouldn't have believed it if she hadn't seen it for herself.

But there it was.

She'd scared him.

Whatever she was to him—which she might never understand—she'd scared him enough that he was trembling with it.

He turned and faced her, a tight, grim look in his eyes and his mouth.

Grace reconsidered. Maybe he was so mad he was shaking. He certainly looked as if he could throttle her any moment.

She was suddenly afraid to move. "What did they leave? What kind of booby traps?"

"Explosives," he said tightly. "Don't you ever disobey one of my orders again. Not while we're here. Not until I have you safely off this island."

"I won't," she said.

"And don't you ever scare me like that again. I swear, I may strangle you myself if you do."

Which seemed odd coming from a man sworn to save her. But she didn't argue the point. She did wonder over the oddness of having someone worry about her. Jane used to, but she'd given up in both frustration and anger, as well.

Did Jane think Grace was reckless and careless, too? Did she think it went deeper than that?

Grace didn't know. She didn't know what to say to him,

either, and she didn't want to think about recklessness or fearlessness or anything like that.

So she stood there just inside the entrance to the cave. Still scared and a bit dazed, she watched the rain beat down, the wind bringing a light spray of moisture far enough inside to get to them. Not that it mattered. They were both soaked to the skin. Water dripped off of her.

She looked down, painfully conscious of the cold that came from being wet and whipped by the wind. Conscious, too, of the way his shirt was plastered to her skin, so that it might as well have been transparent. The shape of her breasts, the way her nipples had bunched up and pushed against the material had her fighting the urge to cross her arms and do her best to cover herself. But really, there was no point and no way to hide.

She would have loved to have the luxury of his big, warm body against hers now. Of having him to hold on to now that her legs threatened to buckle beneath her and the trembling just wouldn't stop.

She was truly sorry for scaring him that way, couldn't help but be touched by the fact that for whatever reason, he cared about her. She didn't even want to ask why anymore, just to be able to savor the feeling. Because Grace had been alone for as long as she could remember.

She wondered if he could possibly know that, too.

Sean, she remembered. He'd finally told her his name.

"Come on," he said raggedly, clearly frustrated and still mad. "We have to get dry."

She followed him back to his stash of supplies. He pulled out a pair of camouflage pants. "Dry off with that." And then a T-shirt like the one he wore. "And then put this on. That's the best I can do."

"Thank you."

"And hurry." He handed her a blanket, as well, which she took with a trembling hand. And then he turned his back to her and started to strip.

Grace was tempted to watch him, because it seemed she'd turned totally shameless and utterly fascinated with him.

She turned her back and hurried, instead. Which was hard when she was shivering so. She stripped and dabbed at the moisture on her skin as best she could, then put on the shirt and wrapped herself in the blanket. She tried to wring the water out of her hair and rubbed it with the cloth as well, but it was hard to get her long, thick hair dry under the best of circumstances.

When she turned back around, she thought he was naked. Magnificently naked as he stood there in the grayish light that was fading fast. Her insides turned to the consistency of mush. Hot, gooey mush. But on closer inspection, she could make out what was either a pair of short pants or boxers. Nothing else.

Her mouth went dry. She knew she should look away, but… She'd never seen such an impressive-looking man. He wasn't much more than a shadowy impression of ropy muscles and wide shoulders, but he made her mouth go dry.

Just a man, she told herself. How many men's bodies had she seen? Seldom any as well-cared-for as his. Certainly none that took her breath away.

Her gaze finally roamed over his face, and she wished so much for just a bit more light. So she could see his expression more clearly. What she could see left her with the impression of a very stern frown and a steely jaw. Or irritation and maybe impatience and maybe anger still. Not that she could blame him.

"I…" She had no idea what to say. "I'm sorry."

He didn't move a muscle, seemed every bit as stern and imposing as before. Finally, he said, "We need to warm you up, Grace."

She nodded. She felt cold to the bone. Residual effects of the drugs that probably still weren't entirely out of her system, maybe of the head injury and dehydration, too, which made it hard for the body to regulate its temperature.

He sat down with his back against his supply pack, legs extended in front of him, feet on the floor, knees up at an angle, thighs open, and motioned for her to sit down in front of him. She did. His hand came around her waist, pulling her against him until her back was flush against his chest. She felt the heat of his thighs closing around hers. Even her cold toes were tucked between his warm feet.

He spread her blanket over them both. One of his big hands stayed around her waist, holding her firmly to him, a broad, warm band at her midsection. His other hand pushed her head back against his shoulder. She turned her head, her face and her cold nose pressed against his warm neck.

Grace sighed, thinking this was the best spot she'd been in in years, enveloped in warmth, held fast against him. His body was hard in all the right places, and he was still warm, even after getting drenched with her.

"Do you ever get cold?" she asked.

"Not often."

"But you do?" Basic physiology aside, she found it very hard to believe.

"I told you, I'm just a man, Grace. All human beings get cold from time to time."

"Tell me. About the coldest you've ever been."

He took a breath. She could feel his chest rise and fall with it, felt warm air passing over her forehead as he exhaled. "Bosnia," he said finally.

She nodded. It had been a cold, desolate place. No power. No heating oil. Absolutely nothing left to burn for heat, either, in the time she'd been there.

"What were you doing there?" she said.

"Did a stint with the UN peacekeeping force, and got into a little trouble with my plane."

So, he was a pilot? That certainly didn't surprise her. He had the ego for it. The nerve.

"I had to ditch," he said. "It wasn't the smoothest forced landing I ever made. Screwed up my knee in the process and ended up hiding in the woods for about thirty-six hours. In November.''

Grace shuddered. Thirty-six hours, while injured, with whatever provisions he could scrounge out of a downed plane, in Bosnia in November?

''You're lucky you survived that little adventure.''

''That's what they told me.''

She laughed a bit, because he said it as if the whole thing had been no big deal. As if he'd hardly broke a sweat while hiding and waiting for thirty-six hours to see if he was rescued or killed.

''And I'm supposed to be reckless?'' she asked.

''Calculated risk, Grace. I'm a damned good pilot. It was a great plane. A mission not without risks, but carefully planned and necessary. We flew a lot of missions there, most all of them without incident.''

''I've never been hurt on the job,'' she bragged.

''Not yet.''

''And I don't have a death wish,'' she insisted.

''Really?''

''Really. Think about it... Sean? Is that really your name?''

''Yes.''

''Sean,'' she said, ''think about it. I'm a doctor. I have access to all sorts of drugs, and I know how to use them. If I really wanted to die, I could. Quickly and painlessly. Any time I wanted.''

''Maybe you don't want to die,'' he conceded. ''But I'm not convinced you really want to live, either.''

''That's not true,'' she insisted.

''You go to the most dangerous spots of all.''

''So do you.''

''I go where I'm sent,'' he said.

''So do I.''

''You volunteer.''

''And you don't?''

"I don't get into the field much these days. I've done my time, and I won't lie to you. I miss it at times. But I've bucked the odds long enough. I let the kids who are twenty years younger handle things, and I boss 'em around."

"You can't keep up with the twenty-somethings? I don't believe that for a minute." He could keep up with anyone.

"It's time to let someone else do the job, Grace."

"Why?"

"What are you afraid of?" he asked. "Sitting still? Too much time to think? Too much time to figure out what's really going on inside your head? Why you've been running all these years?"

"I'm not running from anything."

"Give it up, Grace. You've been running for twenty years."

Twenty? She froze. It *had* been twenty years. The anniversary was coming up.

"I know," he said. "I know all about what happened to your family. And you can't run from it anymore, Grace. I won't let you. I don't want to make it any harder on you, and I don't want to hurt you. But this is a conversation you should have had years ago. If you're not going to talk about it with anyone else, it's going to have to be me."

Grace let the silence stretch painfully between them. He waited her out, damn him. He had more patience than any man she'd ever met, more stubbornness, it seemed.

Finally, she said, "You couldn't possibly know."

"James Evans Porter. Teacher, historian, writer, world traveler, lay minister, outspoken peace activist. Nobel prize winner. Your father."

Grace shuddered, and his arms held her more firmly.

"Anne Wright Porter, nurse, missionary, world traveler, lay minister herself, your mother. John Evans Porter, your older brother, showing all the signs of following in your father's footsteps. All wiped out by a terrorist bomb when you were eleven,'' he said softly. "I *know,* Grace. It'll soon be twenty years. I think it's time for you to start living again.''

She closed her eyes, wishing that was enough to block out his voice, to stop the words. It wasn't.

Grace didn't move, scarcely seemed to breathe. There was pain in the pit of her stomach. A hot, hard ball of it that seemed to expand with every passing second, filling her entire abdominal cavity. Heat and pain. Rushing over her, overtaking her. Spreading all the way to her fingertips and toes. It hurt so badly. She thought she might have slid to the floor in a dead faint, if not for his strong arms around her, his body cradling hers.

She had no energy, no way to even move, no will. And her tears started in earnest again. Hot, angry, useless tears.

He shifted her in his arms, drew her against his chest, her face tucked into the spot at his shoulder against his neck, below his whisker-roughened jaw. She thought it might be the best spot in the entire world. Hot, smooth skin and strong, gentle arms. His hand pressed her face against him and stroked her hair, and he was everywhere. Everything she touched was him. He'd done just what she'd wanted earlier. Enveloped her body in his, in the heat and strength.

"Don't you ever talk about them?'' he asked.

"No,'' she said miserably.

"You can't bury it inside of you forever, sweetheart. Pretending they never existed won't make it go away.''

"Nothing makes it go away.''

"I know.''

"You don't,'' she argued.

"I don't know as much as you do about pain and loss. But I lost one of my brothers in the Gulf War. I think about him every day. Even now.''

"I don't think about them. I don't let myself.''

"No, you just let it sit there inside you like a poison. Eating away at you.''

"Dammit, Sean, if I need a shrink, I know where to find one."

"I don't think you need a shrink as much as you need a life," he argued. "Don't you ever let anyone get close to you, sweetheart? Isn't there anyone who's really important to you? Anyone you can trust and depend on?"

"That is the last thing I need."

"Grace, I know how capable you are. How strong. How stubborn. How brave. But even you need someone—"

"I don't want anyone."

"Because you're scared. Because you think it's all going to blow up in a puff of smoke someday."

"Don't," she said tightly. Because she remembered the smoke, the blast. The heat, the noise. The blood, the terror.

"Oh, baby. I am so sorry. If I could bring them back for you—"

"You can't. No one can. Nothing can change it. But I don't have to talk about it, dammit. I can bury it inside, if that's what I want."

"Until it eats you alive? Until it ruins your life? Until you might as well have died with them yourself? Is that what you want, Grace?"

"I don't know."

"It is. God, that's what scares me the most. I'm afraid that's exactly what you want."

And maybe it was. Maybe it was.

She buried her head against his chest and cried some more, pain racking her, cutting her to shreds. She wept miserably, weakly, until her throat was raw and she could barely lift her head.

"Why couldn't I have gone with them?" she said finally, her face buried against his neck. "We would have been together. Wherever we ended up, we'd have been together."

"And they left you all alone."

So wretchedly alone. She would never have believed it possible for anyone to be so absolutely alone. Her family had been her whole world. They'd always been together. Everywhere.

Wherever her parents went, they'd taken her and her brother. There were pictures of Grace as a baby, strapped in a sling across her mother's chest, somewhere in China. Pictures of her and John in crude classrooms all over the world where her father taught them along with all the other children in all the villages they visited.

Her parents had been so open, so loving, so welcoming, drawing people to them wherever they went. Always surrounded by a crowd, but always, too, the four of them together. They'd been so tight, so strong together. Capable of doing anything, her father always said. People could do anything they set their minds to.

Grace liked to think she'd done all she could, that he would have been proud of her. She'd carried on, buried her identity right from the start because she'd been a very reluctant celebrity then. The sole survivor of the blast that killed her family. She'd been just inside the entrance to the building when it blew up. Someone had grabbed her and gotten her out, and someone had snapped a photo of it. Smoke billowing behind them, fire eating away at everything, Grace limp and scared, her face blackened and bleeding, in her rescuer's arms. She'd been on the cover of every major daily newspaper in the world. The press had followed every aspect of her recovery, sung her father's praises, mourned him, buried him, and she'd been in that awful glare in the media spotlight as it happened.

Anonymity had sounded very good to her after that. She'd taken her father's mother's maiden name and gone to boarding school in an obscure corner of England after the bombing, and she'd never said a word to anyone about what she'd gone through. She'd finished her education early and gone straight into medical school, volunteering with the IRC even then.

It had been a bit like coming home. As close as she'd been

able to come to home—being in the field, doing the kind of work her parents had done. It had challenged her, given her a purpose when she desperately needed one. She would have said it filled her life, but he seemed so sure it hadn't.

"I miss them so much," she whispered. God, even now. So much she could hardly breathe when she thought of them.

Her father had just gotten word that he would be given the Nobel Peace Prize in Norway in December when, two months before, they'd gone to an international peace conference in Rome, where he was scheduled to deliver the keynote address to leaders from all over the world.

They'd all just arrived. He was checking out the hall where he was to speak when terrorists blew it up with him and her mother and brother inside. Grace had run into an old friend, a little girl whose father had been a friend of her father's for years. They'd stopped for a few minutes to catch up with each other, outside in the sunshine, and barely missed getting killed themselves.

Grace could be sick just thinking about it, even now. The noise. The smoke. The heat. The screams.

"I know you miss them," Sean said. "But I can't believe they'd want you to live this way, Grace."

"I'm doing the best I can," she protested. What did he want from her, anyway? She had a job, a very difficult, challenging job. What else did a woman need?

"After twenty years, Grace, I think they'd want you to be happy."

"I…" Oh, hell. She'd started to argue that she was happy.

"Tell it to the rest of the world, sweetheart. Not me. I don't buy it."

So she simply lay there miserably against him. Cried out, it seemed. Exhausted. Drained. So very tired.

"I'm doing the best I can," she said again.

"Well then, we'll just have to find a way for you to do better. You're going to have to trust me a little bit. Listen to me. Let me help."

Grace sighed, thinking that as much as she hated him for saying all these things, he had helped. He soothed with the touch of his hands and his mouth, moving softly down the side of her face, kissing her tears away. He took that bone-deep coldness away. When he held her, she wasn't afraid. In fact, with him she felt more alive than she had in years. Twenty, maybe.

And she couldn't stand it, couldn't let it go on. After all, there was safety in being alone, in depending on no one but herself. She'd never, ever disappointed herself. She could never leave herself all alone. She'd found a way to live her life, and maybe it wasn't the kind of life other people had or the kind he thought she should have. But who the hell was he to tell her what she needed, anyway?

"I don't want anyone to help me," she said.

She felt the smile on his lips, which were somewhere very near her cheek. "Why not?"

"I don't."

"And I don't know how to walk away from this, Grace. I don't think I can anymore. Not until I know you're okay."

"Why?" she said. They'd done enough digging into her, and he hadn't told her anything but his name. "Why do you even care?"

She put her hands against his chest, trying very hard to ignore the way it felt beneath her palms, and pushed against him, enough to put nearly a foot between them. Even this close, the light was so faint, she could scarcely see.

He was still very much her mystery man, the one who came to her in the dark and never showed his face in the light. The picture was hardly any clearer now than it ever had been.

"Why?" she asked. "Give me that at least."

He frowned. She gave in to the urge to confirm that for herself by tracing the flat line of his full, soft lips with her fingertips. She felt the disconcerting heat all around her, coming off his body in waves, was aware all the more of the way they were still pressed together in all those interesting places, the way she was still lying against him. She eased back, until her breasts were pressed against his chest. She felt the change in his slow, even breathing, felt the way his heartbeat kicked up, as well.

His jaw was intriguingly rough, his breath warm against her lips, and already it seemed she was addicted to him in so many ways.

She didn't want to feel this way. Didn't want to need him. But wanting him the way she did—in a purely sexual way— while disconcerting, was something she could handle, she thought.

Could it be just about that? Pure sexual need? Everyone had that instinctive need. At least, that's what she'd been taught in school. She'd dismissed it without much thought at all, having more important things to worry about. Until now. Now she'd been forced into close quarters with an absolutely magnificent, sexually charged man.

She inched closer, her mouth instinctively seeking his. He swore softly and didn't so much as budge. He wasn't going to help her with this.

But she thought she was definitely onto something. He wanted her to live, to feel. Well she felt alive now, and she thought maybe this was the one thing that could burn all those awful memories from her mind. The ones he'd dredged up and dragged out into the open and demanded she deal with.

She didn't want to feel anything to do with her family, her past, but dammit, she could feel this. He owed her, as she saw it.

Take it away, she thought, pressing her lips against his. Take it all away.

Chapter 8

Sean had never fought such a battle to deny himself anything he truly wanted, and he very seldom lost any kind of battle at all. But this one…he *was* lost.

He had a woman he'd only dreamed about for so long in his arms. Had so much of her smooth, soft, bare skin plastered against his, her mouth no more than an inch from his, and he might have managed to do nothing but try to console her and warm her with his body. He might have.

But when she put her hand against the side of his face and traced the pad of her finger across his lips, his body reacted with a jolt of pure, sexual need. Her soft, sweet mouth came down on his. She opened herself completely to him, her arms coming around him, tugging his head down to hers.

She was so soft, so delicate, her shoulders and hips so narrow. He knew if he wasn't very careful, he could hurt her without meaning to, and he would never, ever hurt her. He wouldn't let himself.

''Aah, Grace,'' he groaned.

Her breasts were driving him insane. Those pretty, rounded

mounds, encased in *his* shirt that she was wearing, pressing against his bare chest. And she had the longest legs, the kind he wanted to grab and wrap around his waist while he thrust into her. Outside against the tree...as scared as he'd been, as angry, he'd still wanted her. Right there. Just like that.

She didn't have a thing on except the shirt, and he'd been fighting for what seemed like forever not to slip his hand beneath the hem and tunnel up. To find the smooth globes of her breasts and take them into his palm. Tease at her nipple. Cover it with his mouth. Stroke it with his tongue. Bury his face in that sweet spot between them and then suck greedily, one after another. He could let his hands roam over her back, her belly, her hips, between her thighs. There was nothing in his way except one thin cotton shirt.

And now her mouth was pressed against his, her tongue stroking his. She tasted like no woman he'd ever known. That connection between them was so potent, so charged. It went zipping right through him.

He was instantly, totally, completely aroused. The T-shirt was riding up a bit, and he was sure there was nothing but the dubious cover of his boxers between his painfully tight erection and her belly. She arched against him, and he groaned, making do for the moment with that sweet pressure of his straining erection against her belly and the fact that he was kissing her deeply. Greedily. Like a man who might never stop.

He lied to himself for a moment and told himself he wouldn't. Not at all. Not until he gave into the urge to lift her across his lap and spread her legs and bury himself inside her. The damned hurricane could pick up the whole island and twist it and toss it miles away, and he wouldn't so much as notice and wouldn't care. Not if he could be inside her. Just once.

Her hands were greedy, too, he found. In his still-wet hair. All over his skin. His shoulders, his back, his chest, his jaw, in a feather-light touch that was making him insane. She made little noises deep in her throat, sexy, breathless little sounds, and she kept saying his name as if she was begging. *Begging.* For him.

They were pressed so tightly together, there couldn't have been so much as a molecule between them, and suddenly it seemed there was no air in the room at all. Nothing. Anywhere.

Just him and her.

And he could not let himself do this. He couldn't.

He wouldn't take advantage of her this way, wouldn't use her to scratch an itch or even to satisfy a long-denied need.

"Grace," he protested, his need like a fever, burning him alive.

She shifted against him, breasts rubbing against his chest, her mouth so sweet.

He caught her hands and pulled them off his body, where they'd been stroking his chest and leaving a trail of fire in their wake. He took her by the shoulders next and pushed her firmly away. Her lips he found almost impossible to separate from his. All he had to do was lift his head. He knew that. But he didn't want to give that up. Didn't want to give up anything of her.

But he would. He did.

Finally managing to lift his head, he cursed the darkness himself this time. He knew it was better that he couldn't see her right now, but he wanted to. He wanted her thoroughly disheveled and fighting for breath, wanted to see her nipples and the swell of her breasts, their shape, teasing him through the cotton shirt and begging for his touch. He wanted to see her just like that and knew he had to be grateful that he couldn't.

So he sat there, cursing himself and the darkness and the circumstances, knowing he had to explain somehow and having no idea on earth how to do that.

Finally, he said, "It's not that I don't want you."

"I know that," she said wryly, and he laughed in spite of himself.

"I'm not going to take advantage of you. Of the situation."

"Oh." She was quiet for a moment. "Maybe you didn't notice. I'm the one who had my hands all over you. I kissed you. I didn't want you to stop."

"You don't want to talk about your parents or your brother. Or the fact that you need to get a life, and I happened to be the best distraction at hand." Hell, he hated that thought, but he certainly couldn't dismiss it, either.

"Damn you," she said.

"Yeah, I'm damned all right," he admitted.

Because he was afraid he'd always want her and never, ever have her. How was a man supposed to deal with something like that?

"I don't understand you," she said.

"Then we're even. I certainly don't understand you."

She stayed where she was, staring at him, her breathing still agitated, her lashes dipping low. Finally, her hand came up, her palm landing against his chest. *Dammit.*

"You don't really want this, Grace."

"How do you know?"

"I know you."

That there hadn't been many men in her life. She was almost always working, and he almost always had someone watching her. Not twenty-four hours a day, but enough to know where she was and what was going on in whatever part of the world she was in at the time. He had contacts all over the world, resources at his fingertips. If there'd been any man who'd been a part of her life for any length of time, he'd have known about it. And likely hated it. Especially in the last year and a half. But there hadn't been, which made him happy and sad all at the same time.

He wanted to be the man she trusted. Not just the one who got her out of trouble, but the one who gave her everything she so richly deserved, the man who made her believe in promises once again, made her unafraid of love. And there was no way he could do that.

"What is it?" she said, taking his face between her hands, concern in her voice.

"Nothing."

"Liar. You call me on every one of mine. Did you think I wouldn't call you on yours, too?"

"I can't do this, Grace. I want to. So damned much. But I can't."

"Soldier's ethics? The code by which rescuers of damsels in distress live?" she said lightly. "Because that's the first I've heard of any soldier—"

"My own ethics," he said, but didn't add his own guilt and so many things he hadn't told her. Things he wasn't sure he'd ever have the nerve to tell her. "I don't want to hurt you."

"Then stay out of my head. Hold me. Kiss me. Make love to me, but don't go digging into my soul anymore."

He couldn't help it. He bent his head and kissed her again. As softly and gently as he could. He would move heaven and earth, he thought, if only he could. If only he was that mythical, all-powerful creature she imagined.

He'd do anything for her, give her back her family. She wouldn't need him at all then. She'd be happy and surrounded by people she loved and wouldn't be taking stupid risks with her own life. She wouldn't be wishing she could join them. Everyone she loved. Everyone she'd lost.

He was so sad all of a sudden and so very serious.

His sweetly sensual kiss brought tears to her eyes once again, the regrets in his voice nearly breaking her heart. She'd never imagined that he was hurting, too, or that anything she might do to try to make herself forget might bring on such painful memories for him.

"What did I do?" she asked.

"Nothing."

"I did. I touched a nerve—"

"Grace—"

"What? You're going to tell me to leave it alone?"

"I don't suppose I could," he admitted.

"Not unless you want me to laugh in your face." Except she wouldn't. Not when he seemed so troubled, so... She would have said vulnerable, if the word hadn't seemed utterly out of place in any context around him. She wouldn't have thought he had a vulnerable bone in his body, but it appeared he did.

She felt awful about that. She didn't want to hurt him at all. Not ever.

She liked him much too much. Found him absolutely fascinating. Gorgeous. Strong. Stubborn. She wanted him so badly she could hardly see straight, and despised him for the things he'd said to her, even if he thought he was doing her a favor by saying them.

Worst of all, she was starting to get used to having him around. She was afraid that already she needed him, and she couldn't let herself do that.

She didn't let herself need anyone, couldn't let herself get used to this. Couldn't let herself think he really cared about her or that he'd made any kind of commitment to her at all.

Showing up every couple of years for a few minutes when she was in trouble wasn't exactly a commitment. He'd even told her not to count on him. That he was nothing but a man. That there'd come a day when he couldn't get to her in time. Which, arguably, had already happened. She'd been kidnapped off the streets of San Reino, even if he had rescued her a day and a half later.

So she had to stop this, had to find a way to stay away from him.

She wasn't ever going to love anyone. Not in her whole life. She'd promised herself that. She would never hurt again the way she had when she'd lost her entire family. Those promises—the ones she made herself—were sacred. They were what had kept her sane and maybe what had kept her from popping a bottle of pills the first time she had access to them.

Grace pulled away from him and got to her feet.

"Okay. You're right," she said. "We can't do this. It would be a mistake."

"Yes," he said carefully. "It would."

It sounded perfectly reasonable that evening. It would absolutely have been a mistake. But it wasn't so easy the next morning.

She'd slept on top of him. As if he were her pillow. Grace wasn't sure how that happened. They'd gone to bed with one blanket wrapped around her and another wrapped around the two of them. Close but not...not like this.

She vaguely remembered being uncomfortable in the night, remembered scooting closer and closer to him. And then she remembered her bed growing decidedly more comfortable at some point.

Except, it appeared her bed was him.

Two hundred pounds or so of pure muscle and man.

Her head lay against his chest, her hand as well. He had short, curling hairs on his chest, and she fought the urge to run her fingers through them. His skin was smooth in some places, but scarred in others, just as he'd told her. She wanted to find them all with her fingertips and explore at will, found herself infinitely curious about just what he'd been through, just how badly he'd been hurt over the years.

With her ear pressed to his chest this way, she heard every reassuring beat of his heart, felt every breath. He was softer than the ground, but not by much. There was hardly any give to him at all, just all these intriguing dips and swells. The muscles in his arms and shoulders, that hard, flat stomach. He had a hand splayed wide at her back, holding her firmly to him, and another one playing lazily just beneath the bottom of her T-shirt. With her bottom, actually.

She was practically purring at the exquisitely gentle touch against the soft skin of her bottom, his big, slightly rough palm rubbing absently, round and round, cupping it, as if he were fascinated by the shape.

She shifted a bit, one of her thighs sliding between his, and they both groaned as her leg grazed his erection. It seemed the man stayed hard all over. All the time.

"Morning, Grace," he said, his voice a little rough, the word spoken with a lazy drawl this early in the day.

"Good morning."

He sighed and stroked his palm across her bottom one more time before pulling her shirt down to cover her, his hand falling away. "Right back where we started, huh?"

She nodded, so turned on it was hard to speak and too comfortable to ever want to move.

Men woke up like this. Something about hormone levels and sleep. If she tried hard, she could remember the scientific explanation. But there didn't seem to be anything scientific or casual in his reaction to her. She wanted very much to know this was about her. Not just any woman who happened to crawl on top of him while he slept.

"Should I apologize?" she offered.

"Should I?" he murmured, his one hand still at her back, stroking lightly up and down.

"Only if you mean it. I really can't say that I am sorry. Unless I've made it even harder on you…." Her voice trailed off. She felt the chuckle rising from his chest. "If I've made it more uncomfortable for you. I'm sorry."

"I don't think it could get any harder, Grace. Not my body and not what it's going to take for me to let you go one more time."

He shifted again, his thighs falling apart, her whole body pressed that much more tightly against him. She ached now.

Just ached. She fought the urge not to rub her body shamelessly against his.

Gasping, she said, "Would it really be so bad?"

He put his hand back on her hip. Bringing her just to that spot, the one he wanted. Fooling with the pressure ever so slightly and making her moan. She couldn't help it.

"It would be great," he said. "It would feel exquisite."

She did some stroking of her own. Found his skin fascinating. She'd never been up close and personal with such a well-defined set of muscles in a man's chest, arms and shoulders.

She stroked up his biceps, along his neck, his clavicle, down to his left nipple. He sucked in a breath at that, and she didn't stop to think. She was done thinking.

She wanted a taste of him. Her mouth closed over his nipple and she licked it with her tongue, played with it, explored. His breath took a hard, pained tone. He caught her hair in his hand and tugged hard, trying to pull her away at first and then holding her to him.

His whole body shuddered. She felt it ripple through him, and it flat-out thrilled her. She was molded to him already, might as well have melted and had someone pour her over him, the way every inch of her body was draped along his. His thighs shifted restlessly and his pelvis arched against hers. How could a man possibly be this hard, this big?

She fussed over his nipple again. She'd never, ever done this to a man, never wanted to. But she wanted to taste every inch of him. She used her teeth, gently, and he shuddered yet again.

She kissed every bit of skin she could find. Across his chest, down his rib cage. He moaned, his hand still tangled in her hair. He was rocking his hips against hers now, easing off the pressure, thrusting forward.

She wanted him desperately. Like a madwoman, the kind she'd never been before.

And why should she deny herself this pleasure? There'd

been so little pleasure in her life. Too little life altogether; he'd told her that. He wanted her to live. Surely this was living at its absolute best. She wasn't the kind to give herself to any man easily, casually. In fact, she'd been celibate for years. But there was nothing casual about this. This was absolutely essential to her. And maybe she did need a lesson in living, the sheer joy of it. Maybe she would be more careful of her own safety if there was joy like this in her life.

She could keep herself alive just to be able to make love to him so exquisitely, to feel so beautiful, so free, so startlingly alive.

"I don't care if it's wrong," she said. "I don't even think it is."

"Grace," he groaned.

She scooted down a bit more. Her mouth against his bottom rib, then following that thin line of hair down the middle of his abdomen. She kissed, made little patterns with her tongue.

There was a pulse throbbing wildly in his erection. She could feel it now. She put her hand down and cupped him, rubbed against him, and she heard him swear viciously and softly. His flesh leapt beneath her fingers, thrusting itself into her hand.

She was fascinated by it, the shape, the thickness, the hardness, and she wanted him inside her. Now.

Surely he wouldn't deny her that. Surely she could take him to the point where he simply couldn't.

She set out to do just that. The next thing she knew, he grabbed her by the arms, in a hold that allowed no resistance at all, and swung her around until she was lying on her side, and he was covering her body with his.

She was thrilled, waiting for him to push his way inside her like a man on the absolute edge of control. But instead he whispered into her ear, "Don't move. Not a muscle."

The flat, no-nonsense tone of his voice had her blinking

up at him through the darkness, confused and not happy at all.

She opened her mouth to protest, and he shut it for her, his hand covering it.

"Someone's outside," he whispered into her ear, everything about him different now, his hold on her, his voice, even the way he held his body.

She made no sound. She couldn't. And her thoughts were an awful jumble. From sheer pleasure to out-and-out terror. She tried to figure out what he'd heard, couldn't imagine anything that would have cut through the incessant roar of the wind and the rain. She'd been too caught up in him and the way he felt, the things she wanted from him, to hear anything. The whole world might have come crashing down around them. She wouldn't have known. But he did.

He reached for something behind them. His pistol, which he shoved into her hands. "Do you know how to use this?"

"Of course," she whispered. She hated guns, but she knew how to fire any number of them.

"It's a semiautomatic. You've got ten rounds. Stay right here and try not to shoot me when I come back. If anyone else tries to get in here, kill 'em."

She gulped, not sure that she could.

"Grace, I don't care if you start trying to save the bastard ten seconds later, if that's what you have to do. But shoot him first. Dead center in the chest. It gives you the biggest target, and it'll stop most anything that might come at you."

And then he was gone, silently dissolving into the shadows and the grayish half light, as she'd seen him do so many times.

It unnerved her, how many times she'd seen him disappear like that. How long it had taken for him to come back those times. Not that she thought he was going to abandon her now.

No, he'd promised he wouldn't. He'd promised he'd get her out, and there was just something about him. He said it as if he had no doubts whatsoever, and it made her feel the same way. She had no doubts he would save her or die trying. He'd promised her that, too, and he was a man who delivered on his promises.

Feeling that way about him—about anyone—was almost as unsettling to Grace as the weight of the gun in her hand.

She did know how to use it. She wasn't a fool after all. Neither was her father. Peace was a wonderful thing, but some people simply didn't believe in it. There had been wild animals to consider, as well, in many of the places they'd lived. If threatened, Grace could defend herself. Her father made sure of it. He also convinced her she was capable of doing anything. Anything at all.

So she sat there with the gun clutched in front of her in both hands and thought about him, about all the things he'd taught her and tried to teach others. He believed life was a sacred thing. A gift. He'd always made the most of every moment. Her mother, too.

There'd been such meaning in their lives, such purpose. A lot of hard work, but joy, as well. They'd found joy in each other, in every little moment along the way.

Was Sean right? Had she wasted so much of the last twenty years? He'd made it sound like a cowardly thing, and she hated thinking of herself as a coward in any way. But maybe he was right. Was her father looking down upon her, ashamed? She hated that thought, as well.

And then she thought of regrets. If she died right here in this cave, if this was all the time she got, what would she regret? What would she wish she'd done differently?

So many things, she feared. So many...

She sat there for a long, long time. What seemed an eternity.

As much faith as she had in Sean and his abilities, she kept remembering what he'd told her over and over again. He was just a man. Obviously an exceptional one. But his blood was red as hers and as easily spilled.

She didn't want to ever see him hurt, didn't want to think

about trying to patch him back together, working over his battered body with hands she was sure she'd never be able to keep steady.

And she had no supplies. There was nothing as frustrating as knowing you could save someone, if only you had the proper supplies and equipment. Nothing like watching life slip needlessly away.

She couldn't watch that happen to him. Couldn't.

God, she thought. She cared too much already.

She'd promised herself. Promised. And what had she done?

Grace felt a flash of out-and-out terror and anger directed squarely at herself. She could fight it off, she told herself. It wasn't too late. She was very, very smart, very careful. She knew all about loss. Surely she could fight this and win. Fight both him and her feelings for him.

She was berating herself soundly when she heard something over the roar of the wind and the rain.

She lifted the pistol, pointed it at the passageway leading to the entrance, her arms straight, sighted it at what she thought was chest-high to a man and cursed the ever-present lack of light in her life.

How could she shoot anyone if she couldn't see?

And then Sean called her name.

She was scarcely breathing, thinking maybe she'd simply heard what she so desperately wanted to hear. She sat there and stared at the entrance to the cave until he appeared and only then did she lower the weapon. He gave her an encouraging nod for that and came to her, absolutely dripping wet and still wearing nothing but his boxers. Still he was every inch the soldier, the darkly handsome, dangerous man, capable of doing most anything, it seemed.

Staying alive, even? No matter what?

Of course not. As he'd told her, he was just a man.

"You okay?" he asked.

She nodded and looked away.

"Sure?"

"Yes. What was it?"

"I don't know. I didn't see anything. Except a lot of brush on the ground, a few trees here and there. It may have been one of those. Maybe something blowing down the beach that hit something and then went flying again. But I think the wind's picking up. We need to check on the weather forecast. We won't have a big window in which to operate. If the storm's doing something, we need to know about it. We have to be ready to move."

"What are we going to do?" she asked.

"Find a place to meet the others, and then get the hell out of here."

She nodded. It was for the best.

"Grace..." he began.

She colored profusely, for once grateful for the shallow light.

What was there to say? She'd been all over him.

"It's for the best," he said. "We agreed."

"I know."

"I want to," he groaned.

"I know." So why was he holding back?

"Oh, hell, I don't even have a condom. This is one thing I wasn't prepared for, and you're...you're a doctor. There's nothing I could possibly tell you about stupid sexual risks."

"No. Nothing. Except...because of my job, I came into contact with all sorts of things...I get tested. For everything. Regularly. I'm clean."

She looked up to find him frowning at her yet again. "Go ahead," he said. "Make it even harder."

"Well..." She frowned herself, taking his words like a dare. "I take birth control shots."

"What?"

"It's like the pill. Except in a shot. Just once every three months," she said. She wouldn't get pregnant. "It's standard procedure. For any woman going into hostile territory for the IRC…just in case. I won't get pregnant.''

He went as still as a statue then, a look of pure disgust on his face.

''What?'' she asked.

He came to her and grabbed her and kissed her. Hard and deep and hot, soaking her through and through and leaving her digging her hands into his shoulders to hang on to him, to keep him there.

''Why the hell did you have to tell me that?'' he muttered against her mouth.

''I don't know.''

''I need all the help I can get resisting you,'' he complained. ''The thought of making you pregnant might have been enough to keep my hands off you.''

''And that's a good thing?'' she dared.

''Yes. It's a very good thing.'' He kissed her yet again, was working hard for each breath by the time he lifted his head. ''Because I don't have anything, either, sweetheart. I have to get tested for all sorts of things myself from time to time, and I… Oh, hell. I haven't been with a woman in a year and half.''

She blinked up at him, trying to make sense of the idea. Him? ''Not for a year and a half?''

''Not since I kissed you. Which means my self-control isn't what it should be at the moment, and you… Grace, how the hell am I supposed to keep my hands off you now?''

Chapter 9

Grace decided it was the sexiest thing any man had ever said to her. A compliment and a source of frustration all at the same time.

Why did he have to keep his hands off her? They'd worked their way through most all the objections she knew of. She would not get pregnant, and neither one of them had any diseases. They were both adults, both free as a bird. He couldn't have a girlfriend or a wife he'd been ignoring sexually for a year and a half.

She got excited all over again just thinking about that part.

He hadn't been with anyone. Not since her. And all he'd done was kiss her. Granted, it had been an astonishingly good kiss. And she'd ached for him afterward. Somehow, she just couldn't see him as the kind of man who'd lie in his bed alone every night aching for her. She thought he was a man who'd do something about it.

"Something tells me," he groaned, so close his breath brushed past her right ear, "that you don't appreciate the seriousness of my predicament. That you're not going to be cooperative at all.''

"I'm just trying to understand," she said.

He wanted her. He didn't seem to want anyone else, and yet he wouldn't make love to her? It didn't make any sense at all.

"You're not married."

"No!"

"I didn't think so, but…a woman has to ask these days. And you don't have a girlfriend?"

"No, Grace. I meant it. I haven't touched a woman in too damned long. Except you."

"And you don't want to touch me again. I mean…you want to, but you're not going to let yourself?"

"That's right."

"Why?"

"What the hell kind of question is that?"

"I'm just curious. I've found that most men aren't interested in exercising restraint where a woman's concerned. Certainly not a willing one."

He swore viciously, and she laughed.

"You're trying to make me crazy," he said.

"No. I'm trying to understand you. I don't—well, I'm not the most experienced woman on earth, but…''

He was still frowning, but put his hand on her arm and stroked it lightly. Up and down with a fingertip on her upper arm. "I know, sweetheart. That's one of the reasons I'm trying to be a gentleman."

She stroked a fingertip of her own down his chest, felt the skin ripple in reaction to her touch. She thought about teasing him, about telling him she'd still respect him in the morning.

But she was starting to worry. She liked him too much already.

She was actually worrying that they'd get off this island soon, and he'd be gone. She found she wanted to stay here. Quite happily, she could live with him in this cave. She could use him for a bed and even learn to put up with the hurricane outside and eating MREs all the time. For him.

Which meant it was likely time to think seriously about slowing this down. Before it was too late. Before she fell in love with him.

She felt another twinge in the region of her heart, something for which she had no medical explanation. Not pain, like the kind she'd felt when he'd explained he truly did know what had happened to her family and insisted on talking to her about it. This was different. This was…pleasant. Warm and tingly. Something she suspected could put a giddy, silly smile on her face, if she let it.

She had that ridiculous schoolgirl feeling again. As if he was going to be her first serious boyfriend, except she was way too old for that. He could be her first outrageously sexy lover. Other women had those. She wasn't totally out of it. Women gossiped everywhere, a campfire in the middle of nowhere being no exception.

The talk would turn to sex, and Grace always felt as if they were speaking a different language at times. She knew a bit of a lot of languages, but not the man-woman one. It was pure gibberish to her. Grown women would be giggling and swapping stories; she'd smile and nod and hope no one ever noticed that she didn't have any stories of her own to contribute.

Looking at him, she couldn't help but think he could give her stories. He could explain every sexual thing in the world to her, could likely demonstrate it all in great detail, and he'd be so good at it. She knew. There was something so wickedly sexy about him. His scent, his look, his touch. Those big, hot hands and all those muscles. He was so gentle with her, so careful, but she knew instinctively that he could be wild, as well.

She wanted all of that. The gentleness. The wildness.

"Grace," he complained.

She looked up to find him staring at her, in that hotly

sexual way that had her shivering and even more curious about him than before.

Okay, so they weren't going to have wild, wicked sex at the moment. She fought off her disappointment at that and remembered they'd left out a big chunk of the conversation somewhere yesterday, in the middle of her running out of the cave and then, scaring him and herself, finding sheer bliss in his arms. Somehow she'd forgotten about the way he watched over her and all that he knew about her family.

"You never told me how you know all these things about me," she said. "You watch me? All the time?"

"When I think you're in a spot that has the potential to turn ugly fast, someone's keeping track of you," he said.

"Who? And why?"

"I think you deserve to live a long, healthy, happy life."

"Because of what happened to my family?"

He nodded. "And because of who your father was. I think his country owes you a debt that I intend to see repaid."

"But…how? Why?"

"The United States government keeps track of all sorts of people. For all sorts of reasons," he said evasively.

"So someone's always been there? Watching me?" She hated that idea.

"Well, we didn't think you could get into that much trouble in boarding school in Kent. But later, when you started in relief work… You kept showing up in places that make people nervous on your behalf."

"But how?"

"It's not difficult to put a trace on a passport," he said. "Or to find out where an IRC medical team is going."

"And when I show up someplace dangerous, there you are?"

"Someone sees where you're going. Someone puts a little red flag somewhere on a map, watches the situation. Maybe alerts the military commander in the area that we have Americans there. Relief workers. We'd appreciate being able to get them out in time, if the situation turns ugly.''

''Professional courtesy? Among warring factions?''

''We watch all kinds of hot spots, for all kinds of things. All the time.''

''So you're in military intelligence.''

He nodded.

''And I just happened to be your person to watch over?''

''Actually, I think I found you, remember?'' He grinned. ''You looked about sixteen, like a kid playing dress-up with that stethoscope around your neck. I remember trying to kick you out of Kuwait while your patient was insisting on knowing exactly how old you were at the time, because he was sure you couldn't possibly be a doctor.''

''So you just happened to be in the area….''

''I was working there,'' he said. ''I'd seen you, and…you reminded me of someone.''

''Who?''

''My baby sister. She's about your age and nearly as reckless.''

''So you just happened to see me, and I reminded you of your sister—''

''At first. You were so young back then,'' he whispered. ''Or you seemed so young.''

Which reminded her of something else. ''How old are you?''

''Forty-three,'' he said with a slight grimace.

She frowned at him. ''Practically decrepit.''

''You want me to kiss you again, Grace?'' he said, as a dare.

She took him up on it. ''Yes.''

He swore yet again.

She forgot for a moment that she was finally getting some answers out of him. ''So I just got to be…what? Your person to watch?''

''Let's just say I tend to make the most of my opportunities," he said. "Watched that little flag of yours hopscotch across the map. And I worried. And I let myself get too close. At the church."

"Not close enough," she contended.

"And then in San Reino, I didn't watch carefully enough."

"Oh, Sean. You don't think I blame you for what happened here, do you? Because I don't. You've saved me so many times. Me and the friends who work with me, and I'm so grateful for that," she said, then wondered if she'd embarrassed him. "Everybody wants to work with me. Did I tell you that?"

"No. Although I'm not surprised people love being around you."

"It's because of you. They've all heard stories about you. The most outlandish stories. You're a legend among the volunteers. They trust you, too. Or maybe we're just superstitious about some things. I haven't ever lost a member of my team in the field, and everybody thinks it's because of you. They see you and me as a package deal. Being with me, they get your protection, too."

He opened his mouth to say something, and she shut it for him. She closed it and brushed her fingertips across his lips and then her mouth. Softly, thankfully, almost reverently. "Thank you."

He stepped back and took her hands away. She'd definitely made him uncomfortable.

"I'm not allowed to thank you?" she asked.

"I'm just doing my job," he said.

"That's it? It's just a job to you?"

"No, dammit. It's not. You're not. But I have a job to do here. I have to keep you safe, and you're damned distracting," he complained.

"Sorry." She grinned. This was sounding better and better all the time.

"This is serious, Grace," he growled. "Our situation is incredibly precarious. I think I can handle it. I promised you

I would, and I don't make promises lightly. Which means I need to be able to think, to pay attention to what's going on around us, and I can't do that if I have my hands all over you all the time.''

"Oh. I'm sorry."

He groaned yet again. "I would never forgive myself if anything happened to you."

"I wouldn't forgive you if anything happened to you, either," she said.

"Grace—"

"I mean it."

She had to step back, to think, suddenly finding it hard to catch her breath. If anything happened to him… The thought scared the hell out of her. She cared about him already, she realized. As she hadn't allowed herself to care about anyone in a long, long time. And *caring* seemed like a totally washed-out, watered-down word for her feelings.

She looked up at him and felt that little lurch in her heart once again. It had only been a few days, she told herself. Surely it wasn't too late to back away, to slam on the brakes.

She'd lost too many people she loved. She knew how that felt. She wouldn't do it again.

Obviously, she hadn't realized just how dangerous he was to her peace of mind, to her very existence, the carefully controlled chaos of her life.

"I suppose you're right," she admitted. "We really shouldn't do this."

He studied her face, looking very stern, as if he didn't like hearing her say it at all. But he agreed with her. "No, we shouldn't. We can't."

She nodded. "Okay. I…" Damn, she'd been the one who'd pushed. She'd had her hands and her mouth all over him. "I'm sorry."

He shrugged, as if it didn't matter at all. "We're both grown-ups. We can handle this."

Of course they could. She glanced around the cave, look-

ing once again for something to do and seeing nothing. Stuck
here, she thought once again. For days. Just her and him.
They might as well be locked in a cell together, and all the
time trying to keep their hands off each other.

This was going to be interesting.

He pulled out a very sturdy-looking radio and a GPS, a
global positioning satellite link. Grace was seriously envious
of that little gadget. It beamed a signal to a series of satellites
and could tell a person exactly where he was—to within a
few feet—anywhere in the world. There were times when
Grace had a serious interest in knowing exactly where she
was, as well.

He took a reading, then pulled out a set of maps and began
plotting. When he was done, he said, "I think it's time to
get ready to go."

"Where?"

"To meet Duncan and Reed," he said. "The other two
agents on the island. And their hostage. The hurricane's finally moving. It looks like we'll get the eye sometime within
the next few hours. The eye's wide enough and moving
slowly enough that we should have enough time to get to
them before the backside of the storm comes through."

"You want to go traipsing across this island in the eye of
a hurricane?" she said, not liking the sound of that at all.

He grinned. "What do you know about hurricanes?"

"That it's damned hard to clean up after one."

"We won't have to clean up after this one. We just have
to use it to our best advantage."

"How can you possibly take advantage of something like
a hurricane?"

"It's worked in our favor so far, Grace. It kept Milero's
men pinned down enough that no one came looking for us
for the last four days."

"It's what kept us on this island," she reminded him.

Here's a **HOT** offer for you!

The Silhouette Reader Service™ —Here's how it works:

Accepting your 2 free books and gift places you under no obligation to buy anything. You may keep the books and gift and return the shipping statement marked "cancel." If you do not cancel, about a month later we'll send you 6 additional novels and bill you just $3.80 each in the U.S., or $4.21 each in Canada, plus 25¢ delivery per book and applicable taxes if any.* That's the complete price and — compared to cover prices of $4.50 each in the U.S. and $5.25 each in Canada — it's quite a bargain! You may cancel at any time, but if you choose to continue, every month we'll send you 6 more books, which you may either purchase at the discount price or return to us and cancel your subscription.

*Terms and prices subject to change without notice. Sales tax applicable in N.Y. Canadian residents will be charged applicable provincial taxes and GST.

If offer card is missing write to: Silhouette Reader Service, 3010 Walden Ave., P.O. Box 1867, Buffalo, NY 14240-1867

BUSINESS REPLY MAIL
FIRST-CLASS MAIL   PERMIT NO. 717   BUFFALO, NY

POSTAGE WILL BE PAID BY ADDRESSEE

SILHOUETTE READER SERVICE
3010 WALDEN AVE
PO BOX 1867
BUFFALO NY 14240-9952

NO POSTAGE
NECESSARY
IF MAILED
IN THE
UNITED STATES

''True. But we would have had trouble getting off even without the storm.''

''How are we going to get off?''

''Stealing one of Milero's supply boats would be my first choice. He has boats going back and forth from here to the mainland regularly. We'll grab one and take off.''

''Which the storm kept you from doing before now,'' she reminded him. It had caused some trouble.

''Only partially, the storm. You were a mess, and Duncan has a bullet in his shoulder and a very whiny, wimpy hostage who's making their lives miserable. I don't think we would have been able to move fast enough to steal the boat and get away before now.''

''There's a colleague of yours on this island who got shot four days ago?''

''Yes.''

''And you didn't tell me?''

''I knew if I did you'd want to get to him, and you weren't strong enough to make the trip, and we were all better off— Duncan included—by staying where we were and remaining undetected. I also didn't want to argue with you about it. Duncan's in good hands.''

''Whose?''

''Reed's.''

''He's a doctor?''

''No, but he knows what to do. It's a flesh wound, Grace. They're handling it. We're trained in what to do in cases like this.''

''This is my area of expertise,'' she argued. ''Maybe you could let me be the judge of that?''

''Okay. When we get there, you're in charge of Duncan and his bullet wound.''

''Thank you,'' she said.

Sean laughed at her again.

''You must be worried about him if we're going out in the middle of the hurricane,'' she said.

"No. I'm thinking of getting us off this island. As soon as the storm lessens enough, Milero's men are going to be out gunning for us. We need to get the boat and go at the first possible moment. The others are a lot closer to Milero's compound than we are. It makes sense to leave from there, and I want to see what kind of shape Duncan's in for myself before we make our final plans."

"Okay. If you say we can travel in the middle of a hurricane…"

"You know how one works? As long as it has forward motion, you see a slow, steady buildup of the winds and rain as the front side of the hurricane comes ashore. Same thing on the back end in reverse. It starts out howling and gradually lessens until the storm is gone. In the middle, in the eye, it's dead calm. No winds. No rain. If it came during the day, we'd see sunshine. This is a big storm. The eye's wide enough and the storm's forward motion is slow enough that we should have about forty-five minutes to travel. We'll have to push, but we can make it." He frowned. "Do you trust me, Grace?"

"Of course I do," she said. She didn't even have to think about it. She trusted him.

"We'll have to watch for downed trees and debris on the ground. For flooding and for snakes. But that's about it. No wind. No rain. Probably not any of Milero's men, either."

"Okay. We'll do whatever you say."

"Good."

"When is this all going to happen?"

"I'll have to listen to the radio. Right now, it looks like about six hours from now."

Six hours, she thought. And then they would no longer be alone. Surely she could resist him for six hours.

Grace cleaned up a bit, then put on a pair of his camouflage pants, tied at her waist with a string and rolled up about six times on each leg, in preparation of hiking through the junglelike terrain of the island.

Sean put their things into a single pack he intended to wear on his back. She offered to help carry them. She was a woman used to lugging her own supplies, after all. But he gave her a look that said he thought it was ridiculous and insulting to even suggest he'd have any trouble with the pack at all. It only weighed about seventy-five pounds, he claimed.

So he was in full tough-guy mode.

It would be nearly midnight before they made their move, and he intended to blacken her face and his when the time came.

She was beginning to think she truly would never see his face in broad daylight, might never actually have that kind of picture of him to carry in her memory. Which made her think there were still so many things she didn't know about him. So later, when they had nothing to do but sit and wait, she asked, "Where were you born?"

"Italy, but my family's originally from Virginia."

She nodded. That's what she heard in his voice. "So why all the different languages? The accents? With me?"

"Not just with you. In this line of work, you have to learn to blend into different places, different cultures, not to call attention to yourself. It's second nature to me, to protect my identity when I'm in the field. My face, my voice, even the languages I speak and the accents I use."

Grace considered that. CIA? Naval Intelligence? Or another of the military's special ops units?

Oh, yes, she realized. He was a real tough guy.

"My father was career army. A general, before he retired. It took him all over the world. If we could go with him, we did. If not, we were in Virginia."

"So you grew up all over the place? Like me?"

He nodded.

"Brothers or sisters?"

"I told you about Rich."

She remembered. The brother he lost.

"I have another brother who's in the air force. A test pilot. My baby sister is a Naval Academy graduate, like me. She did some time in the navy and then in...other things."

"Other things?" Now Grace was curious. Even his baby sister was tough.

"I don't suppose it would tell you anything, since I'm not going to tell you any more about Duncan and Reed, but my sister used to work with them."

"She used to do things like this?"

"God." He shook his head at the thought. "Probably."

"Wow." Grace wondered if he was as protective of his sister as he seemed to be of her. "What did you think of that?"

"What do you think I thought about it?"

"I think you didn't like it very much."

"I didn't. But she's stubborn as hell, and she didn't bother to ask what I thought, and she doesn't take kindly to being ordered around. I told her not to, but she did it, anyway."

"And now?"

"She's home in Virginia making babies with a guy who used to try to boss her around at the agency. I'm still not sure who's winning that little battle, but I'm a lot happier that she's not sticking her neck out anymore. Although she tells me raising little boys is proving as potentially hazardous as any duty assignment she ever had."

Grace laughed and fought off the odd pangs of envy. She'd quickly dismissed any thoughts she ever had of having children. To do that, she really should have a man, and she really ought to love him. No doubt, she would love her children a great deal, and with loving there was always that potential for loss. Which she'd sworn off totally. But for the last year or so, every time she delivered a baby, every time she held a newborn baby in her arms, it got a little harder to slam the door so tightly on the whole idea. No children. Not ever.

Lately, it hurt too much to think about it, left her with that annoying unsettled feeling that seemed to eat away at her at times.

Questions like, what did she really want? Like…was this it? Was this all life had to offer? As much as she did for the people who showed up at her clinics throughout the world, at times it seemed there just had to be more to a woman's life.

"Do you think your sister's happy?" she asked.

"I know she is," he said.

"And you? Are you happy?"

"I don't know, Grace." He stared at her for a long moment. "My life is different now. I'm in Washington most of the time. I sit behind a desk a whole lot more than I'd like. If I wanted to, I have enough years in to retire, but I'm not sure what else I'd like to do. What about you?"

She drew her knees up to her chest and wrapped her arms around them, rested her chin on her knees. "Before this, I would have said I was content. Which is not such a bad thing."

A lot of people didn't even have an element of contentment.

"You could have so much more, Grace. You deserve it."

"I'm thinking about it," she admitted.

It was an odd idea after all this time of simply not thinking. She'd wanted to be a doctor for as long as she could remember, probably from watching her mother with her own patients and helping out in the clinics. She'd grown up telling her mother and her father what she was going to be, and she'd never questioned that later when the time came to start her training.

For years after that, she'd gone where the IRC sent her, much like he must have as a soldier. It had given order to her life when she craved it, when she'd have been lost without it.

But now…it seemed odd to think about having so much of her life still ahead of her. To think that she could do anything she wanted, make anything of herself that suited her. She had no idea what she wanted to do.

"If you could do anything with the rest of your life," she asked, "anything at all, what would it be?"

He frowned, then got the oddest look on his face. He was watching her so intently for so long. She thought she sensed longing in his expression and frustration and something else. Regrets, maybe?

Which was ridiculous. She could hardly see him, although she felt as if she'd gotten adept at reading his moods without actually seeing the expression on his face.

Right now, his emotions seemed to radiate from him. Agitation, anger and then a deep, deep sadness.

"Sometimes I think your life has been as full of regrets as mine has," she told him.

He didn't say anything. Pushed to his feet and walked toward the mouth of the cave. Grace scrambled after him, found him, seeming as immovable as any mountain she'd ever scaled, standing right at the edge, staring out into the fierce rain and wind.

She put her hand against his arm and stood beside him, wishing he'd pull her close. He didn't.

"What do you regret?" she said.

"I could make you a list, but I don't think we have time for that. We have to get moving soon."

She panicked a bit then, thinking her time with him was almost up. From here, they might not be alone again, between the other two agents and the other hostage. There were so many things she wanted to say to him, so many things she still wanted to know about him.

He turned to go back, and she grabbed him by his arms and stopped him. She begged, "Just a minute. I can't let you go like this. Things are going to get crazy from here on out, right? It won't be just you and me."

"No," he admitted. "It won't."

"Believe it or not, I'm going to miss that."

"So am I."

"I'm not sure I thanked you—"

"You did."

"For the other things, too. Before this."

"It's my job, Grace."

"Is that all this is to you?" She had to ask. "Because I can't help but think there's something I'm missing about you and me. Something you haven't told me."

He hesitated.

"Please," she said. "I need to understand."

"My father knew your father."

"Oh." That certainly came out of the blue. "They were friends?"

"Not what I'd call close friends. They ran into each other from time to time. My father did a stint with the UN at the time your father was involved with the group. He even remembers you, from when you were a little girl."

"Oh." So when Sean ran across her, later, when she'd started with the IRC... "You felt an obligation, of sorts."

"Of sorts," he admitted.

"Oh." It was all she could say. She felt as if someone had forced all the air from her lungs. From the mention of her father, she supposed. No one else mentioned him even casually to her, because no one knew.

"Grace?" He finally turned to her, pulled her into a loose embrace, tantalizingly close but not nearly close enough. "Before we go our separate ways, I'm going to tell you how to contact me. Anytime, anywhere. Day or night. Someone can always reach me. I want you to know that if you ever need me, for anything, all you have to do is call."

Which was an awfully big promise to make. Even more significant was the fact that she had no doubt he meant it. That he would drop everything and come to her, anywhere, anytime.

She'd already known that about him, before she even knew

his name, before they'd ever come to this island. From the start, somehow, she'd believed that about him.

"Promise me you'll do that. If you ever get in trouble. If you even think you're in trouble, Grace."

She shook her head, felt a bit dizzy.

So, she had to be in trouble, did she? His words told her that, but his body said something else all together.

She remembered again the moments after he dragged her back into the cave, after she'd scared him so badly and made him so angry he was shaking. The time she'd sensed he had deep, dark scars on his soul, as well.

He'd uncovered all of hers, but she hadn't found any of his.

And there was that little sting that came from the fact that he wouldn't make love to her. She knew it was for the best, and she had her reasons for believing it, but no idea what his reasons were.

His hands cupped her elbows. He bent his forehead until it was against hers, and she felt his warm breath pass over her face. She wanted to kiss him so badly, she was shaking.

"Are you afraid?" he asked.

"No."

"You don't think I can get you out of here safely?"

"No. It's not that at all," she admitted. "I'm afraid I'm going to miss you. And I know I'm not supposed to do that."

He dipped his head and kissed her, so softly, so gently. Giving her nothing but an elusive taste of him.

"We agreed," he said, pulling back to the spot he had before, their bodies barely brushing.

"I know."

"It's for the best, Grace."

"Why?" she asked. "I mean, I know it is. I know why. At least as far as I'm concerned. But I don't know what's holding you back. Do you think I might be making a mistake? Circumstances and adrenaline and fear, and all that stuff? Are you trying to protect me even now?"

"I think that has to be taken into consideration."

"But what about you? Can't you tell me a little bit of what's inside you?"

Very slowly, he pulled her fully against him. Didn't even hold her tightly, although she found it was the most powerful embrace of all. That same luxurious warmth and strength, but an incredible sense of homecoming, too. As if someone had made a place on this earth for her, and it might just be in his arms. Where he seemed so reluctant to have her stay for any length of time.

How could that be? If this was her place? Made for her? How could he not want her here?

Grace buried her face against his chest, afraid she would start to cry. Until he came along, she'd never cried. But there was something about this feeling, the sweet yearning, the kindness, the caring. His hands stroked gently up and down her back, and she nuzzled the tip of her nose against his shirt, wishing it was his skin. Wishing they were skin to skin.

Her arms wrapped around his shoulders so tightly, and she felt once again the sheer might of the man. It was because he made her feel so safe. That's why she thought she needed him so badly, why she found the whole idea of him so attractive.

"I'm not a man to fall in love with, Grace," he said sadly.

"Why not? You wouldn't love me back?"

"I don't think I've ever been in love with any woman."

"You don't believe in it?"

"No. It's not that."

"You couldn't love me?"

"Oh, sweetheart. I could love you." He kissed her again, deeper this time, with more hunger, more urgency. "I don't think I could do it very well. I don't think it would be the best thing for you or that I could make you happy in the end. But I could love you. And I'm not talking about making love to you, either. Although I could very easily do that, as well."

"But you'd regret it," she said, cursed tears falling down her cheeks.

"Yes, I would. And I know you would."

"How do you know?"

"Because I know you, Grace. Wouldn't you regret it?"

"Yes," she said, growing more miserable with every passing moment and just wishing she never had to stray from his arms. "And I want to tell you why. I need to."

He cradled her closer. "Okay."

"I've lost too many people," she said. "You know that. Everyone who ever mattered to me, and you were right. I push people away. I keep them at a distance. I'm always trying to protect myself, and maybe I've taken that too far. Because I don't want to get hurt again. And the easiest way to make sure that doesn't happen is to never let anyone get too close. Never let anyone be important to me. Which is why you scare me to death."

"Oh, baby. I'm sorry."

"Because you make me want to take every risk. Every one I swore I'd never take again. To me, it's the same thing as jumping off a cliff. It would be that hard. I'd be so sure I'd fall."

"Don't do it, Grace. Don't jump. Not with me."

Which was the same as him saying, *don't love me. Don't.* She still didn't know why. And she supposed it really didn't matter.

"I didn't want to live after they died," she told him. "You were right about that. I was in the hospital for a while, and I kept thinking there had to be all sorts of things I could do to myself. To make me die. I didn't realize they didn't leave helpful little drugs around like that for people to pick up. I thought if I stayed in that hospital long enough, I'd slip away from everybody and find what I needed and just do it. Just be gone. I thought I'd be happy again, that I'd be with my family again. I closed my eyes and saw them, pictured them calling my name. Waiting for me, so we could all go off together.''

His hold was fierce then. Absolutely fierce. She held him back just as tightly, because she sensed he needed it, too.

''Anyway, they didn't just leave drugs like that around, and I never seemed to find myself alone. Not the whole time I was there. I wonder if they knew somehow what I wanted to do. If someone was watching over me, even then,'' she said. ''I always felt like someone was. Isn't that silly?''

''No. I don't. I'm glad you felt that way.''

''So when you came along, when I started to suspect the man who kept coming to my rescue was the same person, it all seemed to fit. I thought you'd been there all along, just keeping your distance more at first.''

She let go of him long enough to wipe her tears away, then bury her face against his chest once again.

''You've always been a magical man to me,'' she said, smiling through her tears. ''You've always seemed like the person I always knew was there.''

He backed up an inch or so. Took her face in one of his hands. Brushed away her tears, and kissed her once more, a world full of sadness in that kiss.

''If I had any magical powers at all,'' he whispered against her mouth, ''you would lead a truly charmed life. I would take every bit of sadness away. Every hurt. Every fear. I would give everything I had to you, Grace. Everything in this world.''

''But you don't think you could? You don't think you could do that for me?''

''I know I couldn't. Dammit, if there was any way I could... But I can't. I'm so sorry. I just can't.''

Chapter 10

Sean thought he might have to pry his own hands off her in order to let her go. She just didn't understand. He was not a hero, especially not to her, and he used to be amused by her whimsical idea that there was something magical about him. Not any longer. He'd never felt more simply a man than he did with her, never felt so horribly inadequate.

His whole life, he'd gotten things done, fixed things, made them right, and in typically arrogant fashion, he'd thought he could make things better for her. Not fix them. No one could do that. But make them better. He was starting to worry he'd make things worse instead. Getting her out of here was one thing. Leaving her better off than she was before Milero grabbed her was another thing altogether.

Sean was a man who'd always found a way to get what he wanted. Always. And he wanted her to be happy, wanted that desperately. But he couldn't give it to her. There'd been so many things he simply didn't have to give over the years. The power to erase the past. To bring her family back to her. To make her happy. None of it was within his reach.

Unfortunately, she was. He held her even more tightly, his mouth brushing light kisses along the side of her face. She was trembling, as he was, and he thought she was still crying. He hated seeing her cry. It had always torn him apart. And she was starting to care for him, more than he could ever let her. He was scaring her now, because she was afraid of falling for him.

"Aah, Grace," he groaned. *If only you knew...* He supposed he'd been half in love with her from the very beginning, impossible as it always had been.

And he didn't think he had the courage to tell her the whole truth about why he had spent the better part of his life watching over her, why he always would, or why he couldn't let himself love her and wouldn't let her love him. It wasn't an easy admission for him to make—that he was too much a coward to tell her. He liked to think he wasn't afraid of anything, but there it was. He couldn't hide from it any longer, either. He couldn't stand the look he feared he'd bring to her eyes by telling her the truth.

So he just stood there and held her, in the most bittersweet moment of his life. He wanted her desperately. Not just sexually. On every level imaginable.

He'd lost a lot of people, too, over the years. Not the kind of loss she'd experienced. But he knew what it was like for someone to be there one minute, gone the next. He'd always found it so hard when there'd been no time for goodbyes. No time to say all the things he wanted to say.

But this...having her here in his arms and knowing he had to let her go, that there was nothing he could say that wouldn't make it even worse... This seemed to be the hardest thing of all.

With what had to be superhuman effort, he loosened his hold on her.

'Don't," she cried. "Don't let me go."

"Oh, baby. It's the last thing in the world I want to do."

* * *

Grace thought it was something of a miracle when the wind just died, as did the rain. One minute it was roaring, and the next, she could look up and see stars. She'd forgotten what it was like to live in a world that wasn't battered by howling winds. Her ears had forgotten how quiet silence could be.

It was eerily quiet now. She couldn't quite get used to it. It unnerved her, as did the whole situation.

She'd cried her eyes out earlier. Over him and the whole situation. Over knowing she had to pull away from him, as quickly as she could, even though she couldn't seem to let go or stop crying.

Finally, they'd done it somehow. It had felt horrible to back away, to lose the feel of his strong, reassuring arms around her.

He'd been all business after that. A bit brusque, working quickly and efficiently, ordering her around. She hadn't argued, had simply done what he'd asked and found herself traipsing behind him through the dense, junglelike foliage.

There were downed trees here and there, tons of branches and leaves and debris. She jumped at every little noise that interrupted the odd stillness, kept waiting for the wind and the rain to attack them once more.

She didn't see how he could possibly know where they were or where they were going. There was no discernible trail at all, but he kept right on moving like a man who knew his direction in life instinctively, unmistakably.

He was in his warrior gear, armed to the teeth and looking like he was ready for anything, and she remembered once more that he'd killed a man for her. To save her.

How could he be so gentle with her, she wondered, and be so deadly at the same time? How did the two sides coexist inside the same man? There had to be depths to him she'd never understand. She'd likely always find herself fascinated with him, and she feared after another day or so, she might not see him again. Or that maybe it would only be those quick, tantalizing glimpses he'd allowed over the years. That he'd always be slipping in and out of her life that quickly, and she'd spend years just hoping for a glimpse of him. That she'd always be wishing, maybe even begging him to stay.

She had no idea why he wouldn't, why he felt he couldn't. Her gut said he cared, that he could love her. He said it as if it made him ache, as it did her, thinking she could love him completely, without a hint of reservation, of self-preservation.

Why would that scare him as much as it scared her?

They walked for what seemed like hours, though she knew it couldn't have been that long. He'd told her when they left the cave that they only had forty-five minutes or so to get to the other agents' location. Otherwise they'd get caught in the back side of the hurricane. He'd asked her to trust him to get her there safely, asked her not to be afraid.

She marveled at the fact that he even had to ask. How could he not know that? She'd follow him to the ends of the earth, if he said that's where he thought they needed to go.

As it was, the storm was closing in on them before he pulled out his flashlight and gave three short bursts of light into what seemed like absolute nothingness to her. But she saw the answering signal come back.

The next thing she knew, they were entering yet another cave. There was a man standing just inside the entrance, a tall man with dark blond hair and a ready smile. He and Sean greeted each other, and then Sean introduced her.

"Reed, this is Dr. Grace Evans."

The man shook her hand and looked her over from head to toe. "Doctor. I'm glad to see you. My hostage has been getting nastier every minute, and I'd pay you any sum of money you name if you have some kind of drug to knock him unconscious. Or maybe just to render him mute."

"What?"

"If he doesn't stop whining soon, Duncan and I are going to put him back in his cell in Milero's compound."

"You wouldn't do that," she said, smiling up at him.

"We got him out—barely. We could put him back," Reed claimed.

"I think I should check on your patient," Grace said, because Sean had her by the arm, drawing her deeper into the cave, and he didn't look happy. "Something wrong?"

"Not a thing," he claimed.

She found a very frightened, very unhappy-looking man sitting on the floor about fifteen feet back. He had his knees drawn up against his chest, his arms wrapped around them, and he looked at Sean as if he expected Sean to blow him away at any second.

"This is George Roberts," Reed said, coming up behind them. "He's not happy to be here."

George merely lifted his eyes and frowned.

"We've never rescued such an ungrateful little prick," Reed whispered into her ear as he directed them to the other passageway, where Grace would see another man sitting against the cave wall. "Duncan," Reed said. "We've got company."

The third man was pale and perspiring, smiling up at her but leaning weakly against the cave wall. Grace knelt beside him and put the back of her fingers against his cheek, his forehead, then felt for a pulse in his wrist.

"Dr. Evans, I presume," he said. "Good to see you."

"Call me Grace, please."

"Movin' a little slowly these days, Duncan?" asked Sean, who was somewhere behind her.

Duncan made a face that said he didn't appreciate that at all. "I'm moving just fine. It's my friend George who's a little slow. Silly me, I decided to do my job and save his sorry ass. But if I'd known him a little better, I doubt I'd have made the sacrifice."

Grace heard it all, but she was concentrating on her patient's condition. Someone—Reed, she presumed—had tucked Duncan's right arm against his chest and rigged up a sling. There was a pad of gauze beneath it, blood that had seeped through.

"The bullet's in your shoulder?" she asked.

"Yeah."

Duncan barely winced as she freed his arm and started peeling back the gauze. "Sean?" he said. "Next time, Reed and I get to go after the woman."

He gave her an unabashedly appreciative look. Grace couldn't believe he was flirting with her at a time like this. He was feverish, his skin clammy, and he'd had a bullet in his shoulder for four days.

"You must not feel that bad," Grace said.

"I've had worse," he said, still grinning.

She thought about telling him she'd seen the tough-guy routine before. If his aim was to impress her, it wasn't necessary. But she saved her breath. Men like him seldom listened, she'd found. If at all possible, their ego would stop them from ever admitting they were in pain.

She was just uncovering the wound, and he was still talking, still making her laugh, when Sean brought her two small packs of supplies.

"I'm afraid that's all we've got," he said.

"Thanks."

Duncan looked up at Sean. "You two heading out?"

Grace turned, found him nodding and handing Duncan his pistol. "Grace tells me she knows how to use it," he said.

"I do," she said, trying to fight off a flare of panic. "Where are you going?"

"To check out the boats."

"Reed's going, too?" Duncan asked.

Sean frowned, looked to Grace. She didn't want to be separated from him.

"We don't have much time," he said. "We need to know the situation at the dock. The condition of the boats. The best path to take. I think we both need to go, but..."

"Go ahead. We'll be fine," Duncan claimed. "We haven't

seen any movement at all from them in more than twenty-four hours. They've got to know we'd be stupid to move during this storm. No reason for them not to wait us out.''

''Still...the eye,'' Sean said.

''If they were coming, they'd have been here by now. Or you'll run into them on your way to the dock. If that happens, you'll stop them before they ever get to us, and you don't need to do that alone. Take Reed.''

Another few moments, and they'd all agreed. Sean and Reed were both going. Over her own protests, they helped Duncan to the mouth of the cave and sat him down there. George scrambled to the back, looking scared even of Grace and muttering under his breath some things that sounded ungrateful indeed. They all ignored him when he kept asking questions about where they were going and when they'd be back.

All too soon, Grace found herself standing in front of Sean, as he was ready to leave, standing in the front of the cave with two men hovering nearby.

''Don't worry,'' he said. ''It's not far. I've got a radio. I can be back in minutes. And Duncan...he's a good shot. He's alert enough to keep watch.''

''Okay,'' she said, a bit dizzy at the notion of Sean heading into Milero's territory. At letting him go already. ''Be careful.''

He nodded, drawing himself up even straighter, looking even more warriorlike.

''Remember,'' she whispered. ''You're just a man.''

Cut him, and he'd bleed. Shoot him, and... Grace shuddered at the thought.

He pulled her close for a moment. The two men behind them fell silent, and she knew they were watching, found she didn't care.

He kissed her quickly, fiercely. ''I'll be right back.''

And then she had to stand and watch him go into the blackness once again.

* * *

She forgot all about the fact that she wasn't alone until Duncan said, "So that's the way it is with you and him."

"What?"

"You and Sean."

He must think they were lovers, Grace decided. She started to deny it, but didn't see the point. She couldn't begin to explain exactly what they were. More than they should be, as two people who were practically strangers in so many ways, but much, much less than she wanted them to be.

"That…that was nothing," she said.

"Sean practically growls at me every time I look at you. He's jealous, and that kiss was a blatant hands-off-she's-mine warning."

Was he jealous? True, in the brief time they'd been here, Sean had seemed even more stern than ever. But she'd taken that for concentration on the job at hand, at him maybe being a bit worried, something she didn't think he let people see too often.

"It's not like that with us," she said.

"If that's what you say, Doc."

She did what she could for his wounded shoulder, which was not as bad as she feared for someone who'd had a bullet inside of him for so long.

"So," he teased. "Am I going to live?"

"Get me something that passes for an operating room and some instruments, and I could fix you up in no time," she said. "But you'll keep for another day or so."

He just grinned at her. He was handsome, she supposed, with dark hair and pretty blue eyes. She guessed he must be close to her own age of thirty-one, and he didn't seem worried at all at the predicament in which they found themselves.

"I suppose this is just another day at the office for you?" she suggested.

"Well, we wouldn't normally head out in the face of a hurricane, but it's going to work out. We'll be fine," he said. "And now that I've seen you…now that I've seen Sean with you, I can't blame him for insisting that we move when we did.''

"He said your…agency was already coming. To get George.''

"We were. But George had been here for weeks, and if they'd put up with him without killing him in that amount of time, we could have left him a few more days, for the storm to pass. Sean wasn't going to leave you here for another minute.''

"Oh.''

"It's none of my business, but I'm dying to know who you are.''

"He didn't tell you?''

"Just that you were a doctor with the IRC and that this was personal. We didn't exactly have time to chitchat.''

"Oh,'' she said, feeling a blush rising in her cheeks. That's how it had always felt to her. Highly personal.

"I've known the man for years, and I've never seen him even close to losing control. But he almost did over you. And I have to say, I find that and you fascinating, Doctor.''

She ignored that and gave into her own curiosity once more. "Who is he?''

Duncan laughed. "You don't know?''

"Not really.'' She saw the doubt on his face. "It's…complicated.''

"He's a complicated man.''

"Secretive,'' she said.

"Definitely.''

"He told me you're…well, that you're with the U.S. government. That the agency's top secret, that his sister used to work with you and Reed, and that he used to be a soldier. A pilot.''

"That's right.''

"I won't ask you anything about who you work for, but Sean…''

"I really don't know, Grace. He's tight-lipped about everything. I know he's one hell of a chopper pilot, because he pulled a friend of mine out of a tight spot with one not long ago. I heard he used to be a jet jockey. That's how he messed up his knee. And I think at one time he was a Navy Seal and that he did a stint with Naval Intelligence. I've seen people salute him and call him Captain, but not even that all the time. Which makes me think he's no longer a part of the navy. At least not in any capacity that would be acknowledged publicly. If you ask him, he'll tell you he sits behind a desk most every day. At the Pentagon, I've heard. But I have trouble believing the desk bit. At least, not on a regular basis.''

''He told me that. About the desk.'' Grace had trouble imagining him being so still. She saw him as pure energy and power, couldn't imagine him doing anything so tame.

''But he's a great guy to know. Somebody you can count on when you're in trouble. He and his guys have helped us out of jams more than once in the past few years.''

''His guys?''

''Soldiers of some kind. He seems to have teams at his disposal, whenever he needs them. But I don't even know exactly who they are or where he gets them.''

''How odd,'' she said.

''We help each other when we need it. Sorry I can't tell you more than that. I really don't know.''

He'd told her enough. Sean was every bit as mysterious as she imagined, as closemouthed with this man as he'd been with her. And Duncan said he'd known him for years.

Why would a man keep so many secrets? What drove him on? What kept him a part of her life, year after year, when he'd drawn a line with their involvement that he didn't intend to cross? He could love her, he'd said, as if it just about ripped his heart in two to admit it. But he wasn't going to let himself.

She should be grateful; she knew that. Instead it was one more thing that left her dying to know everything about him.

It made her wish he wasn't so good at keeping secrets. Made her wish he wasn't likely to disappear again very soon, leaving her with no idea when she might see him again.

Sean was gone too long to suit her. Worry ate away at her. Dug into her. The air took on that odd sense of expectancy. As if the atmosphere were going to explode any minute. She wanted him back before that happened.

Duncan kept talking, she suspected because he knew she was worried, and George was indeed a very annoying and ungrateful man. He must have been nervous, and normally Grace would have been sympathetic to his plight. But he kept coming to stand beside them every few minutes, just long enough to complain. He questioned every decision their rescuers had made, complained about all the hardships he'd endured since being rescued and whined about the fact that he was unaccustomed to being treated with so little respect.

Grace was spitting mad by the third time she'd been treated to one of his tirades. "Reed told me not to let you have a gun anywhere near him," she told Duncan. "I can see why."

"Hey, I'm a man of incredible self-control. After all, I haven't shot him yet, and we've been cooped up with him for days."

She laughed. She did like Duncan, wondered what he would be like back in the real world. More polished, she suspected. Smooth. Elegant.

"You can stop worrying, Grace," he said, nodding into the darkness. "There they are."

She didn't see a thing at first, but they did indeed appear. Reed followed by Sean. She forced a smile across her face, didn't want him to see the sheer relief flooding through her. She wasn't supposed to care that much, after all.

Sean smiled at her, took her hand and squeezed it. "Nothing to it, see?"

"I'm glad you're back," she said. It was so much better,

just having him by her side, and she fought the urge to snuggle against him.

"How does it look at the docks?" Duncan asked.

"Doable. We just need to know when to make our move," Sean said.

"When?" she asked.

"Soon."

Grace looked outside. She had heard the wind, sounding like it was coming closer and closer with each passing minute. "We can't get out in the ocean in a boat in that."

"No," he admitted. "But the storm's forward motion is picking up. It's going to move out. We'll go around dawn."

That soon? she thought, wishing she could simply stop time, hang on to the moment, on to him.

But she couldn't. It was time to exercise some restraint where he was concerned. She had to, for her own sake. She slipped away from him and excused herself, walking deeper into the cave, ignoring George altogether and sitting in the blackness in the back corner, needing to be alone.

She sat there and listened to the wind, knowing that as soon as it died down, they'd be going. To steal a boat and get off this island.

From there, it would likely be a whirlwind journey. She'd be home in London in no time, and God, she was going to miss Sean. She'd have to think about getting back to her real life. Or what passed for real life with her.

The prospect wasn't that inviting. She had no idea what she wanted to do, she realized. For the first time in her life, she didn't want to go rushing back into the field. In fact, she didn't think she could. She'd been truly frightened for the first time by what happened in San Reino. The thought of going right back into that kind of situation again...

Grace wasn't sure she could do it. It seemed she'd lost her nerve. Or maybe that she realized she had to stop running. That's what it was. He'd been right, she decided. She was running away, running through her work.

If she didn't have that, she couldn't imagine how she'd fill her days. Fill her life.

Loneliness settled in around her. Enveloping her. Seeming to smother her. It had never really bothered her before. She'd always had people around, just not that close to her. And that worked. Being busy had worked, as well.

She had a feeling it wouldn't anymore, and she didn't know what she was going to do. She felt a bit like she had when she'd woken up in the hospital, after the explosion. Once she'd realized everyone she loved was gone. A sense that everything would be different from this moment on. She'd been through it all once. She knew how hard it was, didn't feel any better equipped to deal with it at thirty-one than she had been at eleven. Except, it seemed harder this time.

Sean came and found her. Came to her through the darkness the way he used to, when she could see only the faintest impression of his face. He sat down beside her and slipped his arm around her, drew her against his side. "Want to tell me what's wrong?"

"No."

"We'll get out of here, Grace."

"I know. I trust you. Absolutely and completely. Do you have any idea what an amazing thing that is for me?"

"You don't trust many people?"

"I don't trust anyone. Except myself. I haven't let myself trust anyone else. Not for twenty years," she admitted. "But I trust you. I always have. Even when it made no sense at all. When I didn't even know your name. I knew if I was in trouble, you'd come. You'd save me."

He just sat there for the longest time, his hand rubbing absently at her arm, his breath stirring the hair against her temple. "I won't let you down," he said finally. "Not in this."

"I know, Sean. I do."

"So what's wrong?"

"We're leaving here," she said in the calmest voice she could muster. "We're going to steal a boat and then what?"

"Rendezvous with a ship. There are several in the area. Someone back in the States is finding one right now that's willing to pick us up. From there, we'll get back to the U.S."

"Oh."

"You're coming with us, Grace."

"All right."

She could stay there, maybe have a few days with him while she pulled herself together. Or maybe she shouldn't. Maybe it wouldn't be wise—to be with him, even for a few more days.

They sat there quietly, while she tried to memorize the feel of his body resting reassuringly against hers. She wanted to absorb this feeling, take it inside her and be able to pull it out later when she needed it, when she was once again alone.

"I don't know how to say goodbye to you," she admitted.

He sucked in a harsh-sounding breath, bent his head down closer to hers, and the next thing she knew, he'd lifted her into his arms, onto his lap, and he was kissing her, over and over again.

Her body came instantly alive. There was no other way to describe it. He touched her, and she was suddenly, painfully, startlingly, blindly alive, after merely existing for so long.

The need she had for him was like a fever, consuming her, burning her, making her dizzy and a bit irrational, she thought. Because at times like this, all that seemed to matter was getting even closer to him. Getting as close as humanly possible.

She wanted him inside her, wanted his body to be a part of hers. Wanted him gloriously naked and gasping for breath, a fine sheen of perspiration running down the middle of his back. She wanted him utterly exhausted and spent and lying heavily on top of her. Nothing but a single, straining heartbeat between them as they lay there in each other's arms.

She wanted to know him. Everything about him. Everything he hoped, everything he dreamed. She wanted to give him everything he wanted, everything he said he'd give her, if only he could.

Could she make him happy? Would she be enough for him? Or any man? She'd never worried about that before. That she might want a man so desperately and simply not have the things he needed her to give him.

He broke the kiss on a ragged sigh and eased her away from him. Only then did she realize she had a near death grip on his shoulders and there were tears running down her cheeks, his deep, harsh breath rushing across her mouth, because he was still so close.

"Could I make you happy?" she said. "Would I be enough for you?"

"Grace, you could be everything to me. Absolutely everything."

"Then I don't understand. I know why I can't do this. I know why I shouldn't, but you..."

"It's me, sweetheart. The problem is with me. Me and the things I've done. The things I still carry around inside of me. I wouldn't be any good for you. Not for long. And I would hurt you in the end. I know that, and I'm trying so hard to do the right thing here," he muttered. "But God knows I don't want to let you go."

Chapter 11

Grace didn't sleep. Sean held her for a long time, maybe thinking she was sleeping, but she wasn't. She lay there thinking of what it was like—drifting off in his arms, waking up with him beside her, his body all hot and hard and filled with yearning. For her.

Maybe later, when she was back in London or wherever she went, she could sleep and dream of him, just like that. Maybe she'd see him again from time to time. Maybe she'd find a way to deal with her fears. Maybe someday, she wouldn't get absolutely sick inside at the idea of loving someone, of letting him come to mean nearly everything to her.

Maybe she could trust the world enough to have children of her own, and a man would want her to have his child.

Maybe.

And what about Sean? What was holding him back? What was back there in his past that seemed to torment him so? Grace couldn't imagine. He was the strongest man she'd ever known. She would have sworn he could handle anything. It seemed, if he wanted her badly enough, he could overcome whatever it was. It would seem they both could.

There was a way to overcome everything, if they both wanted it badly enough. Surely she could find the courage to take one more risk. For him. To let herself love him. Believe that they could build something together that would last.

She was dreaming about it. Loving him, about smiling and laughing and being utterly alive with him, when he shook her awake with a hand on her shoulder and told her it was time for them to go.

Grace blinked up at him, seeing his image in the faint light, so like the man she'd seen in her dreams over the years. She had trouble separating the dream from reality for a moment. Dazed, she just lay there with her hand against the side of his face, wanting to hold him there, never wanting to let him go.

"Grace? Are you okay?"

"No," she said, fighting panic now. "I don't want to lose you."

"Nothing's going to happen to me," he promised. "Or to you. We're going to get out of here. Right now."

She nodded, letting him think what he would. But she was talking about later, when they were safe. When she had to let him go. There were no easy choices here. Either she jumped off that tall, dizzying cliff and into the mist and let herself love him, tried to grab onto any bit of happiness they could find together. Or she had to let him go. There was no middle ground.

Grace knew all about hard choices, situations where there were no good options, merely the lesser of two difficult ones. She wasn't the kind of woman to sit around and whine about why things had to be so difficult. She just coped.

Which it seemed she had to do one more time.

They hurriedly readied themselves for their escape. George was whining and sniffling and Reed was about to smack him. Grace checked the bindings on Duncan's arm and shoulder.

She helped him to his feet and winced at the pain that rippled across his face before he gritted his teeth and smiled at her.

"Oh, yeah. A real tough guy, aren't you," she said, needing any kind of distraction she could find this morning.

"Anything to impress a lady," he claimed.

"I'm impressed. I swear. But I don't know how you're going to make it to the boat."

"He'll get there," Sean said. "Reed is going to baby-sit our buddy George. You two take care of each other, and I'm going to guide us to the boat. We need to stay low. To stay together and to move. Grace, I don't need to tell you to get your butt down if anybody starts shooting, do I?"

"I've been shot at before," she reminded him.

He didn't seem reassured at all by the fact, and he shot Duncan a look she wasn't quite able to decipher, probably something about Duncan keeping a close eye on her.

"I'll be careful," she promised him, wondering if he was thinking about that old reckless streak of hers. She wasn't the fearless creature she'd once been. Maybe she'd tell him that, once they got out of here.

There wasn't a spare moment to be had for her and Sean from then on. She donned her rain poncho, because while the storm had lessened a great deal, it was still nasty out, and off they went. It was slick, muddy, the path strewn with a thick layer of leaves and branches and limbs. As if someone had shaken every tree on the island at once and all of those things had showered down upon the ground. The wind was still fierce, the rain coming down hard enough to hurt.

It seemed to take forever, but once they reached the edge of the clearing, she wished it had taken even longer. Milero's compound, a huge stone fortress, loomed in the background, carved into the side of a hill to the right. His marina was below them, in a cove that was anything but peaceful today.

Boats were strewn everywhere. The storm, like a child throwing a tantrum with his toys, had tossed them all around and left them discarded here and there like trash. One was broken in two, one smashed against a line of palm trees. One was lying on top of another.

Grace gasped when she saw the devastation. The dock had ripples and bulges in it, simply disappearing into the water at some points, and the ocean was gray and positively churning and swirling angrily, relentlessly. She didn't see how they could leave in that. It seemed suicidal to even try it.

Sean signaled for them to stay put. They crouched behind the trees. Holding her breath, she watched the expanse of beach between them and the boat, looking immense, as he crept down to the dock. He went into the water, swimming a bit when he had to, then climbing out onto the next section of dock. There at the end, bobbing in the water and looking still seaworthy, was one boat. A big, sport-fishing vessel that seemed their only hope.

She watched him disappear inside of it, and then held her breath when he didn't come out. Her nerves ate away at her.

Reed said something into his radio, then crept back to her and Duncan.

"Looks like we've got a ride," he said. "All we have to do is get to the dock. Sean's gong to start the boat. I don't think any of Milero's men are out here right now, but if they're close enough, they'll hear it. So we have to move. When the engine starts, we head for the dock. All the way up to the section that's collapsed. Sean will pick us up there. Got it?"

Grace nodded numbly.

"If I tell you to take cover, do it. If I tell you to go, you go."

"I will," she said. She could do this. To get to Sean.

Duncan, his face ashen, gave her a grim smile. She hoped he could make it to the boat, and knew that if he did, it would be on sheer guts and determination alone.

Time seemed to stretch endlessly then, each heartbeat like an eternity. She'd forgotten what it was like to be moving in the face of fear, to truly care whether she made it to see the sunrise once again. She didn't remember the last time she had anything she truly wanted to live for. Except Sean.

He'd been that one bright spot in her life for so long. That one bit of magic and intrigue. She'd always believed he'd come to her one day, that somehow she'd get him to stay, finally get him to talk to her so she would understand everything about him. If getting kidnapped was what it took, she couldn't even regret that. At least, not if they all came out of it alive.

But she thought of all the time she'd wasted, too, time she'd thrown away. She'd give anything to have just a bit of it back now. To live those days over again and make something of them. With him. She simply couldn't lose him now. Not yet. Not when they'd had so little time together.

A rumbling sound shot across the water, seeming amazingly loud, even above the roar of the storm. She thought anyone for miles must have heard it and went to look behind her and see, but Duncan grabbed her by the arm.

"Go," he said.

She felt so exposed, so vulnerable, thinking any minute something would come drilling into her back. She was thinking of the expression she'd seen on so many dead people's faces, that look of utter surprise. Not even pain. There'd obviously been no time for that. Just surprise. She could go just like that.

Grace ran faster. She was on the dock, which was swaying alarmingly, the wrenching sound probably coming from the waves trying to pry the dock loose from its moorings. She had to fight to keep her balance. Duncan was beside her. They were almost to the point where they were supposed to meet Sean. He was fighting to hold the craft there, close enough to the dock without slamming into it.

When they reached him, Duncan told her to jump. She got dizzy just looking at the boat bobbing there in the water. He yelled at her again to go, and she did, landing hard on her hands and knees on the deck of the boat. Duncan came right after her, rolling on his side as he hit and swearing at what the impact must have done to his injured shoulder.

Somehow, he got to his feet and went to take the wheel from Sean, who came to make sure she was okay. He'd just turned around to see where the others were when the first shots rang out.

"Down." Sean shoved her hard onto the deck of the boat.

He had a submachine gun in his hand and was already firing back. She didn't see much after that, just listened. There were shots. Everywhere. She was right beside him, could see his feet, his legs and not much else, as she lay on the deck of the rocking boat. She covered her ears, like a frightened child, and curled up into a little ball, trying to make herself a smaller target.

And she was doing okay, was handling it, until Sean disappeared.

She screamed and got up, thinking he'd fallen overboard in the rough water, maybe after getting hit by a bullet. She didn't see him anywhere.

A moment later George came sprawling onto the boat, howling and screaming himself. Reed came right after him. The minute he landed on the deck, he grabbed Grace and shoved her.

"Down!" he barked.

"Sean's gone! He disappeared!"

"He's over there," Reed said, "trying to buy us some time and to slow them down."

Reed was shooting, too. It seemed everyone was shooting. She got to her hands and knees, then her knees alone, and peered over the side of the rocking boat. She could see him, barely, between two boats.

Why didn't he come? she wondered. All they had to do now was leave.

But obviously, Milero's men weren't going to let them go easily. She heard the rat-a-tat of weapons spraying bullets everywhere.

"Grace," Reed yelled. "Down on the deck!"

She couldn't. There was nothing reckless about it. She simply had to know where Sean was.

She stared through the blinding storm. There he was.

She was watching.

One minute he was there.

The next minute something exploded.

It seemed to move right through her. The fire, the heat, the rush of wind. She remembered it so well. The world turned to orange fire and billowing black smoke for a moment. Grace recoiled in shock, in horror.

One minute he'd been there. The next, he was simply gone.

She screamed. Not like the first time, when she was eleven. She didn't think she'd made a sound then. It had happened too fast, and she'd been right in the middle of it. Just inside the building, actually. She'd scarcely been aware of the blast before she'd been knocked down by it, mercifully knocked out.

The next thing she remembered was being carried out of there. More smoke. Her chest hurting. Her head. All the noise. The crying. The chaos.

This time...this time she just screamed.

He was gone, and all she could do was scream his name.

She must have fainted.

The next thing she knew, she was on the boat, which was racing along, rocking sickeningly from side to side.

She was lying down, out of the wind and the rain. There were no more gunshots, but her throat felt raw, and she knew why.

Grace closed her eyes, a fresh rush of tears coming on. *Sean. Oh, God. Sean.*

And when she opened her eyes, he was there.

She whimpered. He looked so real, standing there dripping wet, a smudge of soot on his jaw, a reddish spot on his forehead, a bit of blood on the arm he had extended to the right, bracing himself against the cabin wall.

It was such an odd kind of vision, she thought. Soot, abraded skin, blood, him fighting to keep his balance.

Tears poured down her cheeks, and she curled her lip over her bottom teeth and bit down hard. He was not real.

Still, he kept coming toward her, slowly and carefully. His gaze locked on hers, a tightly controlled expression on his face. He looked as if he was scared to get too close. Just as she was scared to have him here.

Because when she touched him, she'd know.

He carefully eased himself down on the bench seat she was lying upon. She could swear she felt his hip pressed against her side, and he looked so sad.

He never looked sad in her dreams. She'd imagined him all sorts of ways, tall and strong. Invincible. Magical. All-powerful. He'd suffered from none of those nasty human frailties of regular men. Cut them and they'll bleed. Blow them up and they'll die. Not him. Not her mysterious savior.

"I know you're not real," she whispered, her throat painfully strained.

And then he put his hand against the side of her face. His big, warm, slightly roughened palm.

"We've had this conversation before, Grace. Nothing magical about me at all. I'm just a man."

"I saw you die," she sobbed. "I saw you standing there, and then the explosion, and then you were gone."

He shook his head back and forth, and she thought she saw the faint sheen of tears in his eyes. She put both her hands on his face. The rock-hard line of his jaw, the shadowy stubble on his cheeks, his nose, his mouth.

"Grace. I'm so sorry. I didn't even think of it until I threw the grenade."

"What?"

"You and explosions. I didn't even think. I just...reacted. I needed to slow down Milero's men and make sure they couldn't follow us. I blew up the boats. I threw a couple of grenades and jumped into the water.''

Grace listened to him. She watched his lips move to form the words, but she still had trouble comprehending the meaning.

He'd done it? He'd set off the explosion?

She ran her fingers through his hair, feeling the soft texture of it, the wetness. It curled a bit when it was wet, and it was a deep, rich black. Thick with the slightest bit of gray at his temples. A person had to get very, very close to him, to even see it. This was the clearest look she'd ever had at him, and she saw tiny lines at the corners of his eyes and his mouth. A scar or two on his forehead and at the corner of his cheek. She was sure his nose had been broken at one point or another. His eyes were a deep, warm, chocolaty brown, and his mouth… She pressed her mouth to his, and then pulled away just as quickly, staring at him and rendered mute by the shock.

''I'm real, Grace. I've always been real.''

''I thought you were dead,'' she cried, sobs coming now. ''I was so sure you were dead. Just like…just like everyone else.''

He hauled her into his arms, his glorious strong, sure arms, and crushed her to him. ''I know, baby. I know. I'm so sorry.''

Scan held her for a long, long time, soothing her as best he could, knowing it simply wasn't enough. With her, it seemed nothing he did was ever enough.

He'd told her the truth. He simply hadn't thought about what being that close to another explosion might do to her. He'd certainly never imagined she might be staring over the railing of the boat, with bullets flying, seeing what looked like him disappearing into a ball of flames and black smoke.

He'd heard her scream his name over and over again, once he surfaced and the noise from the blast quieted down, and he'd imagined the worst. He'd forgotten everything else, just gone tearing through the water to get to her. But long before he reached her side, she'd fallen silent, and then he'd imagined something even worse.

She slid into a dead faint before he got to her, and he was surprised she wasn't hysterical when she finally came to. Even though she wasn't, she'd been so confused, so dazed.

She'd never had any counseling at all, as far as he knew, after the explosion that killed her family and nearly killed her as well. He was afraid all the grief, fear and pain she'd buried inside of her for twenty years might come tumbling out after that little stunt he'd pulled to get them off the island.

He'd known it was possible there might be some kind of explosion during their getaway, and he'd had grenades. They were standard equipment for him. And he hadn't said a word to her, had worried about frightening her so badly with just the prospect of explosions that she wouldn't be able to function at all while they tried to get away. He knew her scars went deep.

When the time came, he'd just tossed a few grenades, thinking to put a lot of smoke and fire between them and Milero's men. And to keep anyone from following them by boat. No big deal. It wasn't until he hit the water and the explosion sent him rolling that he'd thought of her. What would she be thinking in that moment? What kind of demons would he bring back to her?

Sean grimaced. How much was he going to hurt this woman before he was through? It seemed there was no end to the pain he might inflict upon her.

He'd lowered her back down onto the cushions and was rubbing her cold hands between his when Duncan came into the cabin.

"How is she?"

"Exhausted. Scared to death."

"She thought you'd bought it, buddy."

He nodded, hating himself. Absolutely hating himself.

"Hey. Come on," Duncan said. "It's over. We got off the damned island, and we're all alive. She'll have a few nightmares, but—"

"It's more than that. Her entire family got blown to bits right in front of her when she was eleven," he said grimly. "Remember James Evans Porter? Nobel Peace Prize? Awarded posthumously? The bomb in Rome? Grace is his daughter."

"Damn. I remember the picture of a solider carrying her out of the building. She was so little, so thin. I looked at her and thought, that girl is dead."

Sean nodded. He remembered that day all too clearly. He'd looked down at her as he carried her in his arms and thought the exact same thing.

Grace woke up again, and he was still there. Still by her side. Still gloriously alive. She didn't feel like she was. She was numb, wrapped in a nothingness that was both very attractive and much worse, all at the same time.

So many times, she wanted to be numb, to simply not hurt anymore. Now that she was, she found it left her feeling empty and disconcertingly disconnected. He sat beside her, touched her, held her, even kissed her softly, gently, and she felt nothing. Except the need to draw away from him and deeper inside herself.

She knew it hurt him. No matter how quickly he covered the reaction, she could see it in him, in the way he held himself so carefully, the way he was so careful with her, tiptoeing all around her, as they all were. But she'd reached her limit. Gone beyond it, even. She couldn't do anything except lie there and breathe, and sometimes even that seemed like too much effort to make.

So she let him fuss over her, let all of them, and sometimes she tried to smile. But that was it.

They were taken aboard a container ship of some kind. Once they reached land, they boarded a plane. She was unaware of much of the journey until she was sitting beside Sean in the first-class cabin of a plane. He held her hand in his, and when the lights were dimmed in the cabin, he wrapped a blanket around her. Then he pushed the armrest between them out of the way and tucked her against his side.

She finally thought to ask, "Where are we going?"

"D.C.," he said.

Grace felt the breath he took, practically felt the words coming from deep inside of him. They'd done this before, she remembered. She lay with her head against his chest, feeling the words form there, then hearing them come out. Back when she wasn't even sure if he was real.

In many ways, she still wasn't sure. Odd, how little she knew about him, and how important he'd become to her. Or how important he might have been. Before he'd exploded before her eyes. Before she'd been shown so viciously what it would be like to lose him and how easily it could happen again.

"Is that where you live?" she asked, so she wouldn't have to think about the other part, so maybe it wouldn't hurt so much. "In D.C.?"

"Yes."

She coughed a bit, her throat still scratchy. Because she'd screamed too much, thinking he was dead.

"Does your throat still hurt?"

"Yes," she said. Now that she let herself think about it, her throat did hurt. Somewhere deep inside her was a world of hurt hidden away, waiting for the walls to come tumbling down and for it to come spilling out.

He got her some juice for her throat, drew her back down to his chest and urged her to sleep while she could, and she tried to do that. He brushed his hand lightly up and down her back, through her hair, sometimes touched his lips so softly against the side of her face, and she let him do that, too.

But for the moment, she didn't feel anything at all. She

was safe from everything and everyone in this cocoon of hers, and she was never, ever going to love anyone. Especially not him.

A tall, dark, imposing-looking man leaning a bit on a cane met them at the gate. He reminded her of Sean and turned out to be his brother-in-law, Dan Reese. She was absently trying to figure out what he might have done to himself to have that kind of a limp while Dan got them through Customs, despite the fact that they had no passports and no ID. It wasn't until then, as they made their way through Customs, that she finally knew Sean's full name.

Sean Patrick Douglass.

She'd come so close to loving him and hadn't even known his full name.

Grace found the airport crowded and noisy, overwhelming, even. They were hustling her out when she could have sworn she heard her name...

She turned and stared in the direction of the voice, saw an anchorwoman on the TV mounted on the wall.

"Manuel Milero," the anchorwoman said, "one of San Reino's most notorious military dictators, claims to be holding the daughter of slain civil rights activist and Nobel Prize-winner James Evans Porter, and is demanding three million dollars for her release.

"Porter's daughter, who hasn't been seen in public in years, would now be thirty-one years old. The sole survivor of the blast that killed her father, mother and brother, at an international peace conference in Rome twenty years ago, she was the subject of this now famous Pulitzer prize-winning photograph shot only moments after the blast."

And then there she was on the screen, eleven years old and lying limply in the arms of a soldier who was carrying her out of the smoldering wreckage.

Grace stumbled. Sean caught her. His gaze went from the image on the screen, to her face, and his expression seemed to reach right down inside her, shoving aside all the barriers she'd so carefully erected.

He looked every bit as tormented as she did. She fought against seeing the compassion in his eyes, the tight hold he seemed to have on his own emotions. He hated this, maybe as much as she did, and whatever feelings he had for her were very strong indeed. Even if it would never work out— even if she didn't want it to anymore—obviously he felt so much for her.

For a moment, Grace felt it all herself. Every bit of fear and dread and hope and need, and then she put up the wall once again. That protective shell she'd woven together after the blast on Milero's island.

Sean swore softly, and Grace sensed his tension—he was holding her arm so tightly it hurt.

"Sean?"

"Yes."

"My arm. You're hurting me."

He looked down at his hand on her arm and swore yet again as he unwrapped his fingers. Looking as dazed as she felt, he said, "I'm sorry."

"It's all right," she said, knowing he must not have even been aware of it. He would never deliberately hurt her.

"God, Grace." He went to touch her again, his hand hovering near the spot on her arm, then falling to his side.

"It's nothing."

But she reached for him, taking his hand and holding it between both of hers. Needing to reassure him as he'd done for her so many times, wishing she could ease his pain. What in the world was wrong with him? He was hurting, too. She hated that, hated the look on his face.

Maybe he pitied her, she thought. Maybe he looked at that girl on the screen and felt sorry for her. Maybe it hurt him just to look at her, and he'd been so kind out of sheer pity.

Grace didn't want anyone's pity. She didn't want anyone looking at her that way. That I-know-what-you've-been-through-and-I'm-so-sorry look. She'd seen it enough over the years, from friends of her parents who'd tracked her down at boarding school or who she ran into in her relief work, and she'd come to hate it.

She did not want this man's pity.

She dropped his hand and took a step back, the wall firmly in place. He stayed there, grim-faced and frozen to the spot. She didn't think she'd ever seen him hesitate in the least, never seen him look unsure of himself. But he did now.

It made her mildly curious. She stamped out that feeling as well. She'd stamp out them all. She'd stop wanting just to look at him, now that she could finally see him clearly and in perfectly pristine light. She'd stop needing his touch and could forget how reassuring it was, merely to be in his presence.

She could forget it all, and maybe, just maybe, she would survive.

"Let's go," he said. He didn't take her arm, didn't touch her in any way, though he stayed close to her side in the crowd, leading her out of the mass of bodies and into the bright October sunshine.

His brother-in-law stood beside a big four-wheeler at the curb. Sean opened the back door for her, and she climbed in. He sat beside her. Dan drove.

"Where are we going?"

"It's going to take a few days to get you a new passport and ID," Sean said. "Before you can travel again, if that's what you want."

She nodded, wanting to go home. To put this all behind her.

"You saw the TV at the airport. You're all over the news, I'm afraid. Milero couldn't resist bragging. Or the publicity, I suppose. It would probably be good to lay low for a while, Grace. If the media people find you..."

She shuddered at the thought, had no desire to be news.

"I told you about my sister, Jamie. She and Dan live in

Maryland. On the bay. Practically in the middle of nowhere. Easy to stay out of sight there.''

"We have plenty of room," Dan said. "We'd be happy to have you."

"Just for a few days," Sean said. "Let everything die down."

She supposed it didn't matter where she was, who was with her, who wasn't... She could let him go right now. She'd have to very soon, anyway.

He took her hand, held it very gently in his, making it even harder.

"It's going to be all right," he said.

She didn't believe him anymore, but then again, she didn't really care, either. Nothing mattered. There was nothing that had happened that she could change. Her life was her own, her past simply her past. She'd accepted that long ago, had given up on railing against the universe for the cards it had dealt her. She'd deal with this, too. With everything. With him and explosions and all those nasty memories. She'd bury it all deep inside, as well, and go on. Like she had before she'd ever known his name or seen his face.

Chapter 12

Sean held her hand until he was sure she was asleep. Glancing to the front of the vehicle, he caught his brother-in-law's gaze in the rearview mirror. He'd barged into Dan's office a week ago like a madman and literally demanded to be in on the mission to free George Roberts from Milero, so he could get Grace at the same time.

He'd started by simply demanding to go. He'd refused to wait another day, even in the face of a hurricane, trading on friendship and family ties. His brother-in-law happened to run Division One, the highly secretive counterterrorist organization for which his sister once worked. Sean had called in every favor he'd done for the organization over the years. When that hadn't worked, when it was down to just him and Dan, he'd simply said it was personal and asked what Dan would have done if Jamie was the one in trouble. Which had worked, because it hadn't been that long ago that his sister had been in a too-similar situation, and Dan Reese was the one who'd gone after her.

Now he owed Dan an explanation.

He climbed into the front passenger seat, the knot in his gut getting worse every minute. Finally, he said, "Sorry about the mess down there."

Dan shrugged easily. "Duncan's going to be fine. He and Reed said their only problem was their hostage, not you or Dr. Evans. We'll handle the rest with Milero and the San Reino government."

"I appreciate you letting me go."

Dan shook his head and said, "You said you had to."

As if that were all that mattered.

And then, because explanations might be a moot point now, Sean said, "Did you pull the file?" He'd told Dan who Grace was when he argued that they had to go and get her. But he hadn't said anything else.

"I pulled it," Dan said. "Didn't have much time to do more than glance at about ten years' worth of information. We've been keeping close tabs on the lady. Because of your father?"

Sean nodded. His father had the clout to do that, and later when Sean did himself, he'd taken care of it.

"You want me to pull this out of you?" Dan offered. "I'm willing. Or you could just tell me what you want me to know."

Sean winced. They turned onto a smaller road and the sun nearly blinded him. He shielded his eyes with his hand, dug into his aching head with his fingers and felt the sickness deep inside once again.

"I don't know what I want," he said. Then he admitted, "I haven't told anyone about it in twenty years."

"Just so you know, Jamie knows you were down there and who you went to get. I don't keep things from her now. It's one of the few promises she asked for, and I gave it to her. So if you don't want her to know any more, stop now."

Sean nodded, accepting that. He owed them both. "I think Jamie was too young to remember much of it."

"She was old enough to notice the change in you and your

father, and to worry. She knew you were hurt in the blast. She knew your father felt responsible in some way, that it weighed on him for years to come.''

"It happened when he was with the UN. The Italians insisted for the longest time that they had everything under control, but as the peace conference got closer and bigger and the threats escalated, they panicked and asked the UN to step in at the last minute. My father ended up in charge of security," Sean said, then got to the heart of it. "Grace doesn't know any of this. She has no idea I was there."

Dan nodded once again, and Sean thought he could almost hear his brother-in-law's thinking process. Sean was obviously involved with her, and she didn't know anything about him or his father being there when the bomb exploded and her whole family was blown to bits.

"I've seen countless news reports since Milero started bragging about having her," Dan said. "But when they flashed that old photo onto the screen, my eyes were always glued to the little girl, to Grace, and I suppose the wreckage behind her. I never looked at the soldier who hauled her out of there. Not until I saw the two of you staring at it in the airport."

Sean sat there still as a statue.

"You're the one in the photo, aren't you?" Dan asked. "You're the one who got her out of there?"

Sean nodded, simply unable to say a word.

"And you're not going to tell her? Not any of this?" Dan asked.

He shook his head yet again. There was no point. He and Grace both agreed. Their relationship had no place to go. She didn't want it to, and he... Well, it didn't matter what he wanted, because it all involved changing the past, which was something he hadn't figured out a way to do.

So he wasn't going to tell her. It would serve no purpose, except to make her hate him, and if they weren't going to be together, anyway...

It was a roundabout way of justifying a lie, a luxury he didn't normally allow himself. But there it was. He'd sunk so low as to telling lies, and yes, he'd done it in the beginning with a fairly clear conscience. He'd done it so she would listen to him and let him protect her, something she wouldn't do if she hated him. He'd done it because he honestly and truly wanted her to be safe and thought he could ensure that. But once he'd held her in his arms, the lies had taken on a life of their own. They'd been purely personal, purely selfish on his part. Because of the look of disgust he didn't think he could handle seeing in her eyes when she looked at him, once she knew the truth.

It was too late, he told himself. It had always been too late.

"What are you going to do?" Dan said finally.

"She thought she saw me get blown to bits on the island. She's been in shock ever since it happened, and I'd take her to a hospital for observation, if I thought she'd go. But she won't, and I'm afraid the media people would find her there," Sean said. And that she'd find out the truth somehow. Surely he wouldn't try to lie to himself about that. Not now. "I hope she just needs some rest, some time to process it all. And then she'll go back to London. Probably right back out into the field. It's what she's always done, how she copes."

And he would have to hope that some of what he'd said had gotten through to her. Hope she'd be more careful and maybe build a life for herself. Maybe even find another man. Someone she could count on. Someone who would love her and wouldn't lie to her.

"I have to let her go," he said, and found himself staring right into the sunlight, feeling more exposed in the harsh light than he'd ever been in his life, more desperate, more lost, more ashamed.

He had to let her go. He'd known that from the beginning. He just hadn't understood what it would mean, what she'd come to mean to him.

Everything, he thought. She was everything to him, and in a day or two or three, he would have to stand here and watch her go.

Grace woke as they pulled into a gravel driveway amid a tall stand of trees. The drive led to a beautiful old three-story white house with a porch that wrapped around the entire front and along the side she could see. She'd bet it went to the back as well, for a view of the bay. She glimpsed water through the dense trees. Birds flew away, no doubt disturbed by the sound of the vehicle, and she saw a few toys scattered along the porch and the front lawn.

Her throat went a little tight at the sight, the house so solid, so enduring. There were climbing roses encompassing one entire side of it, intertwined along the columns of the porch, as if they'd never let go. There was a child's swing hanging from a massive tree on the left side of the house, flowers everywhere, and a dog, a golden-colored cocker spaniel, who came bounding around the corner.

It was so obviously a home. That was what got to her. Grace had never had anything of a lasting home. Hers had been with her family, wherever their travels took them. Which made this something totally out of her experience.

This was a home. His sister's and the man who had to be about Sean's age and had a tendency to look a bit too stern for her own comfort. He and Sean seemed comfortable with each other, but she found Dan Reese thoroughly intimidating.

He climbed out of the vehicle and shushed the dog, commanding him to stay down. Sean took her hand and helped her out of the tall vehicle. She was standing there edging closer to him, looking for that sense of reassurance that always came from being near him, when the front door of the house burst open and a little boy came flying out.

Dan swore softly. He dropped his cane and ran awkwardly the five strides to the bottom of the steps leading up to the porch, snatching the little boy out of thin air as he tripped coming down them.

The boy, absolutely adorable with blondish-brown hair and big brown eyes, couldn't have been more than two. He obviously thought it was a game. He laughed as he swung into the arms of the man trying to stifle a curse.

"You said a bad word, Daddy," the boy said, obviously delighting in catching him.

"Rich, I swear—"

"You said a bad word."

"You're going to crack your head open coming off the steps like that one day when I'm not around to catch you," he warned, with what Grace thought was admirable sternness in the face of such beauty, charm and enthusiasm.

At that moment, a woman appeared in the doorway. A stunning, dark-haired, dark-eyed woman with a baby in her arms.

"Your son can still get the front door open," she complained. "Even with all the locks in place and those silly childproof things, I couldn't keep Houdini in."

Dan walked up onto the porch and kissed the woman, Jamie. He kissed her quickly, deeply, and when he turned around—his wayward son still in his arms, their baby in his wife's—the smile on his face was absolutely dazzling.

Grace didn't find him intimidating at all in that moment. In fact, she felt an altogether painful twist, deep in her heart. What in the world was going on with her? How could it hurt that much just to see the four of them together? She'd seen thousands of families over the years, some intact, some not. It never hurt that much.

This one nearly blinded her. She had to look away, felt ridiculous tears sting her eyes, had no defenses at all that could combat this.

"Come on," Sean said, taking her hand. "Come meet the rug rats."

The little boy yelled "Uncle Sean!" and then Sean grabbed him before the steps did him in again.

"You're in luck, Rich," Sean said. "This lady is a doctor. You can get into all kinds of scrapes while she's here, and I bet she can fix you right up."

"Please, don't encourage him," Jamie said.

Sean just grinned. "Rich, this is my friend, Grace. She's going to be staying here for a few days, and I want you to be very, very nice to her."

The boy grinned. Grace saw that he had a bruise on his cheek, a scrape on his knee, a bandage on his finger. He was obviously in the midst of that into-everything phase. The phase where kids moved too quickly and had no understanding whatsoever of gravity or heights or risks.

"Grace," Sean said, "this hellion is my very first and best nephew, Richard Douglass Reese."

He said it with obvious pride and such affection, a look she'd simply never seen on his face. He was happy in the moment, she realized. Relaxed. Off guard, here with this beautiful little boy and surrounded by his family.

Sean had always been handsome. He absolutely took her breath away now.

She fought the feeling, instead taking the little boy's hand and shaking it. "How do you do?"

Suddenly shy, he giggled again and threw his arms around his uncle, burying his face in Sean's neck.

Grace had to look away completely. Seeing them together... There was definitely a strong family resemblance between the two. It was too easy to imagine this was his son. That he'd stand there just like this one day with his own child, and maybe then he'd smile more often. Maybe then he'd be happy.

Grace wanted him happy, she realized. She wanted him smiling and dazzling and carefree. Not blown to bits on some island an ocean away.

And just like that, she closed the door once again. On all

the possibilities, all the nasty little risks associated with loving someone and letting him into her life. It would get easier with time, she told herself. She'd only been trying since she'd woken up on the boat and realized one more time that Sean was indeed real. A bit battered and bruised, but heartbreakingly real. She wasn't going to let him anywhere near her heart again.

So Grace politely shook hands with his sister, smiled at the baby and just as quickly looked away. Jamie showed her to a pretty bedroom in a quiet corner of the house, where Grace sat and stared at the bay and counted the hours until she could go back to her real life. Back to days in a too-hot or too-cold climate, where the pace was frantic, the work never done. No time to do anything but work.

Work had always gotten her through. She was counting on it doing it again, making her forget all about him, all about the idea of loving him, and remember her utter certainty that no matter what, she would lose him, too.

Sean put her off for three days. She stayed in her room at Dan and Jamie's most of the time and stayed away from him, being unfailingly polite and determinedly distant. He couldn't get through the wall, couldn't get to her, and honestly, he was afraid to try too hard. She seemed too fragile, as if one strong push would send her toppling over the edge.

He didn't want to let her go like this, but it seemed pointless to make her stay. After all, he had no claim on her, no rights whatsoever where she was concerned. He'd have to settle for doing what he always had—worrying from afar and watching out for her as best he could, hoping to God that would be enough.

He walked out onto the back porch of his sister's home that afternoon with her new passport in his hand. There was a wrought-iron patio set there, lined with big, fat floral cushions, and Grace was sitting in one of the chairs, her legs drawn up to her chest, her chin resting on her knees. She barely looked at him, just stared at the water, looking so fragile and lost and alone.

It hurt him just to see her now, hurt so much he had to concentrate hard on staying quiet, staying in control, when he wanted to tear something apart with his bare hands. To scream and yell and pound on something. On himself, actually. How the hell was he supposed to deal with this, when the person he absolutely despised for doing this to her was himself?

But at he moment, he buried all that inside of him and sat down beside her. Handing her the envelope, he said, "A present from my brother-in-law."

Grace took it with the merest bit of interest and opened it. He might have seen something flicker across her face for an instant, before she buried that as well.

They were a real pair, he and Grace.

"I suppose you want to go to London?"

She nodded.

"I checked with the airlines before I came over. There's space on an overnight flight leaving tonight, if that's what you want. They're holding a ticket for you."

She seemed torn at first, looking this way and that, anywhere but at him. *Come back to me, Grace,* he thought. Just for a day. For an hour. So he wouldn't worry so much. So he would know she was going to be okay.

"It's for the best, isn't it?" she said finally. "There's nothing else for me to do."

"I know." And then it was his turn to look away. He stood up, shoved his hands into his pockets and closed his eyes, tried to keep his voice steady and to give nothing away. "I understand."

"Then there's no point in drawing this out."

He nodded, not knowing if he could stand it even now. "You're going right back out into the field, aren't you?"

She hedged, saying nothing except "There are never enough doctors to go around."

Sean's breathing became more difficult, more strained. He bit back a half a dozen things he wanted to say, and settled for simply asking, "Will you be careful, Grace? Please? For me?"

"Yes."

"And if you need me..." He couldn't go on. Absolutely couldn't. Bleak eyes stared out into the water. He was shaking, he found. Absolutely shaking with the need to grab her and hold her and never let her go.

She got to her feet. For a moment, he thought she was coming to him. He braced himself for it, yearned for it, nearly died a thousand times waiting for it.

But she didn't come to him. She stood up and said, "I should pack."

He nodded. "Jamie has some things to do in town. She'll take you to the airport. I'll call the airline for you."

"Thank you. For everything."

He nodded, thinking, *cut me, Grace. Go ahead and cut me to shreds.* He'd put the knife into her hands himself, felt as if he were already bleeding all over the place. As if he simply couldn't contain the utter misery pouring out of him, but he didn't want her to see it. He didn't want her to know or to ask why.

He just had to let her go.

She disappeared, and Sean called the airline. Behind him, the door opened and he braced himself as best he could, in case she'd come back. But when he turned around he saw his sister standing there.

She didn't say anything at first, just walked up behind him and put her arms around his waist, leaning her face against his shoulder. And just her attempt at comforting him was almost more than he could bear.

He wanted Grace. He wanted her so badly he felt as if he could tear his own body limb by limb to get to her.

And he had to pull himself together. If he could just make

it past the next few moments, he'd be gone. Maybe he'd find the strength to get through that without begging her to stay, knowing it would only make things harder in the end, once she knew, once she left him for good.

Because she would go, once she knew. He had no doubt.

"Would you do me a favor?" he asked his sister.

"Of course."

"Take her to the airport?"

"I thought—"

"I can't, Jamie."

"I don't think I've ever heard you say those words," she said, holding him more tightly. "About anything. I've always known you could do anything—"

"Not this," he said raggedly. "I can't fix this."

"You're in love with her."

He didn't waste his breath denying it.

"Have you even told her? That you love her?"

"She doesn't want me to love her. She told me so, and she has good reasons for feeling that way."

He had to be thankful they'd never crossed any of those uncrossable lines. They'd never said the words to each other, had never actually made love. That had to make it easier, didn't it? Eventually, he'd be grateful for those two small things.

"Sean, please. I've never seen you like this."

"I'll be okay," he insisted. He'd be a hermit. Or maybe he'd bury himself in his work like she did. Maybe he'd start working out with the teams every morning, maybe every evening, too, instead of the three days a week he gave it now, when he was in town. Maybe he'd try to burn off every bit of frustration and energy he had there. Until he was too tired to think and could sleep at night and maybe forget how it felt to have her in his arms.

"I love you," Jamie said. "And I want you to be happy."

Sean swore softly, bitterly. He loved his little sister, but she knew him too well, saw too much.

"You're going to have to let me help you for a change," she argued. "Let me take care of you."

He turned around and grabbed her tightly and just held on to her for a moment. "You can fuss over me when she's gone, okay? Just a little bit."

She kissed him, and said, "Okay."

"Now, get her out of here. Please," he begged, tearing himself away before he said any more.

The next time the back door opened, he knew who it was, and he knew what he had to do. Sean faced her, saw her face already wet with tears. She was trying in vain to stop them, the only outward show of emotion he'd seen from her in days.

He wasn't sure if it made him feel better, that the shock of the explosion seemed to have worn off, or if it just made it worse to see her crying. But it was an excuse to touch her, and he'd been praying for that for days, too. That he might take her in his arms and have her feel something. Anger, fear, frustration, anything but that awful numbness in which she'd wrapped herself for days.

If anything, that's what convinced him to let her go. He'd hurt her this badly, had taken her this close to the edge when he blew up the boats. And she didn't even love him. She hadn't let herself. She'd stopped in time.

What would have happened to her if she ever let herself love him and then lost him? He understood the risks to her now, how closely to the edge she lived, and he could only hope that one day she'd overcome those fears. But he couldn't force her, shouldn't even try to make her, not when they couldn't ever really have anything together. She'd have to do that for some other man. He had to hope that she would, because he honestly wanted her to be happy. He was afraid she would always be alone.

But all he could do now was say goodbye.

He went to her. She lifted her hands to his side, to hold

on to him tightly. He brought his arms up alongside hers, holding her elbows in his palms, thinking to keep some distance between them now, that it was important, necessary. And then he bent his head, his forehead resting against hers, and fought with everything inside of him not to kiss her the way he was dying to. She'd freeze up on him again, put up those walls of hers so firmly, and he didn't have the heart to try to break through them. If there was a chance that this could work out somehow, he would. But it was impossible. He'd always known that.

"Am I ever going to see you again?" she whispered.

His hands tightened on her arms. He felt the heat of her body, the vaguest impression of it against his, and from somewhere deep inside of him, he found a way to speak without every bit of his emotions in his voice.

"Are you going to get in trouble again, Doc?"

"Probably," she admitted.

"Then I'll be there," he vowed.

"Still? Even after all this?"

"I told you I'd always be there for you, Grace. That I'd always be watching out for you, and I keep my promises."

"I know. I just…"

"Just wait. If you need me, I'll come walking around the corner one night. If you're not in trouble, if you just need to see me, for any reason at all, all you ever have to do is call. You have the number. The phone's manned twenty-four, seven. Someone can always find me, and I'll be there. Anywhere. Anytime."

She buried her face against his chest and sobbed, "I wish things could have been different."

He held her there, not nearly long enough. "So do I."

"You do?"

"God, yes."

And he kissed her then. One last time. One too-brief moment.

Very, very nearly, he told her he loved her, choking back the words at the last minute.

"I'll never forget you," she said, breaking his heart all over again.

He swore softly, frustration pouring out, along with the hardest bit of advice he could ever imagine giving in his life.

"Forget me, Grace. Forget what I've done to you and the way I've scared you, and find someone else. Find someone you're not afraid to love and...be happy, sweetheart. *Live.*"

"If I was brave enough for that, I'd do it with you."

To which he could say nothing.

She stayed in his arms for another moment, kissed him hungrily, desperately, one last time, and then said, "I have to go."

He pried his hands off of her and let her slip away. He didn't look back, didn't so much as move, until he heard the car drive away.

Jamie didn't say anything when Grace, her face drenched in tears, came around the side of the house and climbed into the car. She just handed Grace a tissue and started to drive.

They were nearly at the airport when Grace said, "What is it that makes him so sad?"

Jamie's eyes turned to look at Grace, then back to the road. "He's never talked to me about it."

"But you see it in him, don't you?"

"He doesn't often let people see it. I'm ashamed to say that for the longest time, I never imagined he might be hurting so badly. I barely even see him as human. He's always been so much more than that to me. So much bigger, stronger, all-powerful. As if nothing could hurt him," Jamie said. "He's my oldest brother, older by ten years. In my first memories of him, he's already so tall, so strong, so capable. I used to think he could make anything better. I used to run to him with my scraped knees or when something scared me in the dark. My father was gone a lot when I was a baby, and mother used to joke that I was as much Sean's baby as hers. I've admired everything about him for so long. He's always taken care of the rest of us. I forget that he's human, too, that there are things that hurt him, too.''

Grace nodded. She'd seen all of those qualities in him. Perfect. More than human. Capable of anything.

''He hasn't told me much of what's going on here, and I don't know how much he let you see,'' Jamie said, ''but it's killing him to let you go. It doesn't seem to be any easier for you, either. And it's none of my business. Except that I love him, and I don't want to see him hurt.''

''I'm terrified of loving him,'' she confessed. ''And losing him.''

''So you're going to accept it as a sure thing—that you're definitely going to lose him. You're going to give him up, without ever taking the chance that you could have him? That it could work?''

''No. Not that,'' she argued. ''Not that at all.''

She was protecting herself. She was making one last-ditch effort at self-preservation.

Jamie didn't look convinced, but she let it go, walked Grace all the way to her gate at the airport, although Grace swore that was unnecessary.

''You'll look out for him, won't you?'' Grace asked.

''As much as he'll let me.''

Which would have to be enough, Grace supposed. And then she found herself alone, tears in her eyes once again, as she was standing in line to board the plane to take her far, far away from him.

She'd thought she could get through this without feeling much of anything, that she had her shell firmly in place. Until he'd handed her the passport a few hours ago and told her she could be on a plane almost instantly.

Something seemed to have cracked inside of her then, something that scared her. She'd fought it, tried to push all the feelings away. If only she could get away fast enough...but she hadn't.

She was shivering with cold, and everyone around her seemed just fine. As if the room weren't an icebox at all.

She kept hearing the explosion ringing in her ears, kept being blinded by the flames, and it was as if she was still screaming his name, over and over again, deep inside.

She could close her eyes and see him, coming to her out of the darkness, giving her one of those seductively charming smiles. She could feel his arms around her, could feel his body very, very close.

And then the bomb went off again.

Sometimes she was eleven again, but back on the floor of that cell at Milero's fortress, and he'd come to her in the night and was soothing her and making all those sweet promises in the dark. And she wasn't afraid. Not with him. She shouldn't be afraid, now, leaving him, escaping. But she'd so counted on simply being numb.

It wasn't working.

Maybe when she got back to London. When she simply erased him from her senses. It might be years before she so much as caught a glimpse of him again.

Grace gasped, the pain spreading again.

"Ma'am," the man behind her said. "Are you all right?"

She lied and said she was.

She was a survivor, after all. She was saving herself once again.

But for what? What was she saving herself for? The empty, desolate life she'd always known? Where she worked and seemed fearless in the face of danger and just never stopped moving, tried to never even think?

Was that life really so important to her that she couldn't risk losing it? Losing her sanity and protecting her so-called life?

For so long, that's what she thought. One more blow like the one she'd suffered at eleven and she'd either lose her mind or take her own life. That little eleven-year-old girl still lived inside of her somewhere. The one who'd wanted to go be with her parents, any way possible. She thought about the pact she'd made with herself—that she'd never suffer that kind of pain again. The promise had let her go on by holding herself apart from everyone and everything in this world.

But that wasn't living. That's what Sean had been trying to tell her. That she had no life. That life was a gift, and she was wasting hers.

Her father *would* have been ashamed of her, she realized. After all, he'd placed a great value on life, and she'd been throwing hers away.

In the name of protecting herself, she was nearly killing herself trying to walk away from a man who...a man who was simply everything to her.

Even tucked deep inside that thick shell of hers, the pain crept in. Making her feel as if she were a hundred years old and that there would never be anything good in her life from this point on. Making her so tired she didn't want to go on. There was no point. Not if she went on living the way she had been. Not if she was living without him.

She'd been so stupid. All this time, she'd thought to save herself by getting away before she fell madly, deeply, irrevocably in love with him, and it seemed it had been too late from the start. She knew it was too late now.

She loved him.

If she lost him someday it just *might* kill her, but leaving him right now most definitely *was*. Which meant it was certainly too late to protect herself, but maybe not too late to save herself.

Time to jump. To close her eyes and take a leap of faith like none she'd ever made before.

She loved him. Grace smiled through her tears and told the startled ticket agent that she'd changed her mind. She wouldn't be going to London tonight. And then she turned around and ran.

Chapter 13

Sean poured himself a shot of whiskey, then another, and then gave up on that. He didn't get drunk easily, and even if he did, what he needed was oblivion. He'd never found that in a bottle.

He prowled his apartment in Georgetown, hearing nothing but the clock, which seemed to be taunting him with every passing minute, every one taking her that much farther away from him.

Staring at the bottle again, he dismissed it once more.

There was a gym around the corner. Not a prissy one. A real one. For men. He could hit the punching bag for a while. At least he'd be tired, and maybe then he could sleep. By the time he woke up, she'd be in London.

He didn't want to think about how many miles away that was.

He paced some more, thinking it was too hot. Much too hot for October. He was sweaty and tired and aching. All over. He flicked on the air conditioner, and then there really wasn't anything he could do. Not to escape.

He knew about pain, about hating himself, about the rawness of a freshly made wound. There was nothing to do but endure. Let it hurt. Let the time pass and hope it brought some measure of relief.

Finally, he stripped and got into the shower, just stood there under the spray, his hands in front of him pressed against the wall. He stood there for so long thinking about her, wet from the rain on the island. Her face, her long, glorious hair, his shirt clinging to her like a second skin, more erotic than anything he could imagine.

He stood there for so long, he could swear he heard her calling his name.

God, he was losing it.

He leaned against the wall, his forehead resting there, his hands knotted into fists. He was so oblivious, he didn't even realize he wasn't alone anymore until someone pulled open the shower door and said, "Sean."

In Grace's voice, someone said his name.

He turned around, dazed, and he could have sworn she was standing there, looking a bit lost but not quite so sad. Looking so very real.

"Hi," she said.

He frowned at the image. It talked, too.

"I know you're not real," he said.

She looked sad for a moment, and then said, "I think that's my line."

"No." He was going to argue with an illusion. He felt so stupid for it, but it was that or reach out and touch her.

He thought about every time he'd shown up out of the shadows, thinking to keep her from ever getting a clear look at him, just in case she might recognize him. Every time he'd tried to sound different and look different, so he could watch over her without becoming a person to her, without being real.

It had all played into the silly idea of hers that even when she saw him standing right in front of her, he might not be real. He understood completely now just how disconcerting that could be.

"Grace," he said.

"I got all the way to the gate and realized it was too late."

"Too late for what?"

"To stop myself from falling in love with you."

He felt the words ripple through him. *Love.* She was not supposed to love him. He would never have asked that of her, even though he selfishly wanted just that, wanted it more than he wanted to breathe.

"You said you could love me, too, if you just let yourself," his beautiful illusion said. "I found out I didn't have a choice in the matter. I couldn't stop it at all. I love you."

"Grace—"

"Could you really stop yourself?" she asked. "Are you going to tell me you're strong enough, powerful enough to control even that? That you could stop yourself from loving me?"

"I'm telling you I can't quite believe you're here. Because I want that so desperately."

"I got all the way to the gate," she said again, crying now, smiling through the tears. "I had to chase Jamie through the terminal, barely caught her outside, and she brought me to find you. We knocked and knocked, but you didn't answer. She had a key, so here I am."

He just stood there, his heart banging like a jackhammer. *Touch her,* he told himself. *Reach out and touch her.*

His hand came up, water dripping off it, and hesitated there with a good six inches between them. He was scared to try it.

"Do you still have your knife?" she suggested finally. "You could—"

That was it. He grabbed her, his hand closing around warm, soft flesh.

"Grace," he said, the sound ripped from him.

He pulled her to him, thinking, *never, never, never let her go*.

She laughed a bit as the water hit her. "It's cold."

If it was, he didn't notice. But the air conditioner was on, and there was a draft coming in. He closed the shower door, adjusted the knob for warmer water, and then pulled back just enough to see her, and he could very easily have laughed until he cried, if he let himself. He'd pulled her into the shower fully dressed, and now she was drenched. But she was here. She was right here with him and there wasn't an ounce of conscience inside of him capable of making him let her go. He'd denied his need for this woman for years, but no more.

"I don't deserve you," he said, his hands on her arms, her shoulders, in her hair, at the side of her face.

"I can't imagine anything I ever did to deserve you," she claimed.

"Oh, baby. You just don't know."

She ran her hands along his shoulders, his chest, the way she had that one night in the cave. When she'd stroked him so sweetly, so innocently. He'd never forget the feel of her delicate, innocent hands on him.

They'd been soaked then, as well. Every truly erotic picture he had of her featured her soaking wet.

He peeled off her shirt and found her bare beneath it. His eyes feasted on her breasts, those nicely rounded curves. His hands did, too. His mouth. He licked the water off of her, sucked it, finding all that smooth, creamy skin he'd so longed to touch, to taste.

He fell to his knees in front of her and pulled off her slacks. He'd ruined her shoes, and he threw them onto the bathroom floor. She laughed over that until he planted a kiss on the inside of her knee and started working his way up her left thigh. Then she shuddered and clutched at his shoulders, his head, his hair.

Water cascaded down her body. He drank it straight from

her body, wanted her absolutely drenched from wanting him. There was a storm raging inside of him, a need, and he wanted it inside of her, as well. He wanted to give it to her, to take her there. He wanted her dazed and gasping for breath and hanging on to him with every bit of strength she had left. He never wanted this night to end, and there was no way he was going to make this last. Not when every nerve ending in his body was screaming for him to take her. Right now. Hard and fast and so deep. To be so far up inside of her. To claim her as his.

For now, she was going to be his.

His body was throbbing painfully already. He felt as if he were perilously close to exploding, and he couldn't imagine the sheer pleasure of joining his body to hers, of driving inside of her, struggling to overcome the physical limits of what their bodies could do, could take.

He simply wanted to be a part of her in every way possible. He wanted her heart and her soul and all of the love inside of her that he absolutely did not deserve.

He wanted to feel her, stroke her, kiss her, taste her, and make her so ready for him she couldn't stand it anymore. He wanted her begging and pleading and exploding around him, the first minute he thrust inside her.

He pushed her up against the wall, had his face buried between her thighs, urging her to open herself up to him, and her legs were trembling. All of her was.

"Like this," he said. "I'll hold you."

And he lifted one of her thighs, draping it over his shoulder, pressing more deeply with his mouth and his tongue, stroking her relentlessly, tasting her, making her cry out and quiver and sink her nails into his shoulders.

He made her come again and again. It went on and on. He loved knowing he could give her this, that he could make her as crazy for him as he was for her.

Finally, he worked his way up her body, loving the taste of her breasts, wet and soft, her nipples sweet and so hard.

"You're perfect, Grace," he said, his face buried against the side of her neck. "I've dreamed about you too many nights to even count, and you're absolutely perfect and so beautiful. You take my breath away."

"You're beautiful," she insisted.

And he laughed, feeling as if he were absolutely on top of the world.

He still had her pinned against the wall, but she was straining against his body, writhing, rubbing herself against him. He had indeed made her ache.

"Are you trying to torment me?" she asked.

"Maybe I am." He pressed his erection against the softness of her belly. "Payback for the island. It's a miracle I didn't take you there."

"You seemed quite capable of resisting me," she said, kissing him deeply now. Great, gasping, desperate kisses.

"No," he said. "Not at all. I was dying to have you. And I'm going to. Right now."

He reached for her thighs, lifted them, hooked her legs around his hips and slid against her, back and forth against the wet, swollen opening of her body, thinking he might manage to tease her a bit more.

They both gasped. She looped her arms around his shoulders, found some leverage from the wall at her back and the hold she had on him with her legs, and angled herself up to him.

He was right on the brink then. Right there.

"Are you really going to make me beg?" she asked.

"I don't have the strength."

He slid inside her barely, testing, measuring at first, and then once he was sure she was ready, he let go of all that iron self-control. Gave in to all the sensations bombarding him.

Grace, he said, over and over again in his head and maybe to her, as well.

He could feel her body working to accommodate him. All

those little contractions deep within her, her body gripping and releasing, holding him so tightly, trying to find room for all he had to give her.

"Am I hurting you?" he said tightly.

"No. I just... It's too much."

"You're too much," he muttered against her lips. "You did this to me. You."

"No. It's you," she said. "It's all you."

She slid her legs even farther apart, arched her body against his, and he sank so deeply inside of her. She held him tightly within her, squeezed him, burned him, drenched him.

He was lost. Just lost.

He couldn't resist the sweet, hot fire any longer. The feel of being inside of her, stroking in and out, going deeper, striving for that point where he simply ceased to be, where there was no more him and her and they were one, in a way that no one could ever deny.

"You're mine," he said fiercely. "You belong to me. You always have."

She held on to him so tightly, for that hard, fast, wild ride, and she gave herself to him, beautifully. Holding nothing back. Clinging to him and moving with him and crying out his name.

Her climax seemed to ripple through her and straight into him. He shuddered so deeply he wasn't sure how he could stand it and still hang on to her and stay on his feet.

They hadn't used a condom, so there was literally nothing between them. They were skin to skin. Heat and fire and need.

"Take me," he said. "Me."

And she did.

When he came inside her, he was so turned on by the idea that she would carry just a bit of him around with her forever. For an instant, he thought about doing this with no precautions at all, thought about the idea of making her pregnant, seeing her with his baby growing inside of her, a bond between them that could never, ever be broken.

"Grace," he said raggedly.

"I know," she said, soothing him now, kissing his neck, his jaw, his cheek, his mouth. "I know."

Grace had tears seeping out of her eyes when it was over. He didn't seem to notice at first, with all that water raining down upon them.

Who would have guessed that water could be such an erotic thing? But it made his body, which was so impressive all by itself, that much more touchable. Her fingers slid so easily along his skin. Along all those lovely muscles. She liked tasting the water on him, tasting his wet skin, rubbing up against it, loved the water on her, too. It made her feel so absolutely bare and at the same time, caressed all over.

It made her think of the island. Of being with him in the rain, there against the tree, when she'd wanted him so badly already, and he'd been so strong, so invincible.

She couldn't quite believe what it had been like to finally be with him. So raw, so intense, so powerful.

He'd claimed her. Primitively. Forcefully. Told her she was his. She shivered a bit now, just remembering the words, the feeling. How delicious it was to be *his*. She couldn't imagine ever wanting to be anything at all in this world but *his*. If she could just have that, she'd be the luckiest woman alive.

"Are you okay?" he asked.

"Yes."

She could still barely find enough oxygen to satisfy her, couldn't get it inside of her body fast enough. Her heart was still thundering, as was his. His shoulders were heaving with each deep, harsh breath. She was still pinned against him and the wall. He was still inside of her somehow.

Her legs had turned to mush. They were so heavy. Her body sagged against his, totally at his mercy. Her face was buried against his shoulder, and she couldn't have moved an inch, not if her life depended on it.

He eased his upper body back, enough that she could breathe a bit easier and she could see him. Water cascaded down him everywhere. She wanted to kiss it off his mouth, drink it off his body, as he'd drunk from hers. When she'd opened the shower door and seen him standing there, so magnificently naked, she'd wondered if she might collapse in a puddle right there on his bathroom floor. It seemed she'd waited forever for him to pull her inside, pull her against him.

Although she understood his reticence. She'd seen just a bit of the hurt in his face, the way he'd suffered that day as well. Seen the confusion, the need, the fear to believe that what he wanted so badly was truly standing right there in front of him. After all, she'd felt that way so many times about him.

He kissed her mouth, her cheek. "I think it's time we made it to the bed."

And she shivered yet again. She wouldn't have believed it was possible to want him again so quickly. Not as blown away as she'd been by the first time. But there it was. He mentioned a bed, and she was ready. Eager. For everything he had to give her.

He gently separated himself from her. She hung on.

"I swear, I'll fall down if I don't have you to hold me up."

So he lifted her, carried her to the vanity and set her down on top of it. He shut off the shower and grabbed a big, blue towel. She went to take it from him, but he wouldn't let her. He dried her himself. Slowly. Sensuously. Rubbing the cloth against her and kissing her. Then rubbing some more.

"There," he said, then grabbed another towel.

When he went to dry himself, she took it from him, shaking her head back and forth. Kissing his wet chest.

"I want you just like this," she said.

He hesitated, and then she saw that dark, dangerous glint come into his eyes.

"Is that all right?" she murmured, still drinking from his skin.

"Grace, you can have me any way you want me. You might kill me one of these days, but you can have me."

"You said something about a bed?"

He lifted her into his arms and carried her to the soft sheets. She pushed him down flat on his back and just admired him for a long moment.

"You're the most beautiful man I've ever seen," she said, and she could have sworn he couldn't have looked any better. But he fought a grin and lost, and it seemed she'd actually made him blush. And she was dazzled by him all over again.

He reached for her, would have drawn her against him, but she pushed him back down onto the bed.

"You said I could have anything I wanted."

"And I meant it." He took her breast in the palm of his hand, cupping it, stroking it with his thumb. "Do you really not want me to touch you?"

"I want to touch you. And kiss you. All over."

"You want to torment me," he said, stroking her still.

"Maybe. I want to make you tremble for me. And shudder. And shake. And beg. All the things you make me do."

"You do, sweetheart. Believe me, you do," he said softly. "But if you feel the need to prove the point, be my guest."

She stroked. She teased. Kissed and licked and rubbed her breasts against him, and he did as she asked. He lay back and let her. Groaning at times, shaking, shuddering, swearing. She found out exactly what he liked—everything. And what she liked—everything, as well. He was amazing to touch, and it was amazing to think of him as hers. He was so very big, so powerful, so controlled, so amazing when she took him to the point where he just lost it.

She loved the way his body felt against hers, the way it

moved, the sureness of his touch, the confidence in it. The need. He made her so greedy, so very alive.

She'd explored nearly every bit of him, except the big, throbbing part of him between his legs. That, she'd merely teased, a glancing touch here and there, just to hear that sweet catch in his breath when she did it. There was the merest sheen of water left on his body. A bit in his hair, but most of it smeared by the touch of her hands and brush of her body against his. And he tasted so clean, his skin so hot.

She nudged his legs apart and knelt between them, wanting to taste him there.

"Grace?"

She leaned over him, wondering where to start. "You said I could have anything I wanted."

She felt him tense, found him fascinating. His skin—there—was so soft. Like baby skin. So delicate. She rubbed her cheek against him, the tip of her nose, and was rewarded with a shudder.

His hands were clenched into fists by his side, and he swore softly as she teased, barely touching him with her mouth, her tongue. Every muscle in his body went even tighter than before.

She touched him even more softly, slowly. And when he moaned a bit more and his hand tangled in her hair, she gave him what he wanted, what she'd come to crave herself. Him. Inside of her. Like this.

She had to struggle to take him, just as her body had struggled the other way. He was just too large, but he felt so right, too. Hot and slick and big. She found herself greedy now, as well. Could not get enough.

He tasted so good. She wanted to take him so deep, give him so much, and there was a place between her legs that was suddenly so achy, so empty, a place only he could fill.

His body started to move, thrusting gently beneath her. She sucked harder. He shuddered, swore, groaned.

"Grace, you're going to have to make a decision. Now."

She knew what he meant. A decision about how she wanted it. How she wanted him.

"Because this cannot go on," he said. "Not like this."

How did she want it? She loved the whole idea. Of what he was going to give her and all the possibilities for how she could have it, have him.

She lifted her head, found him lying there, his dark eyes no more than dangerous slits, his jaw rock-hard, all the muscles in his body trembling.

"Now," he demanded. "You decide. Or I will."

She shivered herself. At the command in his voice, one born of a need every bit as strong as hers.

She rolled over onto her back and pulled him to her. Her thighs fell apart and he was right there, so deep up inside of her in an instant. Every bit as powerfully as before. Just as tight. Just as hot. Just as overwhelming.

He lay there heavily on top of her, still somehow, and he kissed her again and again and again, just letting the heat rush even higher between them, the urgency, too. She wrapped her arms around him. Found his back was straining, a fine sheen of perspiration running down his spine.

Finally he lifted his head and said, "I'm afraid I'll crush you. You're so delicate, sweetheart. Are you sure you want it like this?"

"Yes. I want to feel your body on top of mine. Hot and heavy. Surrounding me. Inside of me. Everywhere. I don't want you to hold anything back at all."

He looked skeptical, worried.

She took it as a challenge. "I could make you lose control," she boasted.

"I know you could," he admitted.

And it was only then that she felt the full weight of his body pressing down upon hers. The bulk, the heat. Her bare breasts pushing up against his chest. All those lovely muscles in his flat stomach, his thighs. He had her surrounded. He was everything she could see, everywhere she could reach.

And he was moving inside of her, steadily, then strongly, then urgently.

It was everything she'd never understood about being with a man. Everything she'd thought was nothing but silly, sentimental songs and carefully scripted scenes in a movie made to look like things no one had in real life. It was that first giddy feeling in the pit of her stomach at the thought that a boy was attractive. A first kiss. First embrace.

It was magic and power and raw, sexual need, and everything. Just everything.

He took her out of her body, out of his world. To a place where all she could do was feel. Where everything was so much more intense than it had ever been, than she'd ever imagined it could be.

And all she had to do was hang on to him. Just hang on for that wild, wild ride.

"I've never felt anything like that in my life," she confessed later when he was lying sprawled on his back with her curled against his side. He'd tugged a sheet over the two of them, to ward off the chill when the air conditioner kicked on, and he had one arm around her, lazily stroking up and down her back.

"Never?" he asked.

"Nothing's ever come close," she said. "I suppose you find that hard to believe."

She was thirty-one years old, and she felt like a novice with him. He was obviously so experienced. He'd shown her a completely different side of making love. An incredible mix of love and sheer skill, of experience, patience, determination and eagerness to please. She knew she'd pleased him, as well. But a part of her thought there must have been so many other women, so much more experienced than she was.

"It's never been that urgent for me," she said. "That overwhelming. That necessary."

"For me, neither, sweetheart."

She pulled away from him, just enough that she could look at him. He seemed deliciously tired and so very relaxed, still so gorgeous. That was part of it, of course. He was absolutely gorgeous, and at forty-three he was most definitely a man in the prime of his life. He'd probably spent decades pleasing legions of women who'd come before her.

"You don't believe me?" he asked, clearly offended.

"I think women must have been crawling all over you from the time you hit puberty, and I have trouble believing you were discouraging them."

"Oh."

"There must have been so many women."

"None that mattered," he insisted.

She frowned at him. "You just know exactly what to say, don't you?"

"You think I'm feeding you a line? Are you really that inexperienced, Grace?"

She colored profusely.

"You are," he said, a goofy grin coming across his face. He looked pleased, she thought. *Pleased?*

"You can't think it's always like that," he said. "You have to know how incredible it was."

"For me."

"And for me." He took her chin in his hand, turning her face to his. "Don't you ever doubt that. You're it for me, Grace. There'll never be another woman in the world to come close to you, to what we have together."

And if that wasn't enough, he set out to prove it to her. There in the darkness that settled in around them, in the quiet and the comfort of his bed.

Chapter 14

Every time he woke her, he told himself. One *last* time. By dawn, that wonderful sensual storm of the night before had eased, and in its place, his conscience was giving him hell. All those insurmountable obstacles he'd always seen between them, the ones that had been seared away last night by the first touch of her in his arms, were creeping back into his head.

Last night, he'd pulled her to him and stripped off her clothes, vowing that there had to be a way, that he would find it. And in the cold light of day, he hadn't found anything except what he'd wanted, what he'd taken that she'd so generously given, what he wanted to take still.

Which meant if he had a decent bone in his body, he would leave her alone now, would take this time while she was still asleep to think about what he had to say to her, what he owed her.

But he would never have his fill of her, would likely never have more than this. He woke for the last time to find her sprawled on top of him, her body warm and soft and absolutely limp, draped over him like a blanket. Her head was on his shoulder, her hair spread out across his chest, one of her thighs tucked between his, her toes, somehow cold, inching along his leg. He captured that foot between his legs to warm it and wondered how she managed to stay warm without him, wondering if another man would warm her this way.

His hand stroked lightly through her hair, and she murmured, "Mmm. What time is it?"

"Early."

She lifted her head just enough to press a kiss over the top of his heart. "We don't have to get up, do we?"

"Not yet. Go back to sleep. I remembered I never fed you last night. I was going to grab breakfast for us from a little shop around the corner."

Maybe if he wasn't lying naked beside her, he could clear his head. Think. Plan. Find the nerve to come back and confess. Get ready to see the look of disgust and likely hatred in her eyes. Especially after the way they'd spent the night. The lines they'd not just crossed, but obliterated. There was absolutely no excuse for that, except that for the first time in his life, he'd absolutely lost control. He'd pushed his sense of what was right and fair totally aside and simply taken what he'd so desperately wanted for so long.

But even that was no excuse. Especially for letting her tell him she loved him.

God, she loved him.

"Are you okay?"

He turned to find her staring up at him and nodded, still wanting to believe there had to be a way and finding none. He just had to hold it together for a little longer, say what he had to say and then watch her go once again. Twice within twenty-four hours seemed like more than the world should demand of any man, but there it was.

"I should go," he said.

"It can wait," she said, pressing her mouth to his, drawing

him down into that sinfully sweet, dark pool of desire, drowning him in it.

Not that he fought against it. She was just too perfect, too beautiful, too eager, too soft and sweet-smelling. He would take all of her he could get. Take and take and take, it seemed. She was already lying on top of him, boneless and so willing, and he was hard once again.

He ran his hands over her body, wanting to memorize every detail, savor every touch. And then he put a hand on either of her thighs and pulled them into position on either side of his body. He palmed her hips and settled her on top of him. She kissed him deeply, hungrily, and with one little move of his hips he was inside her once again. In that place that seemed to have been made just for him. He thrust gently, just once.

"You must be sore," he said.

"A little. But I don't care," she admitted, pushing herself up until she was sitting astride him, looking so wild with her hair hanging down her back and her pretty breasts filling his hands.

"You are so beautiful, Grace."

"You make me feel beautiful," she confided.

His hands went back to her hips, spanning them, cupping them, urging her down harder against him, taking him deeper, setting a rhythm that would have this over in no time.

"Like this?" she said, always so eager to please.

"Yes," he said through clenched teeth. "Just like that."

Grace woke up alone, the bed gone cold without him.

So, she thought, this was love. This was what it was all about. Losing herself completely in a man. Thinking the sun rose and set in his eyes, in his smile, his laughter. She was absolutely dazzled by him, by all he'd shown her, all he'd given her. By the sweet, seductive promise of tomorrow and the next day and all the ones after that. With him.

She was so very happy she could cry, and she fought off

an attack of sheer nerves, which had no place in the face of such happiness. She didn't always have to expect the worst. It was one habit she could break. Starting right now.

She showered quickly, blushing at the thought of what they'd done right here in his shower. The way he'd looked, so sleek, so powerful, so beautiful. The way he'd felt. Her whole body was trembling, just thinking about it.

Dressing quickly in one of his T-shirts and a matching pair of sweats with a drawstring waist, which he'd left out for her, she only gave herself a minute to stare into the bathroom mirror wishing she was indeed beautiful, that she could look that way for him.

Then she went into the kitchen and absently turned on the small TV in the corner, looking for one of the all-news channels. She was a news junkie, after all, and wondering how bad the hurricane had been to the people of San Reino. She'd just found the right channel when he walked into the apartment with a bag that smelled of baked goods and coffee.

"Good morning." She pulled him to her for a brief kiss as she took her coffee and followed him to the little table by the window where he unpacked still-hot croissants, muffins, bagels and fruit, a mountain of food.

"Expecting company?" she asked.

"Just you. I didn't know what you liked."

"Oh." She blushed a bit. He didn't even know what she liked for breakfast, and she'd done things with him that she'd never dared with another man.

She was sitting down to join him when she heard her own name, then the name San Reino, coming from the TV she'd left on. She turned to the screen and saw one more time that photo of her at eleven being pulled from the wreckage in Rome.

"So, I'm still news," she said, turning to Sean.

He stood unmoving, staring at the screen, and when his gaze came back to hers he looked... She couldn't say exactly. Worried? Nervous, maybe?

That was odd. She'd never seen a hint of nerves in him. Bombs, bullets, dungeons, Central American madmen…none of that had him so much as breaking a sweat. So whatever was bothering him, it must be bad.

Grace took a sip of her coffee, which was black and strong and helped a bit to settle her nerves. "Has something happened?"

"No."

But obviously something had. He stared at her, his expression so odd. He seemed like a man absolutely torn. She put her hand on his arm, thinking to soothe him. He pulled away and abruptly stood up.

"Give me a minute, Grace. I need to…I just remembered a call I have to make."

He flicked off the TV and then went into his bedroom. She fought the urge not to move closer to try to hear what he obviously didn't want to say in front of her. What in the world had gone wrong?

He was back in a moment, his expression as guarded as she'd ever seen it, and it made her even more nervous.

"Please tell me what's wrong," she said.

He gave her a sad half smile and said, "I got up this morning thinking I'd like to take you away somewhere. Just the two of us. Somewhere we could hide away from the rest of the world for as long as you'd stay with me."

She'd stay with him forever, she thought. That's what she'd planned. Forever.

"I'll go," she said. She'd go anywhere with him.

He shook his head. "It's not that simple. I have a bad habit of always thinking I can fix anything, manage everything. I just thought there had to be a way for us to be together."

"We can't?"

He looked hurt, she realized. Bleak. There was something different even about the way he held himself, his back so straight, chin up, expression rigid. As if he were facing a court martial.

"Sean, you're scaring me."

"I'm sorry." He started walking around the room. To the window and back to the sofa and back to her.

"I love you." She decided to lay it all on the line. "I don't care what's wrong. I love you."

And it was only then that she realized he'd never said it back to her. On the island, he'd said he could love her, if he let himself. But that was a far cry from being desperately, madly, passionately in love with her, which was what she felt for him.

"Whatever it is, just say it," she begged.

"God," he groaned. "I don't know how. I haven't talked about this in twenty years."

Twenty years?

It couldn't be a coincidence. She knew of only one significant thing that happened twenty years ago.

"The bombing?"

He nodded and looked away.

"I never meant for any of this to happen, Grace. I thought I could watch out for you and try to make sure you were safe and still keep my distance. I thought if I looked different and sounded different every time, you might never even make the connection that I was the same person. I thought as long as you never got a good look at my face in the daylight..."

"Why wasn't I suppose to see your face?"

"I was afraid you'd recognize me," he said. "Think about it, Grace. Close your eyes for a minute and listen to my voice. This voice. The real one. You've always known me."

She had, it seemed. Always. She didn't know why or from where. But it had always seemed she'd known him all along.

"I don't understand."

"My father was doing a tour of duty with the UN during the peace conference twenty years ago. He was in charge of security for the conference."

"Where my father was killed? My mother and my brother?" Everyone she loved?

"Yes."

He waited, giving her time to try to take that in.

So their fathers hadn't just been friends. His father was there the day her family died. There was the connection she'd always known must be there. None of this had happened by chance. Nothing to do with him and her.

"He's always felt responsible," Sean continued. "Always felt there had to be more he could have done, and I... We both felt we owed you. A debt of honor. He tried to be a part of your life back then, even talked about bringing you here to live with us, but he said your mind was made up. That lots of your family's friends had offered to take you, and you'd been adamant about going to boarding school in England. So he gave up on that idea. But he's always kept track of how you were doing. We both have. When you went on your first IRC mission, he got worried. I was in the area already.

"I hated the whole idea of you being there, but, as he pointed out, neither one of us had any say in the way you chose to live your life. So I did what I could. It wasn't that hard to keep track of your team and what was going on there. I kept hoping you'd all pack up and leave, but the IRC's one of the most stubborn groups I've ever known. When we got word that the UN bombing campaign was starting, I had to get you out of there somehow. So I went to see you, to tell you to go. And you did.

"It wasn't long until you were in the middle of something else. You are so stubborn, so strong, so determined, so committed. As frustrated as you've made me over the years, I can't help but admire all of those things about you."

Which she found didn't mean the least to her now. That he merely admired her? When she loved him? And he'd been keeping things from her. Important things? Things she still didn't fully comprehend?

"So you and your father have watched over me because you think you owe me?"

"We did," he said.

A debt of honor, he'd said.

And she got scared. So scared. He thought he owed her, because his father was in charge of security at the conference where the bomb went off?

Just how seriously did he take his debts? she wondered. How far would he go? He'd tried awfully hard to resist her on the island. He'd taken such tender care of her, been so gentle, so understanding, so strong. But he hadn't wanted to make love to her. He'd told her goodbye just yesterday, would obviously have let her walk out of his life without a word, without ever asking her to stay. So what in the world could she possibly mean to him?

"Just how guilty do you feel?" she asked, thinking that she loved him. Oh, God, she loved him. And he thought he *owed* her something.

"There's more to it than that, Grace. There's...I don't even know if I can say it. I've always been such a coward where this was concerned."

"No," she said, thinking he wasn't. Not about anything. Thinking she didn't want to know. She wanted to go hide away in a cabin in the mountains with him and make love to him until neither one of them could move. She wanted to run. Now. With her illusions firmly in place.

"I was twenty-three," he said. "Just a couple of years out of the Naval Academy. I was... I don't know what I was. Thinking I knew everything, I guess. Thinking I could handle anything. So young and so stupid. So full of myself."

"What did you do?" she asked, finally understanding. This wasn't about his father, but him.

"I was there visiting my family. In Rome. I was in the courtyard when the suicide bomber waltzed in. You were playing with another girl. I heard the two of you laughing—"

"Sean, what did you do?"

"There are some kids... My age, a few years younger maybe, hanging out near one of the barricades around the lecture hall. I didn't like the fact that they were loitering so close to the perimeter. There'd been a number of threats made. Apparently, your father got them wherever he went those days. My father was nervous, thinking he wasn't prepared, didn't have enough troops, hadn't had the time he wanted to plan.

"We'd looked over the area the day before, talked through what we thought were the greatest weakness in the security setup. We had talked about somebody trying to drive through the barricades with a truck full of explosives, and the next thing I knew, there was a truck. Near where those kids were. They started arguing, shouting. One of them pulled a gun, and I thought, this is it. What my father was so afraid of happening right there in front of me. And I thought I could stop it. I thought it was my duty to. That I was going to make my father proud of me, that I was going to be such a hero."

And she'd always thought he was. Always.

"I shouted a warning. There were guards right next to me—at the main entrance. I ran for that pack of kids, and I had the people on duty following me. I was even barking orders at them, I think, as if I had the right. There were shots fired, a lot of smoke. A lot of confusion. And in the middle of it... I don't know. It just felt wrong. I remember I turned around, and I saw someone heading for the entrance to the auditorium. A kid with a backpack on who was...I don't know. There was just something about him.

"And then I knew," he said. "I just knew. That was him. He was the one we should have been worried about. The other was just a diversion, and it worked. Perfectly. Because of me. I started running then, would have shot him right then, but I wasn't even armed. And...and I was too late, anyway. The next thing I knew, the bomb went off. The whole building just exploded. Right in my face."

Grace listened to all he had to say, and when he was done,

he stood in front of the window with his back to her, stood so straight and so tall, looking like a man who could indeed do anything. A magical, all-powerful man.

She'd believed that. Believed everything he'd ever told her, everything he'd ever done for her, that it had been genuine and real and...and she'd loved him. Foolishly, it seemed.

He'd always told her that he was just a man. She'd never quite believed that, but she had believed in him. In all the goodness and the strength and the honor that was him.

And now...

Grace shuddered. She got up, just needing to move, headed for the opposite side of the room from him, thought about just walking out the door, just walking away. But she still couldn't quite believe what he'd done.

She was standing there shivering in his apartment after spending the night in his bed, standing there with his clothes on her body, thinking she'd been so foolish to love him. Wondering why, after being so careful for so long, she would have let her guard down with him.

She sensed movement behind, turned around and found that he was right there, his hand dangerously close to her arm.

She flinched and backed away, her chin coming up as she forced herself to look at him. This man who she thought was going to mean everything to her, the man who'd taken everything she'd had, everything she'd loved, away.

"I'm sorry," he said. "It's totally inadequate, I know. I feel like a fool for even needing to say it to you. But there it is. I'm sorry. I would give anything to be able to go back and change it. I'd give you anything I had, if there was a way to make this up to you. I'd give you my own family, if I could. But we both know there's just nothing that could ever make up for this, Grace."

She stared up at him. The words were rumbling around inside her head, but she couldn't seem to put them together in any way that made sense. It was too much, too overwhelming, and she felt panic rising up inside of her.

She opened her mouth to say something… She had no idea what. Then closed it once again.

She'd never really asked exactly what happened the day of the bombing or why. She'd never been able to make sense of people feeling threatened by her father, people hating a man who preached peace around the world. And she knew that the man who walked into the building with the bomb on his back had died that day, with her family.

End of story. There was no sense to make of it, after all, no changing it. She hadn't felt she needed any of the details.

But this man…he was here, standing in front of her. A living, breathing human being, and he said he could have stopped it. That he should have been able to. That he screwed up, and her family died that day.

"I never had anyone to blame," she blurted out.

He didn't so much as flinch, just stood there as tall and straight as a statue. He looked as if he expected her to hurt him, to wound him. Maybe to scream and cry and hit him.

She wondered if she'd feel better if she did.

There was energy coursing through her veins, an odd, unfocused kind of energy. She felt as if she should be doing something, as if she couldn't just stand here. She wasn't sure if she could be in this room with him.

He could have stopped it? He'd wanted to be a hero?

She thought of lying in the hospital, dazed, confused, scared to death. She thought of when they finally told her that her mother wasn't coming to her bedside. Neither was her father. Or her brother. Because they were all dead.

She thought about how it had always felt, being so absolutely and completely alone, thought of telling him she'd wanted to die, too, but he'd already known that. He'd known she was living like a woman who wasn't really alive, merely existing on the fringes, and he'd wanted to change that. He'd wanted her to care about something or someone. To live.

And here she was. *Living.* And hurting like hell. She didn't quite see the appeal.

"I hate what you've done to me," she said. All that bitterness, all that fear, had a target. Right in front of her. She zeroed in on him. "I hate it."

He nodded, accepting.

"And I think I hate you, too."

And he still didn't say anything, just looked away.

"I don't understand why you ever had to be a part of my life. Why we had to go through all of this...."

"I know," he said. "I should never have touched you."

"No, you shouldn't have."

"I just wanted to protect you—"

"For what? To live to see a day like this? To feel this bad, all over again?"

"I never thought you'd come to care about me. I thought I could talk to you, maybe make you see what you're doing with your life—"

"I thought you were going to *be* my life," she cried. "And you let me think that. All of those things I'd promised myself I'd never want, never risk having, you dangled it in front of my face, and then took it all away."

"Grace—"

He reached for her, and she panicked. She couldn't let him touch her. She knocked his hand away, and when he reached for her again, she slapped him across the face.

They both froze, the sound echoing around the room. All the angry words seemed to do the same, and the images of what they'd done here. The way she'd been in his arms. So hungry, so needy. So damned happy. For all of half a day. One night, actually.

"Why did you let me do those things with you?" She couldn't put a name on it, had no idea what it was now, the things they'd done deep in the night. Except a lie. All of it had been a lie. "When I came back here last night, why didn't you just tell me? Why didn't you send me away?"

"I'm sorry. It was wrong of me not to."

It was like kicking somebody in the stomach and saying "Oops." Like tearing someone's heart out and stomping it on the ground, and thinking there were any words at all that could ever make up for that.

"I can't believe you did this to me," she said.

She couldn't believe she would ever hurt this badly again. She'd thought her whole life was going to begin. Finally. With him.

All those foolish dreams about having someone to love, about having a place to belong. She was going to conquer all her fears, for him, remembered thinking it would be like jumping off a cliff. And it was. She knew because she'd jumped already, and she saw now there was no one to catch her. Just rough, hard ground rising up to meet her, and any minute, she was gong to break into a million pieces. Hopefully not in front of him. In fact she didn't think she could stand to be here. Not one more minute, one more second.

"I have to get out of here," she said, and turned to go.

He caught her at the door, and she glared at him, only to find him holding out her shoes to her. She shoved them onto her feet, and then he handed her her airline ticket and her passport.

"You're going to need these."

She took them, wishing she could throw them back in his face. But she did need them. She needed to get as far away from him as possible.

Thankfully, he didn't try to stop her then. He opened the door for her instead and said, "There's a car waiting at the curb. The driver will take you anywhere you want to go."

Which infuriated her.

"You knew all along what you were going to do? You were going to climb out of that bed this morning and tell me everything, weren't you?"

"I thought maybe there was a way, but...seeing you on the TV screen from that day, I knew I had to tell you."

"You knew I'd find out," she said.

"I knew I owed you the truth," he insisted.

Which sounded suspiciously like it had something to do with honor—his own—and at the moment, she didn't think he had any.

She thought about slapping him again. It had brought her some measure of satisfaction the first time. She wanted to shatter that damned self-control of his, wanted to see him crumble, as she was crumbling before him. She wanted him to admit that he'd done it all wrong. Everything. Every word. Every touch. Every sweet, seductive promise in the dark. But there was simply no point, and she just wanted to be gone.

She walked out the door without another word, climbed into the car that was indeed waiting at the curb and asked the driver to take her to the airport. An hour later, she was in a window seat in the first-class cabin, wrapped up in a blanket, a tiny pillow between her head and the side of the plane, headed for London.

She didn't look at anyone, didn't speak to anyone. She just turned her face into her pillow and let her tears fall, wishing she never even knew his name.

Chapter 15

Two months later

Grace had blood all over her, a fourteen-year-old boy's blood.

Her stoic staff stood all around her, waiting for her to do what she had to do. To give up.

Damn.

She did it. It was her call, and she made it. He'd already been down too long to ever hope he'd come back to them, and it was only through her stubbornness that they'd fought this long. The boy was dead.

A few minutes later, Grace stripped off her blood-stained gloves and stepped outside the classroom—they'd been using an abandoned schoolhouse as a clinic this time—and went to find the boy's parents.

She hadn't even stayed in London for a day after running back there from the States. The hurricane that had so complicated her escape from Milero's island had gone on to do even greater damage to the already-devastated San Reino, and she went back there. Peter Baxter hadn't been happy about it but couldn't deny the overwhelming need, and in the end, she went.

They were in what was left of a little village about fifteen miles from the coast, doing what they could, and as usual, it was never enough.

But the boy... The boy had gotten to her. He'd been in twenty-four hours ago. He'd fallen from a roof of some kind, trying to salvage something of it so his family might have some shelter, but when she'd seen him earlier he'd been talking to her, in that bashful way of still-awkward adolescent boys. He'd been charming, and she'd believed he hadn't done himself any permanent damage.

But he had.

Now he was dead.

The boy's mother started crying right away and begging Grace to tell her it wasn't true, and the boy's father simply exploded.

"How could you do this to him? How could you let him die?"

Grace said nothing. Intellectually, she knew all about being a target of people's anger, and this boy's father just needed to get it out.

"There must have been something you could have done!" he screamed. "He was here this morning. You said he was fine!"

"I'm sorry," she said, thinking a CAT scan would have spotted the slow pooling of blood into his belly. With more space, she could have kept him here, giving her time to continue monitoring his condition. A well-equipped operating room, and she might well have saved him. But more often than not, they had so little, too few staff members, and they simply moved from one impending medical disaster to the next. They lost too many patients.

"You let him die!" the man roared. "My only son—you let him die!"

She touched his arm. "Sir?"

He shoved her away. "Don't you dare touch me."

"I'm sorry."

"Sorry? You let my son die! How does it feel to know you let my son die?"

Fifteen minutes later, Grace was standing outside, staring off into the hills and still shaking, when Jane appeared by her side.

"It wasn't your fault," she said.

Grace merely nodded. The boy was dead, and his father hated her. She hated herself at the moment.

"A whole series of events led to that boy's death," Jane said. "Chief among them the fact that he lives here, in a place where health care is haphazard at best. Where we struggle to meet even the most basic of needs. And then there's the damned hurricane, the mud slides, the lousy construction of most of these people's homes. You were just a little piece of the puzzle, Grace. You happened to be there at the end, and you couldn't save him with the deck stacked against him that way."

"I know. But he's still dead, and I still feel guilty."

Jane frowned at her, gave her a quick squeeze and said, "You're not God, my dear. Just a doctor. Just a woman."

Which, oddly enough, made her think of Sean.

He'd said that to her so many times. That he was just a man. And she'd never believed him. She'd been so convinced he was a truly magical creature come down to earth to save her.

Grace closed her eyes and fought back a rush of tears.

"Is there anything I can do?" Jane asked.

Grace shook her head, and Jane left her alone in the cool December night. It wasn't the first time she'd been the target of someone's anger over the loss of a loved one, and it wouldn't be the last. It normally didn't get to her like this, but everything got to her lately.

She hardly recognized the woman she'd become since she came back here. She'd lost all her objectivity, all the careful distance she'd always maintained between her and her emotions.

She still managed to do her job, most of the time until she was tired enough to sleep, sometimes even tired enough not to dream. When she did dream, it was always about *him*. At times, she thought she could still feel his arms around her, and she had a bad habit of staring into the darkness thinking he might be out there somewhere.

Most of the time, she tried not to think of him at all. She was holding it together. That was all she really had to do. Keep moving. Keep working. Don't think about it. Try not to be afraid.

That was one of the hardest parts, she'd found. So many times now, she was desperately afraid.

Right now, even.

Lately she'd heard rumblings about Milero that left her even more unsettled, and she didn't like to be alone anymore. Especially outside in the dark.

She should be in bed, but here she was, shivering a bit and looking up into the sky, wondering where she could possibly go from here and what she might do. Wondering what, if anything, might make her life just a bit less difficult to bear.

She had no idea, and even her work, the one thing she'd always had, didn't seem to be enough. She just hurt. All over. All the time. And she was so scared.

Grace had turned to go back inside when she felt something—that odd tingling at the base of her spine that told her someone was watching her. She heard the slightest sound, a faint tap against the ground, and whirled around, her heart in her throat.

Maybe she wanted to live after all, she thought, foolishly

and too late. Maybe it truly was important that she live to see another day.

And then she saw him.

In the shadows, in the darkest part of the yard, stood a man. A tall, broad man dressed all in black, his face indistinguishable at this distance and in this poor light.

Grace shivered. Not from fear, but anticipation, hope.

All of a sudden, she just couldn't breathe. She could hardly hear over the pounding of her own heart.

It was *him.*

She had no idea what she was going to say to him or what might have changed between them that could ever matter. But it was him. He'd come back to her, and if the feeling rising up inside of her was any indication, she was glad. As much as he'd hurt her, somehow she still wanted to see him, still needed him.

She stood there waiting as the man took another step toward her, and it was only then that she saw…

He was leaning on a cane, one of his legs obviously not functioning quite the way it should. He stepped into a shallow pool of light, and she knew.

It wasn't Sean.

It was his brother-in-law, Dan Reese.

"Hello, Grace," he said. "I'm afraid it's time to go."

"What?"

"He said you're familiar with the routine."

And then she realized what he meant. "Sean sent you?"

Dan nodded. "Milero's men are going to try to take the capital, if not tomorrow, the day after. He would like very much to have you back in his hands—"

"Milero's been making noises about taking over this country for weeks, and he hasn't done it."

"We have someone inside his compound, Grace. We've had someone there for months. How do you think we knew enough about it to get you out?"

In truth, she hadn't thought of that.

"I've seen the data," he said. "The threat's real. It's time for you to go. If it had been up to me, you'd have been gone at least a week ago."

"It's not up to you," she said. "Or anyone else."

Looking every bit as intimidating as he had when she first met him, none of the man playing with his little boy in him now, he said, "I made a promise to a friend that I would get you out of here. You're going."

She ignored the sheer audacity of any man thinking he could tell her what to do. Normally, it automatically got her back up, but she let it go this time. She was still too stunned thinking that Sean, despite everything that had happened, was still trying to take care of her.

"I can't believe he's still keeping track of me, that…" That he still cared in any way at all.

"Then you don't know him at all," Dan said simply.

Grace closed her eyes and had to look away. Because she had thought she knew him very well, and he'd promised her he'd always be here for her. At one time she would never have thought to question it. But they'd parted in such an ugly way. She'd said awful, hurtful things to him—like that boy's father had said to her—and Sean had hurt her more than she thought she could bear at times. So she couldn't help but be both surprised and touched to find that he was keeping his promise. In her experience, promises weren't worth the breath it took to speak them.

"He'd have come himself," Dan said. "But he's under the distinct impression that you hate him. He was afraid you might not listen to him. So he asked me to come instead."

"Where do you want us to go?" she asked. The lives of her team were in her hands. She wouldn't risk them because of any emotion she might have regarding the man responsible for this warning.

"All the way to the border. I'll see you safely across."

"He doesn't do that," she told Dan. "He just tells us to go, and we do. He doesn't stay to see that we get there."

"Of course he does. He just never let you see him follow-ing you. But I didn't see the point in keeping up that little pretense any longer."

"Oh." She felt so foolish then. Of course Sean wouldn't leave anything like that to chance.

It was nearly dawn by the time they went. She found her-self in the cab of a run-down truck with Dan at the wheel. She'd feared he'd use this time to plead his friend's case, but he hadn't. She was relieved, and yet incredibly curious. She lasted an hour before she asked, "How is he?"

"He hates himself," Dan said simply.

Grace felt another of those annoying little twinges in the region of her heart and thought about Sean, hating himself. In her anger and her shock, she wasn't quite clear on exactly everything she'd said to him that day. She thought it was something along the lines of, *I hate what you've done to me. I think I hate you, too.*

What was any different about him hating himself? Why would that bother her in any way?

She found it did, wondered how bad it was, wondered what it had done to him and what he might do. Nothing, of course. He was too strong a man. He would endure. No matter what. Which might just be worse. Grace knew what it was like to simply endure. Still…

"I don't know what I can do about that," she said.

"Don't you?" Dan reached inside the folds of his black leather jacket and pulled out a sheaf of papers, folded in thirds, and tossed them to her. "I don't know what he told you about that day the bomb went off, but I doubt he made any effort at defending himself or his actions. He certainly didn't when it came to testifying about it at the hearings that followed."

"Hearings?"

Dan nodded. "That's a transcript of the UN Security Council's final report."

She glanced at it in the dim light, saw the red stamp that read Top Secret and Classified across the front.

"Do me a favor. Burn it when you're done," Dan said. "Sean's not a man to make excuses for himself. He's careful and precise and very, very smart. I don't think he's ever made another mistake in his life. Which may be why he didn't recognize this for what it was. A mistake. One little part of what went wrong that day and allowed a crazed man with a bomb strapped to his back to get to your father."

Grace looked down at the paper, thinking she didn't want to know, didn't want to read it. Dan as much as dared her.

"If you want to hate someone for that, Grace, hate them all. Every organization involved. Every soldier there. Not just him. Or maybe you could take that anger and direct it at the man who deserves it. The one who walked in there with the bomb. That's who killed your family, and you know it."

It took time to deal with what equipment they had, to decide what was worth transporting back to London and what they'd leave behind. To make travel arrangements for the staff and get ready to go.

Two days later, Grace was in a hotel in Panama, her travel plans made, when she found herself packing what little she had with her and came across the report Dan Reese had pushed into her unwilling hands.

She hadn't read it, hadn't wanted to.

But her mind kept coming back to the boy who'd died and the father who hated her. Sometimes she replayed the scene in her head, and yet halfway through, it wasn't her and the boy's father anymore. It was her and Sean, and she was the one screaming. At him, Sean, who it seemed hated himself, too.

There were few absolutes in Grace's profession. A patient had this, the doctor did this, and likely everything would be fine. But every patient was different. Some situations weren't so easily read. Procedures weren't so obvious. She could do this or that. One thing might work. One might kill her patient.

There were judgment calls; she made them every day. Sometimes everything worked out. Sometimes it didn't. Had she made wrong calls that left patients to die? She could certainly think of things she wished she'd done differently and patients who'd died. Had she been negligent? Careless? She didn't think so. Had she simply made the wrong decisions at times? Yes, she had. Did she feel guilty? Yes.

Grace stared down at the report in her hand. All of a sudden, as much as she didn't want to know what was inside, she thought she had to look. She had to wonder just how similar her situation and Sean's might have been. She knew about instinct, about split-second decisions. She relied on both. He must, as well. He thought he'd done the wrong thing, that he could have stopped that bomb from killing her family, just as she thought she could have saved that boy.

She ignored the question of the way he'd lied to her, the way he'd let her fall in love with him without telling her the truth. It was a totally separate issue. She was thinking about fairness now. About that boy's father and how lousy he made her feel. And about what she'd said to Sean that day.

Dan said he wasn't the kind of man who made mistakes. Which meant he must be suffering now. Sean told her he'd been living with this for twenty years, and that nothing ever made it better. She knew all about that, too.

She owed him, she realized sadly. He'd saved her life more than once and the lives of the people on her team. He was looking out for them even now, even thinking she hated him and blamed him for the death of her family.

She couldn't let that go on. She realized it wasn't the reason she was so angry with him. She was angry because he'd lied to her. He'd allowed her to fall in love with him without being honest with her. And because what she'd taken as signs of love from him—the kindness, the gentleness, the concern, the intensely personal stake he seemed to have in her own well-being—she now saw as nothing but the actions of a man with a guilty conscience. She couldn't stand the idea of being nothing but a responsibility to him. A wrong to somehow make right. Someone he pitied. Her face burned at the idea even now. At the way she'd gone so eagerly into his arms. All the things she'd felt, things she'd shown him and said to him. Why had he ever let things go so far between them? She would never understand that.

But she owed him the rest. For all he'd done to keep her and her people safe over the years. And it wasn't the kind of message to be delivered by letter or phone. She had to stand in front of him and look him in the eye when she said it.

Maybe she could do it without crying, without yelling at him, without pouring out all the feelings she still had for him. Regardless, she had to go.

When she got to D.C., he wasn't at his apartment or his office. She considered calling the number he'd said was manned twenty-four hours a day, but she wasn't looking for someone to come rescue her, and if she went through that number, he would worry. If she left a message that nothing was wrong, that she merely needed to talk to him, she wondered if he'd come after the way she'd left things between them.

Finally she drove to Dan and Jamie's house. Jamie opened the front door, and all Grace said was "I can't find him."

"He's in Colorado. In the mountains. A family friend has a cabin there. We've been going since we were kids." Jamie brought her inside, pulled a slip of paper from a message pad by the phone and started writing. "It's not the easiest place to find, but he hasn't been answering the phone or returning any messages I've left. If you really want to see him, I'd recommend you just show up."

If Grace wanted to find him still there, she supposed his sister meant.

"All right. Thank you. I just... I have to talk to him."

Jamie nodded and stood there, staring.

"I'm sorry," she said finally. "I just can't get over the fact that you were that little girl I saw in the newspaper photograph all those years ago. I didn't want to say anything before. Sean told me not to dare to bring it up," Jamie said. "But I remember how worried we all were, how close we'd come to losing Sean, and that I just didn't think I could bear that. They kept flashing the picture of you and him on the news. My mother said you'd been hurt, and that you'd lost your whole family. She said we should all say a prayer for you, and I told her that I knew you'd be okay. Because you had Sean with you."

"What?"

"I knew he'd take good care of you."

"Sean?"

"Didn't he even tell you that much?" Jamie asked. "Didn't you recognize him? Didn't you even look at the picture? Or read the report Dan gave you?"

"I... It had a transcript of his testimony. I started it, but..." It had been awful. A startlingly factual, emotionless account of what he'd done that day. A scathingly brutal dissection of all he thought he'd done wrong. "I couldn't stand to finish it."

She couldn't stand the pain etched into those words.

"You never even looked at the photo? It's you and him, Grace. He was going to do everything he could to stop that man from blowing up the building. He was running for him when the bomb went off. God, if he'd been any faster, we'd have lost him, too. As it was, he was close enough to the blast that he spent six days in the hospital himself. He carried you out of that building. You and three others before he collapsed himself."

Grace couldn't say anything. She couldn't.

Every time she'd ever seen that photo, she'd looked away as quickly as possible. She never wanted to remember that day, had steadfastly ignored reading any accounts of it until Dan had shoved that report into her hand. And even that had been an analysis, a dry accounting of the facts and assessment of blame, of which there had been plenty to go around.

But she thought of it now. That day. Deafening noise. Heat. Fire. Smoke.

She'd been terrified, and if she closed her eyes and tried very hard to go back to that day, she thought she remembered being scooped up off the ground. Remembered strong arms around her. A voice, a deeply reassuring voice, promising her that he was going to take care of her, that he would get her out of there. She'd wanted her father, her mother. Told him they were inside. And he'd told her not to worry, that he would go back for them. Obviously, he had. Back into hell to get them, and it seemed he'd lived in that hell ever since.

"I have to go," she said. "I have to find him."

She took a late-night flight to Colorado, then set off in a rented Bronco just as the sun was coming up the next morning.

She thought the drive would give her plenty of time to work out what she had to say to him, but she was too nervous. It meant too much to her. Two months away from the man hadn't made her immune to him at all. Her hands were shaking, her arms, her entire body. Jamie said he'd been here ever since Dan had called to say he'd gotten Grace safely out of San Reino, and Grace was worried.

Right before she'd left, Jamie had said, "He likes to think he's invincible, but he's not."

Just a man, Grace remembered.

She would tell him that. Now that she wasn't so hurt, so shocked, she doubted anyone could have single-handedly stopped a madman with a bomb and saved her father. Maybe if she said it, he'd believe it. Maybe they could both start to put this behind them.

Grace pulled into a small clearing with a cabin in the midst of it, smoke coming from the chimney, a big Ford Expedition parked in front of it. There was snow everywhere, but thankfully none falling from the sky yet today.

She got out of the truck and found silence greeting her, stepped closer to the house, so she could see past the clump of trees to the mountains behind the cabin. And found them breathtaking. She stood, just breathing in the air, taking in the broad expanse of sky and the rocky, snow-covered peaks.

"Grace?" a deep, familiar voice that did odd things to her insides, said tentatively.

It couldn't be him, she thought. He didn't have a tentative bone in his body. But when she turned around, there he was. In a pair of worn jeans, a flannel shirt and no coat, his dark hair damp and curling a bit, his eyes so bright in this sunshine that it hurt to look at them.

It just plain hurt to look at him, she found.

Something squeezed tightly in the pit of her stomach, a knot of pain, unfurling slowly and seeping out, like the smoke curling out of the chimney behind him.

He looked different, she realized. Like he'd lost weight. He'd never be thin, but he looked…thinner, in an unhealthy way. The skin stretched more tightly over the bones in his face and his arms, the lines deeper at the corners of his eyes. From the shadows beneath them, she'd bet he hadn't been sleeping well, either. And he was as still as she was, as cautious as he might be around someone or something he thought might lash out at him at any moment. As she'd done before she left.

Which was why she was here. To make her apologies and go.

Grace nearly laughed at how utterly ridiculous that idea was now. She'd come thousands of miles telling herself that, but one look at him and she knew it wasn't true. Not at all.

"What's so funny, Grace?"

She shook her head back and forth. "I've just been lying to myself again."

"Oh?"

She nodded. She hadn't come here merely to clear up one little thing and go. She'd come here because she wanted desperately to see him. To try to make some sense out of all that had happened. She'd come praying there was an explanation other than the one she'd come to on her own, for what he'd done, for the way he'd hurt her. She'd come because she needed him. Desperately.

Maybe she had no pride, either. Maybe if all he felt for her was a mistaken sense of obligation, a debt of honor, she would take that and all that came with it. Be with him, for as long as he thought it took him to repay the debt. Because he'd been the only bright spot in her life for the last ten years. The only thing she'd looked forward to. The only thing that interested her, intrigued her, excited her. He'd been her reason for wanting to stay alive, and she'd crammed more living into the few days she'd spent with him than she had in the last decade. How in the world could he think he was just a man, if he could do all of that for her? She had to find the courage to tell him, as soon as she cleared up this thing with him and her family.

"Do you think I could come inside?" she asked.

He turned, gestured for her to precede him. She climbed the three steps to the small deck overlooking the mountains, and he reached around her—his hand brushing against hers—to open the door for her. She shivered at the slight touch and felt him stiffen behind her and draw away.

Oh, Sean, she thought. Did it hurt him that much, too? Just to touch her?

He took her coat, carefully avoiding touching her again, and offered her coffee. She wrapped her cold hands around the cup and sipped, all the while looking at him. She could have sworn those were nerves that had him tapping his fingers along the countertop, hardly able to keep still. *Him? Nervous?*

So, it meant something to him, too?

Grace got herself back on track. First things first. The guilt. How could she make him understand? Because if they didn't get past this, they had nowhere to go. No possibilities at all. Except a lifetime without him. And then she remembered how she'd finally seen it herself.

"I lost a patient a couple of days ago," she said.

"Oh?"

"A boy. Fourteen."

He waited, arms folded across his chest now, one hip cocked against the cabinet on which he was leaning.

"He'd taken a fall, slid off the remains of a roof, and when they brought him into the clinic, he seemed okay. I checked him out as best I could, but we don't have the kind of equipment that can look inside people and pick up those subtle signs of bleeding. The slow, seeping kind that can kill people just as effectively, given time. And we were swamped, as usual. His parents took him home, and the next morning, they rushed him back. Turned out he was bleeding internally. By the time he felt bad enough to come back, there was nothing we could do that mattered. We couldn't pump the blood into him fast enough. His pressure crashed, and his heart just gave out. And I felt so guilty—"

"Grace, I'm sure you did everything you could."

"How do you know that?"

"Because I know you. I can't believe you'd ever do anything less than your absolute best. Especially when a teenage boy was concerned."

"It doesn't seem to help," she said.

He looked puzzled, uneasy, oddly reserved. "Why did you come here?"

She held up a hand to silence him. "I'm almost there. I had to tell his parents. His father was so hurt, so angry and in shock. He lashed out at me. Made me think of how I must have been with you when you finally told me what you did in Rome.''

''Why did you come here, Grace?''

''I thought I owed you—''

''You don't owe me anything,'' he said flatly. ''You can get in your car right now and go.''

She flinched at that, at the harsh tone he'd never used with her before. But she hadn't come this far to turn around and run the first time things got difficult.

''I listened to you. You just had to tell me about that day, and I listened,'' she reminded him, because she knew that would work. His sense of honor was unquestionable. ''I think you owe it to me to listen now.''

He let out a harsh, ragged breath and seemed to steel himself for the rest.

Oh, Sean, she thought. Dan was right. He hated himself. He thought she hated him, too, for something that she now realized she could not blame him. She hated the idea that she'd hurt him so badly, that he'd been hurting for as long as she had over this. It seemed they'd both wasted so much time.

''I was shocked by what you told me that day. I was angry, and I was hurt and...'' And she'd thought she was watching every dream she ever had of a life with him disappear. ''I wasn't thinking at all, and I just didn't understand. But I'm afraid I said something about hating you and blaming you for the fact that I lost my family. And that's just not true.''

He gave her a look that said it didn't matter in the least. Of course, it wouldn't. Not when he blamed himself.

''It was like me and that boy, Sean. You have to see that. You have to know it, somewhere deep inside. Sometimes people just die. I've seen it happen too many times. Heard too many stories about it from too many grieving relatives and friends just trying to make sense of it all. And you know what? There's no sense to it. Sometimes it's like we all have to step up to the table and roll the dice, see whose turn it is to go. It's as random as that.''

He shook his head back and forth.

''Why do you think I was so petrified to ever love anyone again? I know how capricious life really is. One minute, you're here. The next minute, you're gone. And sometimes it's just the difference between being in a certain spot now or a split second later. So many times, I've had people drag someone to me who's just taken a bullet. They drag him in hoping I can help, and the whole time they're babbling on about how he was just standing right next to them. How is it that the one man is dead and the other isn't, when all of six inches separated them? Sean, for that boy to die, so many things had to come together in just that way. And on that day, all of them did. He was the one. He died.''

''It's not the same thing,'' he argued.

''For him, I was just one of those pieces, and that's what you were where my family was concerned. You were one of those little pieces.''

''Don't make excuses for me, Grace. It's not necessary.''

''You don't make excuses for anyone. Neither do I, and even if I did, I'm hardly likely to do it for you in this case. This is my family we're talking about,'' she said. ''Did you do the best you could in that moment? Not now that you've had twenty years to analyze it to death and know how it was going to end, but in those seconds when it was happening? Did you do the best you could?''

''It wasn't enough,'' he said raggedly.

''Sometimes our best still isn't enough. Even your best effort, which I know was considerable. Do you think maybe that's the problem? I had trouble believing you were just a man. I think you do, too. We all have limits. We all fall short at times.''

''I know I'm far from perfect, Grace.''

''Not far from it,'' she tried to reassure him. ''Just not absolutely perfect. But you don't have to be perfect for me.''

He closed his eyes, and the hand at his side was balled into a fist. She went to him. It was so good to go to him, to take that fisted hand in hers and try to soothe him just a bit with her touch. She thought she could feel the pain coming out of him, rolling off of his body in waves, and she definitely felt him go even more tense at her touch.

"You said more than once that you'd do anything for me," she reminded him, because he was a man who didn't make promises lightly.

"I would," he said tightly.

"Then I want you to forgive yourself."

"Grace—"

"That's what I want."

"Don't pity me," he said. "That's the last thing I want from you."

"Fine, I won't. Don't you pity me either. It's the last thing I want from you."

"It's not pity. I feel responsible. That I owe you."

"Then consider your debt paid," she said. "You've saved my life more than once. Probably the first time on the day the bomb went off. Were you ever going to tell me that? That you're the one who pulled me out of what was left of that building? And don't you dare try to tell me that didn't matter."

"It was damned little and too late," he said bitterly.

"Saving my life was such a small thing?"

"You were far enough from the bomb that—"

"Don't tell me I wasn't in any danger. Don't tell me there are tons of men who would have gone into that building when it was on fire, smoke pouring out and the walls coming down. I know that's not true. And I know you're what I've always thought you were—"

"Grace—"

"What you've always been, your whole life. An incredibly brave man."

"You can't stand me, sweetheart."

"I can't stand the idea that you pity me. Or maybe that all you feel for me is a sense of obligation, misplaced at that. What a combination, pity, obligation and a bit of sexual attraction thrown in to confuse things even more."

"You think you and me were about nothing but great sex and me trying to pay a debt?" he said incredulously.

"I don't know what it was about," she cried. "Except that I thought you were going to be everything to me."

And then she'd said it all, laid bare her whole heart and done her best to make him believe she no longer blamed him for something for which he insisted on blaming himself.

She waited, hoped, maybe even prayed. He didn't give an inch, looked as determined and as closed-off to her as ever.

God, he was going to let her go again. She could see it in his eyes.

"Dammit." Grace bit her lip and looked to the door. "I don't know what else to say."

And still he said nothing.

She had her hand on the knob, twisting it, tears streaming down her cheeks. She didn't hear him make a sound, could have sworn he was still halfway across the room, when he came up behind her.

"Wait."

He sounded like he might have choked on the word. She leaned against the door for support, her legs shaking, and she couldn't stop crying, stop pleading with the whole universe to stop him from letting her go.

"What are you going to do?" he asked, his voice low and strained.

"I don't know." In truth, she was as lost as she'd ever been in her life.

"God," he muttered. "I've stood here and watched you walk away from me twice already. I thought the first time was going to kill me, and the second time, it hurt so bad I wished it would. I don't think I can do it again, Grace. I don't think I can stand it."

"I told myself that if you loved me, you wouldn't have let me go in the first place," she said, trying to hide from him the fact that she was sobbing.

"I let you go because you told me you couldn't take the risk of loving anyone again, and I understood that."

"And I told myself the second time that it was nothing but sex—"

"It was everything," he said. "Everything, and it was absolutely wrong of me to ever let things go that far. There's no excuse for it, Grace. It was wrong."

"Then why did you let it happen?"

"I didn't have the courage to tell you the truth about who I was. I couldn't stand what I'd see in your eyes when you looked at me once you knew. When you came back to me the first time, when I saw you standing there in my bathroom, I just couldn't believe it. Not until I touched you. Until I knew you were real, and then I just lost it. There was no way I could let you go."

"Why?" she asked, needing to hear him say it.

"It started as guilt," he admitted. "You're right about that. But it's always been so much more than that. Even at eleven, you were so sweet. So brave. You had such spirit. I was amazed by you, even then. And when I finally saw you again, at twenty-one, I wanted you then. I wanted to grab you and carry you out of there and make you swear to me you'd never come back to any place like that. I wanted the *right* to do that where you were concerned. I've lost more sleep over you in the past ten years than I can even begin to count. Worrying about where you were and what you were doing and just trying to get you out of my mind. I've admired you and been absolutely fascinated by you. I've always thought you were so beautiful and so good, and I knew I shouldn't ever put my hands on you. Because before I ever did that, I owed you the truth about who I was first, and I knew you'd hate me then."

"I don't hate you," she said, her tears finally slowing.

"I don't see how you keep from it. I hate what happened. Everything I did to hurt you. All the time when I should have told you the truth and I didn't. But mostly the bombing. I hate it," he said, drawing in a deep, slow, deliberate breath that tickled the back of her neck. "I've hated it every day of my life."

"I know."

"And I could have stopped it."

"Maybe you could have. Maybe," she admitted. "But you didn't cause it. A man with a bomb caused it. Him and everything that went wrong to ever let him that close to my father. Not you. You know that, Sean. And for me to ever hate you, I'd have to dismiss everything I've learned about you, everything you've done for me, everything you've done with your whole life. You'd have me judge you completely by one mistake you made twenty years ago?"

"A mistake that cost you everything."

"No. Not everything. I believed that once. I believed it for years. I lived like I didn't care what I did with my life, because I didn't think anything good could ever happen to me again. And I was wrong about that. You showed me I was wrong."

"Obviously, I didn't," he said, turning her in his arms, his body still pinning her to the door. "Because you went back into San Reino. Right after you left me. Right after that madman kidnapped you, and his guard nearly raped you. How could you do that, Grace? I nearly went crazy thinking about you being back there. Thinking that even if I went to try to get you to leave, you wouldn't go. I was so furious, I could have torn a building apart with my bare hands thinking about you being there all over again."

"I went because I had to go somewhere. Because work has always saved me, when I had nothing else."

"Nothing I said to you on that island made any difference at all?" he groaned.

"It made a difference," she admitted. "Even my job

doesn't work for me anymore. It doesn't stop me from thinking or remembering you or hurting. And I don't think I can do it anymore, anyway. Because I'm too scared now. I was never scared before, because I didn't have anything to lose. Do you know why I'm scared now?''

"No," he said carefully.

"Because I want to live. I finally have a reason, and it's you. It's always been you. You're the only thing I've looked forward to for years. The only thing that interested me, that excited me, that intrigued me. Just thinking that someday, I'd see you again. Someday you'd come for me, and you'd stay. Someday, I'd find out all about you, and you'd be everything I ever imagined. You'd be the man who saved me.''

He swore softly. "Grace—''

"And that's who you are. My own personal savior," she told him. "When you have your arms around me, I feel completely safe, like nothing can ever hurt me. I think it must go back to that first time, when you pulled me out of that building. That on some level, I remember you from then. I dreamed about you. For weeks afterward when I was in the hospital, and even after that, when I was all alone. I imagined you were sitting beside my bed, holding my hand and just talking to me, about anything at all. And I wasn't so scared then. I—''

She looked up and saw his gaze, steady and sure, on hers.

He had always been so familiar to her. And she was missing something. Something that was right there on the edges of her brain, teasing at her and then flitting away.

That day, when he'd told her the truth, he'd started out by saying something she only thought about later, something she hadn't ever understood. *Close your eyes for a minute. Listen to my voice. You've always known me.*

And what had Jamie said? She knew Grace was going to be okay, because Sean was with her. She said they'd nearly lost him, too. Jamie said he'd been in the hospital for days afterward. He'd been hurt.

Grace closed her eyes, and finally, she saw it, saw him. That dark-eyed, dark-haired young man. So tall and so handsome, even with all the bruises he'd had then. She remembered his voice. He'd talked to her for hours on end, somehow helped her fight back her fears, her panic, at the thought of being so alone. He'd single-handedly kept her sane, and he'd been the one who hadn't left her alone. As if he might have known just what she wanted—to be with her family, any way she could.

"It was you, wasn't it? Not just in the picture. Not just pulling me out of that building. You're the one who sat by my side for days in the hospital and held my hand.... It was you."

Slowly, he nodded.

No wonder, she thought. Finally she understood why she'd always reacted to him in just that way, always trusted him.

"God, I've seen you in my dreams for years." She laughed then, as sweet, sad tears fell down her cheeks. "It was as if I took you with me everywhere I went. From that first day in the hospital or maybe the day of the bombing. So much of it I see through a kind of haze. It's never been that clear. But I remember you now. I just spent years thinking you weren't real. I could hear your voice. I imagined I knew what it was like to be in your arms. I thought I knew what you looked like, even when I didn't think you were real. Oh, my God."

She just stared at him, thinking of all that he'd been to her through the years.

"I spent nights at that damned boarding school in Kent, crying myself to sleep and thinking I was more alone than anybody in the whole wide world, and there you'd be. I'd dream of you. You were always with me," she said. "That's why you used all those different accents. All the different languages. Why, for so long, you wouldn't let me see your face. Sean, you just don't know. You can't possibly know what you've meant to me over the years. And as much as it was, it's not a fraction of what I feel for you now. Which means, I'm not leaving. I'm not giving up on you. Or us. I'm not going to let you throw the rest of your life away—''

"Grace—"

"That's what you're doing," she said, seeing it so clearly now. And it hurt her to think of him doing this, maybe every bit as much as it hurt him to watch her. "You're doing just what you accused me of, for the same reason. I couldn't handle what happened to my family twenty years ago. I couldn't handle the thought of loving anyone else, knowing I might lose him, and you can't handle the guilt over the bombing, even if it wasn't your fault.''

He said nothing. Nothing at all.

"I think deep down you know it wasn't your fault and the guilt is something that's…not easy. I know it's not easy for you. But I think you're hanging on to the guilt now because it's easier than dealing with the real issue. That you're human like the rest of us. That you can't control everything, can't fix everything. That the world's a big, scary place, and if you love someone, if you let someone into your life and ever let them mean absolutely everything to you, you might end up like me someday. You might get hurt that badly, too. I think you can't let me into your life—no matter how much you might want to—because you're afraid.''

Still, he said nothing.

"I'm ready, Sean. I'm ready to risk it all. On you and me. If you want that—"

"God, I want it," he said, swaying toward her now.

She wrapped her arms around him. His came around her more slowly, more carefully, as if he expected her to pull away, maybe to disappear into thin air.

She let the tip of her nose rub against his chest, the side of his neck, breathing in his scent. She kissed the side of his neck, his jaw, finally his mouth.

He groaned, shuddered, and then it was like being in the center of a storm. His mouth was greedy, rushing over her so hungrily, his hands lightning fast, tearing at her clothes and his. The passion just exploded between them, and she was laughing as much as she was crying, her heart soaring, as she found herself stripped bare and lying on a soft rug in front of a roaring fire with him on top of her.

She gave herself up to him eagerly, needily. Gasping and clutching at his shoulders and shuddering with pleasure as he lowered his big body down on top of hers, pushed her thighs apart and slowly, so slowly, inched his way inside of her.

It was so powerful, so starkly sexual, yet at the same time, a joining of souls like nothing she'd ever experienced. She knew him. Knew exactly what he was all about, exactly how he'd suffered and what it had cost him to live with what he believed he'd done all these years. He knew how lonely she'd been, how hurt, how empty, and he filled her completely. Every corner of her soul, every molecule in her body.

If she was taking his pain away, he was taking hers. It was a healing, unlike any she ever expected to find in this world. Unlike anything she ever expected any person to be able to give her.

He'd given her back her life. He'd shown her all the possibilities, all the wonder. All about happiness and trust. Everything she needed to silence her demons.

He lay heavily on top of her when it was over, and she clung to him. She was crying and trying to soothe him, trying to make him understand that nothing else mattered anymore but the two of them. That together they could do anything.

They never made it to the bed, but slept on the hard floor in front of the fire with her on top of him. He didn't think he'd loosened his arms a fraction of an inch all night, and he'd been reluctant to even open his eyes when he woke that morning for fear that maybe it had all been a dream.

They had a lot to learn about trusting this new reality of theirs.

He could still hardly believe it, Grace here with him in a

cabin on top of a mountain, snow falling all around them, and it was almost Christmas.

She'd given him a gift beyond anything he'd ever imagined. Forgiveness. A cold, hard dose of reality—that part of his problem was accepting that he couldn't quite control the universe—and an all-too-real understanding of the risks they were about to take by loving each other.

But he'd fallen every bit as hard as she had. There'd been no stopping it, not from the very beginning. Sometimes he thought he'd loved her ever since that first night he'd spent lying by her side in that hospital in Rome. He'd insisted on being there, hadn't left her for the entire time she'd been there, and somewhere along the way what started out as penance had turned into simply everything.

Everything he'd ever wanted, ever needed, ever dreamed about, he could sum up in one word: Grace.

He must have said it aloud, because she stirred in his arms, the afghan he'd thrown around them late last night slipping off one smooth, milky-white shoulder. He kissed it, then tucked the blanket more tightly around her.

Through the windows to the east, over the tops of the mountains, the first hint of dawn was slipping into the darkened sky, and he found he needed to witness the coming of this day, the first of the rest of his life.

He picked Grace up and put her on the sofa in front of the fire, which he built up again until it was roaring. Then he dressed quickly and slipped outside to stand on the deck.

So many years, he thought as he stood there in the cold, spent living in the dark. He'd thought there would be nothing but more of the same, of worrying over her and wanting her and chasing her around the world and back, and he hadn't been sure how he'd find a way to go on. He just didn't see the point.

And now here she was with him....

He looked across the snow-covered peaks, and the sky was warming to a pale, pinkish glow streaked with a bit of purple, a bit of gold. The clouds were lying low against the top of the mountains and the undersides of them were fluffy and soft-looking and glowing, too. Heaven seemed close enough to touch at the moment.

He thought about his brother, Rich, whom he still missed every day of his life, and once again thought of Grace long ago, so little, so alone. Thought that so easily he could have lost her, too, right there in Rome, and then what would his life have ever been? He closed his eyes and offered up silent, heartfelt thanks for her and all that he'd been given.

The door opened behind him, and she stood there staring at him, looking rumpled and very touchable, a little bit shy. Her glorious hair was hanging down her back in a pretty mess, and her cheeks were already chilled pink, her eyes full of sleep, a softly vulnerable smile on her lips.

"Come here," he said, softly, beckoning her to his side.

She slid beneath his arm, and he tucked her against his side.

"What are you doing out here?" she asked.

He kissed the tip of her nose—cold, as he expected—then pushed her face against his chest. "It's the first day of the rest of my life, Grace. I wanted to see the sun come up."

"Oh," she said.

"You're really going to forgive me," he said, awe still in his voice. "And stay here with me and love me?"

She squeezed her arms around his chest. "Yes."

"I think I might need to hear that. Every day."

"Whatever you need," she said.

"I need you," he whispered raggedly, as the sun hit him squarely in the face, nearly blinding him. He could feel it on his skin, warming him through and through, the way she did, the way the idea of loving her forever did, and for the first time, he had nothing to hide. He could stand right here in the sunshine with her.

"I need you every bit as much," she said.

He thought she was crying again, and he promised himself

that one day he was going to put a smile on this woman's face that would never come off.

"You're the only thing I've wanted in ages," he said, taking her face in both of his hands, and sure enough finding those tears. "The only thing. And I think you're right. I have been hiding, too. Just like you, sweetheart. Maybe it was easier to blame it on what happened twenty years ago than deal with the real issues. Like the fact that I wasn't quite as in charge of the world around me as I liked to think, that there were things I simply couldn't prevent from happening, couldn't fix. Things I might lose, as well," he said. "There came a point a few years ago when I knew what my life had become. Nothing but the job, and for a while that was enough. But there comes a time when a man wants more, and when that happened to me, I looked around and all I could see was you. There's never been a woman in my life who was truly important. No one I ever needed the way I need you. No one who felt absolutely essential to my life. And I didn't think I'd ever have you."

"I'm yours," she said. "All yours. You couldn't get rid of me now if you tried. I'm as stubborn as you are."

He rubbed the pad of his thumb along her cheek, kissing her soft, sweet lips. "You're here now. But I've only been waiting for you for half my life. And I just didn't think you were ever coming, sweetheart. I was sitting there feeling sorry for myself and wondering what was the point? In anything? I told you I sit behind a desk most every day, and I don't think anyone who knows me well believes me when I say that, but it's true. I took myself out of the field because I saw myself getting a little too reckless. Taking too many chances. Just not caring. Right around the time I accepted the fact that there would never be another woman for me but you. And when I saw that same recklessness in you... I knew deep down exactly what it was. I tried to deny it, but I knew."

"And you had to come save me from myself," she said.

"Of course I did. I love you," he said, feeling as if the words had been ripped from him, as if he'd torn the bindings off what was once a gaping wound and found that it had healed completely when he wasn't looking. "I love you."

"And I love you."

"And you'll stay with me?"

"Yes."

"I think I could do anything, if I have you in my life."

"Even have a life?" she suggested.

"Even that." He gave her a long, slow, fiercely tender kiss. "I want to make you happy. I want you to have everything. I want to be the man who gives it all to you."

She looked dazed. "It's a little hard to take it all in," she said. "So many times when you're around, I feel like the world's just moving too fast. Like I can't keep up. I feel like…like…"

"Tell me, Grace," he invited. "Anything you want. Anything I have to give."

"Like I've been born again and somehow made whole." She started crying again. "Like every dream I never even let myself have is going to come true."

"Oh, baby. If I have anything to say about it, they will." He held her for the longest time, keeping her close and warming her body with his and waiting until she wasn't shaking so hard.

"I'd given up. Completely," she said. "I didn't expect anything at all anymore, except surviving and this…all the possibilities…it makes my head spin."

"You've been taking my breath away for years," he said. "And I want you with me. Every day of my life, and I don't care where we are. As long as we're together. I know how important your work is to you. I have enough time in to take early retirement, so wherever you want to go…"

"Actually, I was thinking about staying here," she said. "Ever since you and I made national news, I've had people calling and offering me all sorts of things, things to do with my family in one way or another. A former colleague of my father's is an editor in New York. He wants me to write a book about my father and his work. About my family. Not just my recollections, but those of other people who knew him and worked with him, too. I've spent twenty years trying to deny they even existed, and this seems like a way to get to know them all over again. To say to everyone that they did exist, and they were wonderful people. To have other people know them the way I did. I thought I'd give it a try.''

"Right here in the States?" That seemed too good to be true.

"In Washington most of the time. The IRC wants someone there and at times in New York at the UN. A spokesperson for the group. Someone to make people understand the needs the group's trying to address and maybe to get us some more money. Someone to deal with the public, too. To try to raise money and volunteers. Peter Baxter, my boss, thinks I'd be good at that. Or he thinks James Porter's daughter would be. That the name, coupled with my own experiences in the field, would be particularly effective. Peter says I can do more for him in a job like that than I ever could as one doctor.''

"And that's what you want?"

"I want to stop denying who my family was. My father inspired people all over the world, and if I could do that with his memory... I don't want to be him. I don't think I have the energy or the courage, not after the last ten years in the field. But the whole organization of the IRC depends on money and volunteers. If I could give them that, it *would* be important. It would be more than I could do as a single doctor and a volunteer. It would mean some traveling, but—"

"Whatever you want. I mean that."

"I was thinking that it would also let me lead a fairly normal life. A plan, old, boring, ordinary life."

"It won't be boring. I can promise you that. And I meant what I said a year and a half ago. I sleep a whole lot better at night knowing no one's shooting at you, Grace."

"What about you?" she asked. "Are people going to be shooting at you? What exactly do you do?"

He grinned. "I work at the Pentagon. As one of the people coordinating special ops for all branches of the military. The Seal teams. The Rangers. Naval intelligence. Those kinds of people. Planning things. Deciding who's going where to take care of what kind of problems."

"From behind a desk? Because I'm going to worry about you, too."

"I can count on one hand the number of times I've made it out from behind that desk in the last three years, other than training missions and the times I've gone to get you out of trouble. I promise you, Grace. I'm not going to take any chances," he said. "Not with you. Not with us."

"Thank you."

"I want you to be my wife," he said.

"I want that, too."

"I want that because I love you and I have to have you in my life, if I'm ever going to have a life."

"Me, too."

"And I need you to help me forgive myself. I—"

"I'll tell you. Every day," she promised.

It was something no one but her could have ever given him, a gift of understanding and healing he'd never expected to find on this earth.

"You're an incredibly generous woman," he said.

"I'm a scared one," she admitted. "Still. I woke up this morning and you were gone, and—"

"I'm sorry."

"No, I am. It's just going to take some time. To trust in all of this. To convince myself that it's going to last."

"We have time," he said. "All you need."

"I'm afraid I'm going to need a lot. And I want to make you happy, too. I want you to have everything, and when I think about that, I remember you and your nephew. He looks like you," she said. "I just ached, watching him with you and thinking that he made you so happy and that someday you'd have children, that some other woman would give them to you because I was too scared to take the risk. And I'm still scared, Sean. Children are so vulnerable.''

''I'll watch over them,'' he promised, closing his eyes and seeing Grace in miniature, long tangled curls and the sweetest smile on earth. ''As closely as I've watched over you over the years.''

''Oh. Of course,'' she said, smiling a bit through her tears. ''I might need to hear that. Every day of my life.''

He nodded, kissed her. He planned to do that, at least a dozen times. Every day of his life.

He thought about what she needed, what he had to give her, and he found himself smiling at all the days to come, all the pleasures they would share, all the treasures.

''You know,'' he said, ''when you were little and all alone, I thought we might bring you into my family, in a totally different way. My father asked. I don't know if you remember that at all, and I guess we weren't the only ones to offer you a home, and you turned us down then. My family's incredibly strong, Grace, incredibly tight. We'd do anything for each other, and I couldn't imagine any better gift we could have given you back then than all of us. I thought if we could pull you inside of that circle, that somehow you'd be okay. But I guess that wasn't meant to be,'' he said. ''This is the way. With you as my wife. You'll do that, Grace? You'll marry me?''

Grace stared at him, looking so tall and so strong, with the bright sunlight streaming over the mountains and glinting off the new snow.

He had his face to the sun, light pouring over him, and he was truly dazzling in the sunlight. She couldn't quite get used to the sight of him, every bit as handsome and compelling as she'd ever imagined in those long years they spent alone and in the dark.

But not anymore. Never again.

"Yes," she whispered.

They stood there holding each other for a minute as the whole world seemed to come alive with glorious, pure light. He seemed to bask in it this morning, and she couldn't help but think that they were both through hiding. It was finally their time in the sun, to shine each bright, sparking new day after bright, sparkling new day.

"I love you," he said. "I have for years. Nothing's ever changed that. Nothing ever will."

"And I love you," she said.

For everything he was, everything he'd always done for her.

Because he'd always been her hero.

*   *   *   *   *

Celebrate
Silhouette's 20th Anniversary

with *New York Times* bestselling author

LINDA
HOWARD

and the long-awaited story of
CHANCE MACKENZIE
in
A GAME OF
CHANCE

IM #1021
On sale in August 2000

Hot on the trail of a suspected terrorist, covert intelligence officer Chance Mackenzie found, seduced and subtly convinced the man's daughter, Sunny Miller, to lead her father out of hiding. The plan worked, but then Sunny discovered the truth behind Chance's so-called affections. Now the agent who *always* got his man had to figure out a way to get his woman!

Available at your favorite retail outlet.

Where love comes alive™

If you enjoyed what you just read,
then we've got an offer you can't resist!

Take 2 bestselling love stories FREE!
Plus get a FREE surprise gift!

Celebrate
Silhouette's 20th Anniversary
with *New York Times* bestselling author

LINDA
HOWARD

and get reacquainted with
the Mackenzie family in

Test pilot Joe "Breed" Mackenzie was on a

MACKENZIE'S
MISSION

dangerous mission, and he wasn't about to let sexy
civilian Caroline Evans—a woman who looked
too good and knew too much—get in his way....

On sale in July 2000

And don't miss the brand-new, long-awaited story
of Chance Mackenzie in

A GAME OF CHANCE,
Intimate Moments #1021
On sale in August 2000

Available at your favorite retail outlet

Silhouette®
Where love comes alive™

Visit Silhouette at www.eHarlequin.com   PSMACHAN

where love comes alive—online...

Visit the *Author's Alcove*

➢ Find the most complete information anywhere on your favorite Silhouette author.

➢ Try your hand in the Writing Round Robin— contribute a chapter to an online book in the making.

Enter the *Reading Room*

➢ Experience an interactive novel—help determine the fate of a story being created now by one of your favorite authors.

➢ Join one of our reading groups and discuss your favorite book.

Drop into *Shop eHarlequin*

➢ Find the latest releases—read an excerpt or write a review for this month's Silhouette top sellers.

➢ Try out our amazing search feature—tell us your favorite theme, setting or time period and we'll find a book that's perfect for you.

All this and more available at

www.eHarlequin.com
on Women.com Networks

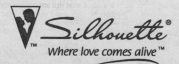

SILHOUETTE'S 20ᵀᴴ ANNIVERSARY CONTEST
OFFICIAL RULES
NO PURCHASE NECESSARY TO ENTER

1. To enter, follow directions published in the offer to which you are responding. Contest begins 1/1/00 and ends on 8/24/00 (the "Promotion Period"). Method of entry may vary. Mailed entries must be postmarked by 8/24/00, and received by 8/31/00.

2. During the Promotion Period, the Contest may be presented via the Internet. Entry via the Internet may be restricted to residents of certain geographic areas that are disclosed on the Web site. To enter via the Internet, if you are a resident of a geographic area in which Internet entry is permissible, follow the directions displayed on line, including typing your essay of 100 words or fewer telling us "Where In The World Your Love Will Come Alive." On-line entries must be received by 11:59 p.m. Eastern Standard time on 8/24/00. Limit one e-mail entry per person, household and e-mail address per day, per presentation. If you are a resident of a geographic area in which entry via the Internet is permissible, you may, in lieu of submitting an entry on-line, enter by mail, by hand-printing your name, address, telephone number and contest number/name on an 8"x 11" plain piece of paper and telling us in 100 words or fewer "Where In The World Your Love Will Come Alive," and mailing via first-class mail to: Silhouette 20ᵗʰ Anniversary Contest, (in the U.S.) P.O. Box 9069, Buffalo, NY 14269-9069; (In Canada) P.O. Box 637, Fort Erie, Ontario, Canada L2A 5X3. Limit one 8"x 11" mailed entry per person, household and e-mail address per day. On-line and/or 8"x 11" mailed entries received from persons residing in geographic areas in which Internet entry is not permissible will be disqualified. No liability is assumed for lost, late, incomplete, inaccurate, nondelivered or misdirected mail, or misdirected e-mail, for technical, hardware or software failures of any kind, lost or unavailable network connection, or failed, incomplete, garbled or delayed computer transmission or any human error which may occur in the receipt or processing of the entries in the contest.

3. Essays will be judged by a panel of members of the Silhouette editorial and marketing staff based on the following criteria:

> Sincerity (believability, credibility)—50%
> Originality (freshness, creativity)—30%
> Aptness (appropriateness to contest ideas)—20%

Purchase or acceptance of a product offer does not improve your chances of winning. In the event of a tie, duplicate prizes will be awarded.

4. All entries become the property of Harlequin Enterprises Ltd., and will not be returned. Winner will be determined no later than 10/31/00 and will be notified by mail. Grand Prize winner will be required to sign and return Affidavit of Eligibility within 15 days of receipt of notification. Noncompliance within the time period may result in disqualification and an alternative winner may be selected. All municipal, provincial, federal, state and local laws and regulations apply. Contest open only to residents of the U.S. and Canada who are 18 years of age or older, and is void wherever prohibited by law. Internet entry is restricted solely to residents of those geographical areas in which Internet entry is permissible. Employees of Torstar Corp., their affiliates, agents and members of their immediate families are not eligible. Taxes on the prizes are the sole responsibility of winners. Entry and acceptance of any prize offered constitutes permission to use winner's name, photograph or other likeness for the purposes of advertising, trade and promotion on behalf of Torstar Corp. without further compensation to the winner, unless prohibited by law. Torstar Corp and D.L. Blair, Inc., their parents, affiliates and subsidiaries, are not responsible for errors in printing or electronic presentation of contest or entries. In the event of printing or other errors which may result in unintended prize values or duplication of prizes, all affected contest materials or entries shall be null and void. If for any reason the Internet portion of the contest is not capable of running as planned, including infection by computer virus, bugs, tampering, unauthorized intervention, fraud, technical failures, or any other causes beyond the control of Torstar Corp. which corrupt or affect the administration, secrecy, fairness, integrity or proper conduct of the contest, Torstar Corp. reserves the right, at its sole discretion, to disqualify any individual who tampers with the entry process and to cancel, terminate, modify or suspend the contest or the Internet portion thereof. In the event of a dispute regarding an on-line entry, the entry will be deemed submitted by the authorized holder of the e-mail account submitted at the time of entry. Authorized account holder is defined as the natural person who is assigned to an e-mail address by an Internet access provider, on-line service provider or other organization that is responsible for arranging e-mail address for the domain associated with the submitted e-mail address.

5. Prizes: Grand Prize—a $10,000 vacation to anywhere in the world. Travelers (at least one must be 18 years of age or older) or parent or guardian if one traveler is a minor, must sign and return a Release of Liability prior to departure. Travel must be completed by December 31, 2001, and is subject to space and accommodations availability. Two hundred (200) Second Prizes—a two-book limited edition autographed collector set from one of the Silhouette Anniversary authors: Nora Roberts, Diana Palmer, Linda Howard or Annette Broadrick (value $10.00 each set). All prizes are valued in U.S. dollars.

6. For a list of winners (available after 10/31/00), send a self-addressed, stamped envelope to: Harlequin Silhouette 20ᵗʰ Anniversary Winners, P.O. Box 4200, Blair, NE 68009-4200.

Contest sponsored by Torstar Corp., P.O. Box 9042, Buffalo, NY 14269-9042.

PS20RULES

ENTER FOR
A CHANCE TO WIN*
Silhouette's 20th Anniversary Contest

Tell Us Where in the World
You Would Like *Your* Love To Come Alive...
And We'll Send the Lucky Winner There!

Silhouette wants to take you wherever
your happy ending can come true.

Here's how to enter: Tell us, in 100 words or less,
where you want to go to make your love come alive!

In addition to the grand prize, there will be 200
runner-up prizes, collector's-edition book sets
autographed by one of the Silhouette anniversary
authors: **Nora Roberts, Diana Palmer,
Linda Howard** or **Annette Broadrick**.

DON'T MISS YOUR CHANCE TO WIN!
ENTER NOW! No Purchase Necessary

Silhouette ®
Where love comes alive ™

Visit Silhouette at www.eHarlequin.com to enter, starting this summer.

Name: _____

Address: _____

City: _____ State/Province: _____

Zip/Postal Code: _____

Mail to Harlequin Books: **In the U.S.**: P.O. Box 9069, Buffalo, NY
14269-9069; **In Canada**: P.O. Box 637, Fort Erie, Ontario, L4A 5X3